The Insane Journey

The Insane Journey

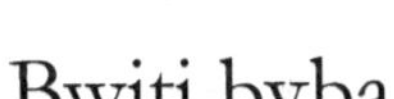

Bwiti bvba

www.bwiti.be
Erps-Kwerps, Belgium

www.insanejourney.com

www.facebook.com/TheInsaneJourney

To my sons,

Alexander and Benjamin

1

Beneath a deep-blue sky scattered with clouds, dashing off towards distant horizon as if late for a very important date, sat the ruins of a small Gothic church. Its crumbling stone walls were first put up nearly a thousand years before and, for the most part, still stood, despite the never-ending wind blowing against them and through their delicate latticework of window frames long since devoid of stained glass – or, indeed, of any glass at all. A headless Jesus nailed to a rotting cross hung from a single, rusty bolt in the remainder of a transept wall and swayed back and forth with a perpetually irritating squeak. One can only assume that Jesus's head, unable to tolerate the godforsaken noise, had long since exploded.

Outside the ruins, an ancient burgundy Bentley was parked. Its modern wheels and tyres attempted to insult the dignity of the bodywork, but the bodywork simply ignored them. Bentleys' bodies are made of stern stuff. It takes more than high-performance alloys to embarrass them.

The sound of the wind whistling round the hills and rustling through the odd tree atop this particular Algarve hill was soon enhanced by a dull roar which increased in volume as the motorcycle to which it belonged drove up the hill, pulled into the churchyard and parked beside the old car.

An athletic woman in her early twenties, wearing what appeared to be a cross between a nun's habit and a designer tracksuit topped off with an aerodynamic carbon-fibre coif, climbed off the bike and walked towards the old car. From the compact rucksack on her back, she pulled out a small electronic device, turned a knob until it clicked and got down on her knees to look under the rear of the Bentley. Finding a suitable space, she tore a plastic cover off the device and stuck it to the underside of the car. She stood and with the tip of her boot brushed away her footprints in the dust as she backed away from the car.

Reaching into her outfit, she pulled out a small, black telephone with a gold cross embedded on the front.

"Sister Alessia," she said into the telephone. A number appeared on the screen and in a second, a dialling tone sounded.

"Good morning," said Sister Alessia, at the receiving end of the call.

"Good morning," said the motorcyclist. "This is Judith. The tracking device is installed and live."

"Very good, Sister Judith. One moment, please." The sound of a computer keyboard being tapped echoed in the phone. "Yes, I've got it on the GPS. Well done. Father Forge will be delighted."

"See you soon, sis," said the motorcyclist with what seemed an almost childlike glee. She remounted her bike and raced back down the road up which she had just come.

This windy, squeaky scene remained largely unchanged until two days later, when a small space cruiser shot across the sky, decelerated to a hovering stop above the churchyard and dropped until it was a scant centimetre or two above the ground, where it bobbed like a boat on a lake. A door hummed open and a pair of steps lowered, enabling Maxwell van Mars, a skinny chap with long curly hair and mismatched eyes, to hop out and take in a deep breath.

"Ah, bliss!" he cried out.

After a week in the tinny, recycled air of a space cruiser, the air of the European countryside was delicious. It reminded him of the first time he had ever taken a breath of Earth's air.

For, you see, Maxwell was a Martian. Not an alien, mind.

Rather, Maxwell was a human born in the hermetically sealed dome-city in the Arimanes Rupes region of the fourth planet, a city which, it should be noted, his family effectively owned through their shareholding in the Martian Mining Company as well as their stakes in dozens of associated companies registered on the Earth, Mars and the solar system's most notorious tax haven, Titan: the methane-ocean-covered moon of Saturn.

His grandfather, a pioneer on Mars, founded the company and changed the family name from something vaguely Germanic and agricultural to one signifying the family's key role in establishing the company and the colony. Grandpa may have been an interplanetary pioneer of the first order – but he utterly lacked class.

Maxwell was nine when his parents brought to him to Mother Earth for the first time. Nevertheless, he could still recall the explosion of incredible smells that attacked his senses when the spaceship doors opened and he was first exposed to the air of Earth. Indeed, the young Maxwell's reaction to standing up and taking in the luscious air of Earth was to pass out – though how much of this was the result of the fragrance-rich air and how much was the result of standing up in a gravity three times more intense than that he had known his entire life is an open question.

In any event, when he came to, he made a vow that one day he would live on the sweet smelling, windy Earth – a vow that, in retrospect, was awfully easy to fulfil when one's family was stinking rich, but one lacked the competence to run the family business or even one of its subsidiaries. Indeed, the family was quite happy to fling him a trust fund or three and keep him tens of millions of kilometres away from the company headquarters.

"Come, Wendy," Maxwell shouted into the space ship. A moment later, a kairuku penguin with a satchel round her neck waddled out and followed Maxwell, who was carrying a couple of rucksacks, to the ancient Bentley. He opened the passenger-side seat, allowing Wendy to hobble in with surprising adroitness, then tossed the rucksacks into the boot.

"Let's get ourselves to Cape City and some creative depravity," Maxwell said to the penguin as he twisted the ignition key. The engine roared to life and settled to a deep throb that suggested significantly more power than what was originally under its bonnet.

"You know I don't do depravity," said the penguin.

"I know, but you should give it a try. It's such fun and I could teach you so much," said Maxwell.

Rather than answer the question, the penguin reached into her satchel, pulled out a battered copy of Kant's *Critique of Pure Reason*, opened it to the bookmarked page and began reading.

"Where would you like to go today?" asked a muffled voice from under a panel in the dashboard.

"Mrs Miller!" cried Maxwell. "I've missed you." He opened the panel to reveal the GPS display screen – also not original equipment on a car of the Bentley's vintage. "Lead us to the Splendouria Hotel in Cape City, please."

"Calculating," replied the GPS unit.

"You do that," said Maxwell as he manoeuvred the car out on to the road and turned left.

"In 1.3 kilometres, veer right," said Mrs Miller, following 30 seconds later with, "in 300 metres, veer right."

Maxwell kept to the left.

"She said to go right," said Wendy.

"Recalculating," said Mrs Miller as the ancient Bentley roared past the suggested exit.

"Yes, but she wants me to take the highway. The road to the left is more fun to drive, if a smidgeon slower," said Maxwell.

"In 3.4 kilometres, turn right," said Mrs Miller.

"I've been thinking, Wendy," said Maxwell.

"That's worrying," said Wendy.

"Don't be cute. It doesn't suit you, old penguin."

"Don't get distracted, Maxwell, or we'll never finish this conversation. What were you thinking?"

"I reckon we should cut our visit to Cape City short and drive back to Erps-Kwerps right after the unveiling," said Maxwell.

"But the unveiling is tomorrow night and you'll drink way too much," said Wendy.

"No, I'll drink just the right amount. Don't be so judgemental."

"I'm not being judgemental. You have a drinking problem."

"Not if the wine cellar is full, I don't. Still, you've got a point. We'll leave first thing next morning."

"In two hundred metres, turn left," said Mrs Miller.

"Oh, good. I don't much like Cape City," said Wendy.

"Turn left," said Mrs Miller.

"I know," said Maxwell to Wendy as he drove straight past the junction that Mrs Miller was referring to.

"Recalculating," said the GPS.

"Good on you, Mrs Miller," said Maxwell.

"Though I sometimes wonder why I bother," said Mrs Miller.

"What?" exclaimed Maxwell.

"Continue for 64 kilometres," said the GPS.

"Okay," said Maxwell pushing the accelerator to the floor. The engine gurgled with delight as it sent horsepower to the wheels. The Bentley picked up speed at an unseemly pace for a car of its size and age. Maxwell tweaked the steering wheel and feathered the accelerator pedal to bring the massive vehicle around the many curves of the winding country road. Occasionally, the tyres let out a screech as Maxwell took a curve too quickly and the tail end of the car considered giving in to centrifugal force and spinning.

Somehow, that never happened.

Meanwhile, in a convent far away, a computer bleeped and its screen came to life, showing the speeding car as a devil's head progressing along a winding line on a digital map.

2

In a roadside café, Maxwell and Wendy stood at the counter drinking coffee and tea respectively.

"Ahhhh! I can feel the caffeine recharging my system," exclaimed Maxwell, extending his arms like superhero preparing for battle.

"No, you can't. It takes 45 minutes for caffeine to enter your bloodstream," said Wendy.

"This is special coffee with fast-acting caffeine," said Maxwell.

"There's no such thing. It's a placebo effect," said Wendy.

"That's good enough for me," said Maxwell, as Wendy rolled her eyes.

"Excuse me," said a tall, thin woman in a billowing white blouse and carefully torn, tight blue jeans. "Are you Maxwell van Mars?"

"That I am," said Maxwell.

"The sculptor?"

"That too."

"I adore your work!"

"Why, thank you, um..." began Maxwell.

"Cynthia."

"Cynthia," said Maxwell.

"I've been studying your work at uni and I think it's great, especially the way you give your figures – those robots – life. When they are dancing, they seem so real," said Cynthia glowingly.

Although he was a failure in business in general and the family business in particular, Maxwell had proven himself capable in the arts. In particular, he had made a name for himself as a leading sculptor of robots. For the past few years, he had been experimenting with robots in the form of nude female figures who performed bizarre dances to any background music or rhythm they detected. If there was nothing suitable in range, the robots would sing from an eclectic collection of music stored in their memories.

The anatomical accuracy of Maxwell's nude dancers and the eroticism of some of their performances were variously a cause for controversy, adulation and erections. Indeed, men attempting sex with the sculptures was not an uncommon cause for concern, though the real problem was that the sculptures' anatomical correctness was only on the surface, making vaginal penetration a penis-bruising impossibility. Since most men who attempted the feat were more than a little intoxicated, they didn't let a little initial resistance – and pain – diminish their determination, though they inevitably felt the consequences the next morning.

"I model them after real women," said Maxwell.

"But lots of artists do that. Why are your figures so much more alive?"

"Because my models do not sit still. They move around, dance and do other things while I watch and make sketches. I do not want merely to capture a still likeness of an attractive woman like you. Rather, I want to capture her life, the way she moves and her feminine sensuality in those movements."

"Wow!" said Cynthia, following with a thoughtful pause. "When you said attractive like me, was that just a compliment?"

"Yes, it was a compliment. But it was a sincere one." Maxwell looked at the young woman more carefully for a moment, scanning her entire body in a professional yet slightly lustful manner.

"I think you would be a great model for a sculpture. Would you be interested?"

Cynthia smiled, but before she could reply, Wendy spoke up.

"He will end up seducing you, you know."

"Wendy!" said Maxwell

"What?" asked Cynthia, startled.

"He ends up having sex with most of his models," said Wendy.

"You say that as if sex with me is a bad thing," said Maxwell. "I have it on good authority that it can be a very, very good thing."

"I wouldn't know. Fortunately, you are not into bestiality," said the penguin.

"Lord love a duck, Wendy!" said Maxwell. "What's got into you?"

"Oh, my!" said Cynthia, now blushing a deep ruby red.

"Oh, don't worry. She's just jealous because I haven't sculpted her," said Maxwell.

"No, I'm not," said Wendy. "We penguins only get jealous when our mates sit on other penguins' eggs. We are not interested in posing for human art."

"Anyway," interrupted Maxwell. "You are an attractive woman with a lithe body, Cynthia. Assuming you can move as elegantly as you look, you'd make a marvellous model. Here's my card. If you really are interested in posing for me, call my assistant and make an appointment to come to my studio. If you pose for me, you will need to get undressed and move around while I watch and sketch you – but, of course, you will not be expected to sleep with me."

"Ha!" said Wendy.

"Thanks," said Cynthia.

"Keep that up, penguin, and I'll throw you into a pool of leopard seals."

"There are no pools of leopard seals anywhere near here," said Wendy firmly.

"I'll improvise," said Maxwell.

"How?" asked Wendy.

"That's for me to know and you to find out," said Maxwell. "Now, let's hit the road. Cape City is still a couple of hours ahead of us. Toodle-oo Cynthia, I hope I'll see you in my studio one day soon!"

Cynthia waved, not quite sure what to make of her brief encounter with a hero who suddenly seemed a little less heroic, but a little more interesting.

"Don't you want to have sex with her?" asked Wendy once they had got into the car.

"Of course I do. She's as cute as a calico kitten playing with a ball of yarn. But you know it's not appropriate to bring the act of sex up so early in an acquaintanceship."

Wendy looked concerned in a penguinish kind of way. "Are you upset with me for bringing up sex?"

"Not at all. Ironically, by your bringing it up, if she shows up at the studio one day, it will likely mean that she wants to sleep with me – or is at least open to the possibility – whereas if I had brought it up, she'd have been upset and walked away then and there."

"Sometimes I just don't understand humans," sighed Wendy.

"No worries, old bird. I don't much understand penguins," said Maxwell, accelerating onto the winding road that twisted between the mountains and would take them to Cape City and some depravity that he hoped would include a sexual component. He had been locked up for a week in a space cruiser with only a penguin for company, albeit one who was his best friend.

3

Into a large stone visitors' chamber in the Cape City Mayoral Mansion walked a tall, well-built man with thick blonde hair plastered back across his head and a substantial matching moustache. He wore a black tailored suit together with the tabbed shirt of the clergy, albeit an expensive silk example.

"May I help you?" asked the young woman sitting at a reception desk beneath a rather drunk-looking gargoyle.

"Why yes, my child. Would you be so kind as to tell the mayor that Reverend Phineas Forge has arrived and is at his service," said the visitor in a deep drawl that immediately identified his origins as being the Southeastern bit of the United Evangelical States of America, or UESA.

Like many who had been born and raised in the vast region of North America that had turned into a Christian evangelical theocracy during the last century, the Revered Phineas Forge had a very specific vision of God and His Son branded into his brain, to the point where it was an unquestionable truth. Indeed, questioning this alleged truth only made the Reverend and his kind deeply uncomfortable and occasionally aggressive.

They had been brought up to believe in faith over facts and prayer over results. That the population of much of the rest of the world, and particularly Europa, failed to appreciate – much less beholden themselves to – the Evangelical vision, was a point of pain and concern among Phineas's countrymen and women. Hence, preachers like Phineas in his early days were sent out with sackfuls of cash as sugar-daddy missionaries to various European cities to share the love of Jesus. Not surprisingly, it was never difficult for these missionaries to find powerful people who would happily profess their love of God, Jesus and the Evangelical Church in exchange for some of that cash. Or better still, a lot of that cash.

Fresh out of the seminary, Phineas was sent as a junior missionary to Cape City on what should have been a temporary assignment. However, he soon came to feel that his beloved Jesus wanted him to stay longer and truly clean up this southern European city of sin. So he stayed on.

That he had taken a fancy to a local girl was doubtless a major influence in this decision, though Phineas would have denied it. She probably also played a part in his signing up to do a master's degree in European history at the University of Cape City, where she happened to be a student herself. Nevertheless, the course enabled Phineas to understand better the country of Europa and her people.

As so often happens with young, idealised love, Phineas's affection for the young local lady was eventually shattered by reality, with some assistance from Maxwell. By then, Europa had become his home as well as his religious mission, and he had stayed on for two decades, transforming from an enthusiastic youth to an obsessive, middle-aged man during those years. Today, he was considered a prominent raving religious madman in Cape City society, albeit a madman who was generous with his church's funding.

Moreover, following the great economic recession of recent years and the resulting wave of social conservatism in what had been Europa's hotbed of naughtiness, a large portion of society was beginning to buy into this whole religious thing. After all, if life is difficult, it's easier to blame it on God's will rather than on one's own actions – or inactions. And praying for solutions is far easier for the simple minded than making solutions happen.

Thus, after a couple of decades, Phineas finally found himself achieving some of the respect he long felt he deserved in this region he had long served.

"Do you have an appointment, Father?" asked the receptionist.

"Of course I have an appointment, young lady."

"One moment, please."

"Bless you, my child."

The receptionist raised an eyebrow while calling the mayor on the internal telephone. She was not sure she wanted to be blessed, particularly not by a loud American with an excessive moustache.

"Reverend Fudge is here to see you, sir," she said into the phone.

"That's Forge, young lady. Forge," said the reverend.

"Yes, of course, Father. The mayor will see you now. Come this way, please," said the receptionist, getting up and opening the door for Phineas.

"Bless you, my child," said Phineas, as he walked into a vast, plush office. One wall was dominated by a massive fireplace that could probably have contained the better part of a forest fire. In the middle of the room was a small conference table surrounded by four chairs. At the other side of the room was a massive oak desk with a massive executive chair reluctantly supporting a massive bald man with pasty complexion and disturbingly large lips.

He stood up, to the relief of the suffering chair.

Jan van den Berg had been voted in as mayor in Cape City a scant few weeks before and was still settling into office. His predecessor had a well-deserved reputation for corruption (participatory, not combating) which was why the local population had turfed him out in favour of a devout – on the surface, anyway – Christian with strong links to the region's powerful Family Values Association, Citizens' Rights Association and several other associations full of members who were certain they were morally far superior to you and I.

Jan had converted to evangelical Christianity some years before, not so much out of belief as opportunism and a keen interest in the American evangelical wealth being showered upon aspiring young politicians.

He had met Phineas once or twice at church functions, but the two men had paid little attention to each other. Jan considered Phineas an annoying American evangelist who talked far too loudly, and until recently, Jan was insufficiently important to interest Phineas. However, with a landslide win in the Cape City mayoral election, the situation had changed.

"Reverend Forge! I am honoured by your visit," the mayor said.

"Mayor van den Berg. The honour is all mine," said Phineas, accepting the offered hand with a firm shake. "More importantly, congratulations on winning the election. The church is proud to have one of our own in charge of Cape City at last."

"Thank you, Reverend," said the mayor.

"Surely this is a sign that the good Lord wishes us to clean up this sinful city," said the reverend with growing emotion.

"Yes, Reverend, but I'm sure it's not..." began Jan.

"No, my son, it is not your fault. Your predecessor allowed the devil's work to run rampant in this once-glorious seaside city, causing it to become a filthy cesspit of sin, debauchery and perversion."

"Well, I don't think it's that..." began Jan.

"But fear not, my son. The church and I are at your service. With the Lord God's most gracious support, we shall rid this city of sin and turn it into a wholesome urban paradise where children can roam freely in the streets without fear."

"Actually, the children can already..." the mayor once again desperately tried to say, before being cut off again.

"And may I remind you that the church's considerable resources are at your disposal. We understand that the war against sin does not come cheap."

"...play in the...Resources, did you say? Does that include money?" asked Jan.

"Of course, my son, of course," said the reverend. "My secretary will be in touch to arrange the details."

"That is most generous of the church," said Jan.

"Don't mention it. It is God's will," said Phineas.

"Now that I think about it, you are right, of course. Cape City is a most sinful place. We will certainly need substantial resources. In fact..."

"Yes, yes. Our Lord has clearly chosen you to lead his fight in Cape City," said Phineas.

"Now, the other reason I am here," he continued, "is that there is a wonderful opportunity for you to make a powerful statement of your commitment to moral goodness."

"There is?" asked Jan.

"There is, Jan. There is. I understand you will be speaking at the unveiling of Maxwell van Mars's new sculpture at the Waterfront tomorrow evening,"

"Yes. It was a three-million-Euro commission by the previous mayor who wanted to bring an interplanetary celebrity to our city," said Jan. "I personally find it a bit, well, too nude for a public sculpture. But the decisions were made before my time in office, of course."

"Nevertheless, that sculpture is a pornographic blot upon your city and Maxwell is a twisted, immoral and evil individual who will surely corrupt your innocent citizens and molest their daughters. Honouring him would be a slap in the face to every upright, moral individual in Cape City, if not the entire country."

"I see, but..."

"Have you seen pictures of Maxwell's abominations pretending to be art?"

"Yes, I am familiar with his work," Jan winced, reflecting on the bruised penis he had acquired some years before when he first came across one of Maxwell's sculptures in a quiet square long after midnight. He flinched at the memory and refocused on the raving reverend.

"It is a robotic set of dancing woman, absolutely naked, displaying their sexual organs for every man, woman and child to see, whether they like it or not. Mark my word: if that sculpture is allowed to present itself as it is, otherwise upstanding men will ravish your women and rape their daughters. It will be an ugly, ungodly scene," said Phineas.

"That bad?" asked Jan.

"Worse!" insisted Phineas.

"What would you have me do about it?" asked Jan.

"I would have you blow it off the map," said Phineas.

"I fear you overestimate my powers as mayor," said Jan.

"I understand, Jan. I understand. That's why I have a more subtle plan to thwart Maxwell's efforts at polluting the moral integrity of your city's fine people."

Phineas explained his plan.

In spite of himself, Jan giggled. The resulting jiggling of his belly and lips was not a pretty sight.

"That is marvellous. I can't wait to see Maxwell's reaction."

"I reckon we'll need some help to pull it off in time for the unveiling tomorrow," said Phineas. "Do you have people who can help out?"

Jan thought a moment.

"Yes, I am sure the Family Values Association, who have protested against this sculpture since the day it was announced, will gladly help."

"Well, that's just marvellous. I knew we could count on you, Jan."

"Thank you, Father," said Jan, hoping his co-operation would make it easier to tap into those church resources Phineas had mentioned earlier.

"Thank *you*, Jan," said Phineas. "Now, there is another thing I would like to ask of you, my son. A more, how shall we say, discreet request."

"Yes?" said the mayor as he looked around and, not surprisingly, saw no one else in his cavernous office. Nevertheless, he bent a little closer.

"I, and a special action team from within the church, intend to..." Phineas paused for a moment, looking in the air for the right words to frame a delicate matter. "...Deal with the Maxwell problem once and for all."

"And how does this affect me?" asked the mayor with some concern.

"It would be to all of our advantages if the authorities do not pay too much attention to our problem-solving actions, if you know what I mean."

"Of course," said the mayor, though he was not entirely sure that he in fact saw what Phineas meant, but suspected he really did not want to be further enlightened.

"Excellent, excellent," said the reverend.

The mayor simply smiled.

"I'm glad we are on the same page regarding morality in Cape City. I won't take up any more of your time." Phineas stood up. "My secretary will be in touch."

Jan stood also.

"Thank you once again, Mr Mayor," said Phineas, shaking Jan's hand. "And you won't forget our little plan for the unveiling, will you?"

"Thank you, Father. I won't," said Jan, walking Phineas to the the lift and pushing the call button.

Phineas could not help but smile as he waited for the lift to bring him to the underground car park. He had long believed that

Maxwell was, if not Satan incarnate, then a very senior demon who was placed upon the Earth to spread evil through pornographic sculptures, ungodly temptation to sin and, worst of all, depraved sexual debauchery of the most vile kind. This last point he knew for a fact – a painful fact.

During Phineas's post-graduate studies in Cape City, a much younger Maxwell had stolen his true love, defiled her body, corrupted her soul and stolen her virginity. Her virginity had been something Phineas was quite sure God had intended him, and not some perverted scion of a notable interplanetary family, to take.

To make matters worse, Cathy, the ex-virgin in question, eventually took to writing a blog detailing her sexual experimentation. Although neither her name nor Maxwell's was associated with the blog, it was a well-known secret on campus she wrote the blog based on experience – experience that Phineas could not bear to read about, and so did not after the first two or three entries. In view of the level of perversion the blog eventually achieved, it was as well Phineas did not read it; the gloriously written detail would doubtless have over-addled his already addled mind.

"Bastard!" said Phineas out loud, remembering that painful event from years ago. Then he reminded himself that his intention to humiliate and kill Maxwell was not about petty revenge. Rather, it was to wipe the demonic man off the face of the planet and save womankind. Phineas was, he assured himself, far too pious and humble to act upon personal feelings. No. He was saving the planet. Whether the planet felt it needed saving through the elimination of one eccentric or not was not a matter that concerned him.

A ping announced that the lift was coming to a halt at the chosen floor. Phineas shook his head to disperse his ugly thoughts about Maxwell. He would soon be burning in Hell, Phineas reminded himself as the door opened. He walked to his car to find his driver, a stocky bald man in a grey suit, waiting by a massive black sport utility vehicle – or SUV, as you surely know – complete with forebodingly tinted windows all around and a shining chrome crucifix bonnet ornament.

"Ivan, drive me to Escher Abbey," said Phineas.

"Certainly, sir," said Ivan, opening the door for his boss before climbing into the driver's seat and starting the engine. He expertly wound his way through the car park and the crowded streets of Cape City before hitting the open road.

Phineas was deep in thought when the telephone rang.

"Hello?"

"Father Forge, Maxwell's car has started driving in the direction of Cape City."

"Excellent, Sister. Thank you."

He rang off and smiled. The demon would soon be in Hell where he belonged.

4

After an hour's drive, Ivan brought the SUV to a halt in front of an old wall surrounding an abbey atop a medium-sized mountain. Unlike most medieval walls, this one was topped with barbed wire, video cameras and automatic guns. At the gate, a small booth was built into the wall and it was here that the monstrous SUV stopped for a moment.

"Good afternoon, Father," said an athletic nun in a black tracksuit and an aerodynamic coif.

"Good afternoon, Sister," said Phineas with a smile.

The gate opened and the SUV rolled in, went round the old church and parked in front of a modern, prefabricated structure behind the church. Ivan let Phineas out and the latter entered the building, where he found his team of ninja nuns, in matching black tracksuits and aerodynamic coifs, hard at work training. Were it not for the coifs, they would have looked like an Olympic gymnastics team, with their boyish figures, short or tied-back hair and femininely muscular limbs.

At first glance, the nuns seemed to be performing some kind of insane, chaotic modern dance involving furniture, weapons and fleeing men, but by the second glance, even the casual observer would realise this was no dance. The nuns were practising elaborate and deadly combat moves, using the furniture to jump off, hide behind and beat the fleeing men — all to the rhythm of church hymns performed on a massive pipe organ.

These dozen ninja nuns were the European contingent of a special force being trained by the church's intelligence arm to solve serious problems. The nuns were slender, fit and fast. The fleeing men, on the other hand, were generally overweight, panicked and slow. That's because they were convicted child molesters, rapists and atheists brought over secretly from the UESA. They had been told that they were being given a second chance; if they could flee the training building, they would be granted their freedom in Europa.

No one had ever fled successfully. Indeed, as Phineas entered the building, he saw a man run up to the door, stop and lose his head. Literally. The head simply rolled down his chest and to the floor. The rest of the body, presumably somewhat surprised by the decapitation, waited a moment before crumpling down beside the head amid a shower of blood.

"They are getting better every time I see them, Sister Alessia," said Phineas to the older nun standing to the side of the action.

"Thanks be to God," said Alessia.

"And thanks to the dedication of you and the ninja nuns," said Phineas.

"Thank you, Father. It is God's will," said Alessia.

"Amen. Are they ready to eliminate Maxwell in the name of God?" asked Phineas.

"More than ready, Father," answered Alessia.

"Excellent. We leave for Cape City tomorrow night as planned," said Phineas.

"Then Maxwell will be burning in Hell tomorrow night," said Alessia.

"Amen," said Phineas.

"Amen," repeated the nun.

"By the way, Sister," said Phineas.

"Yes, Father?"

"This guy seems to be wearing a local mailman's uniform," said Phineas, pointing with his foot at the recently separated head and body that lay on the ground not far away. Sister Alessia looked down and grimaced.

"Mercy me, I believe you are right, Father. He must have been bringing a registered letter. I've told them again and again to leave registered post with Sister Ersilia in the office."

"This is not good, Sister," said Phineas.

"I know. I'll ring the post office first thing tomorrow," said Sister Alessia.

She looked around the room and called out "Sister Gertrude!"

"Yes, Sister Alessia?" said Gertrude.

"Take this body out to the compost pit,"

"Yes, Sister Alessia."

The following night, Phineas climbed again into his SUV, but this time, there were three identical vehicles behind it, each seating four ninja nuns in full battle gear. Each Ninja Nun had in her mind an image of her intended victim: Maxwell van Mars. The SUVs left the abbey and made their way along the winding dark highway to Cape City.

5

The Waterfront Centre was an architectural masterpiece of phenomenal proportions that would have sparked envy in the heart of many a medieval cathedral builder. The building was situated by the ocean and was fronted by a massive hemispherical dome standing 180 metres tall. Branching out from it were three tubular arms stretching over the water. Each arm was bordered by an outdoor walkway rich with cafés, restaurants and pubs; inside each arm were more of the same, together with a truly unbelievable number of shops, several hotels, swimming pools, a zoo and an amusement park.

The massive dome had a wedge taken out of it, opening it up to the mild weather of Cape City. All the poshest shops and eateries lined the dome's first four floors. Above them were prestigious office spaces.

In the centre of the ground floor was a tent-like structure suspended from an overhead gantry and a speaker's podium. Facing the tent and podium were several stands full of people pretending to listen to the mayor of Cape City rabbit on about something of great mutual disinterest. Sitting on either side of the mayor were several forgettably important people in the Cape City political scene, as well as Maxwell, who was wondering what would happen if he put a pin to the mayor: would the obese man burst and sputter crazily around the room like a popped balloon, or would he just get really pissed off? Although Maxwell reckoned the latter would most likely be the case, the former notion amused him.

He was just pulling his notebook out of his pocket in order to sketch the idea when he heard a round of applause and looked up to see the tent over the centre platform being raised to a pop song he absolutely hated.

"Lord love a duck. It can't get worse than that," he said to himself, pushing the notebook back in his pocket. In two seconds, he realised he was terribly wrong.

With the tent raised, Maxwell's dancing robots were clearly visible as they moved to the beat of the horrendous pop song. The music was bad enough, but the robots he had painstakingly crafted to display the nude female form in motion had been dressed! Worse, they had been dressed in luridly coloured, frumpy suits designed for aesthetically challenged middle-aged women.

"What on earth has happened to my sculpture?!" Maxwell demanded, standing up.

"What do you mean?" asked the mayor, with a feigned innocence that fooled no one – with possible exception of himself.

"Some tool has put clothes on my figures – and ghastly clothes at that!" said Maxwell, wishing he had brought some light weaponry to the opening. He suspected that if the person responsible for this aesthetic atrocity was here at the opening, shooting him or her could only make the world a better place. It would certainly make Maxwell feel better.

"Why, yes. I authorised the Family Values Association to dress your figures. You didn't think we could allow our children to see naked dancing women, did you?" said the mayor.

"Of course I did, you twisted excuse for man. It was in the proposal I submitted to your predecessor!"

Maxwell was, as a rule, an easy-going chap – too easy, some would argue – but messing with his artwork was one of the few actions guaranteed not merely to provoke his ire, but to piss him off big time.

"There, there now," said the mayor with painfully patronising assurance. "Your sculpture is still very pretty, but now children can safely look at it without being harmed by its pornographic element."

"Harmed? Pornographic element?" Maxwell sputtered. This was just as bad as when he presented a proposal to the city of Topeka (the capital of UESA), he thought.

He was reminded of that irritatingly pious American at his university, the one who had always glared at him and frequently threatened biblical nastiness of the worst order: Phinny Forge. Since then, the man had from time to time tried to sabotage Maxwell's sculptures and reputation, not realising that every time he did so, he created publicity that only helped Maxwell's reputation.

"Yes, yes. You must understand, Maxwell, that here in Cape City, we treasure family values and decency. I guess it's not the same as in Flanders, but we aren't ashamed to have values, you see," said the mayor.

Yes, thought Maxwell. He could sense Phinny's hand in this.

"That raving Reverend Phinny Forge has put you up to this, hasn't he?" Maxwell demanded.

"Who? What? Good Lord, no!" lied the Mayor. "We are quite capable of looking after our own morals here."

"Wendy!" Maxwell shouted, looking for and spotting his friend in a nearby seat. "Bring me a revolver. This man must be shot. At once!"

With this hint of serious violence, the audience gasped. Would there be a shooting, they collectively wondered? About half were hoping in favour and half against.

When Wendy got up and waddled up the to stage, there was another gasp and several guards pulled their guns out of their holsters; but Wendy simply took Maxwell's hand in her wing and walked him off the stage.

"This is not worth dying over," she said to Maxwell as they walked away from the podium. The audience and security guards relaxed. The mayor started babbling again.

"I think it is," said Maxwell.

"What?! You would die because some small-minded human put clothes on your sculpture?"

"Don't be silly," said Maxwell. "It's certainly not worth *my* dying. But the mayor's dying would be very worthwhile. And the...What was it? Fancy Loonies Foundation?"

"Family Values Association," corrected Wendy.

"Whatever. They could readily die. All of them," said Maxwell. "I would gladly help them to do so."

Wendy led Maxwell to the bar.

"Look, they've got Valpolicella. Have a glass – but go easy on it. We've got a long drive tomorrow," she said, pointing to a several bottles and many filled glasses.

Maxwell smiled. He had led an unstable life that resulted in making and losing many friends on Mars, Earth and other planets over the years, but somehow, this particular Tuscany wine had always remained a reliable friend and curative for troubled times.

"Pour me a generous glass, lad," Maxwell said to the young man behind the bar. "My soul has been savagely bruised today and only red wine will save it."

"Yes, sir," the bartender said. "For what it's worth, I think it is shit what they've done to your sculpture."

"You've summed it up remarkably well," said Maxwell, taking the generous glass of Valpolicella and drinking deeply from it.

"And will you have some wine, madam?" the young man asked Wendy.

"We penguins don't drink alcohol, thank you, but some sparkling water would be nice." Then she said to Maxwell, "remember to take it easy on the wine."

Of course, she knew Maxwell better than to expect him actually to heed her advice, but every now and again he surprised her, and she hoped that with some gentle reminders, he would surprise her this evening.

Meanwhile, the mayor hastily wrapped up the ceremony and the crowd slowly made its way to the open bar.

The young man behind the bar handed Maxwell the remainder of the bottle of Valpolicella.

"I think you could use this, sir," he said.

"You will go to Heaven," said Maxwell. "Thank you."

"But you don't believe in Heaven," scolded Wendy.

"It's just an expression," said Maxwell. "Don't get hung up on it."

"That was just appalling. I am so sorry it had to happen to you," said a brunette of about 40 who clearly took her approaching middle age with a disdain that was more than a little sexy. She wore a flowing, low-cut beige dress that showed off her shoulders and revealed just the right amount of cleavage to be interesting, but not enough to be inappropriate.

But her best feature was her smile, highlighted by a twinkle in her left eye, and gentle crinkling under both. She held a half-full glass of red wine, which Maxwell topped up.

"Thank you," said Maxwell. "I've never experienced anything like that before. Aesthetically challenged nincompoops seldom commission sculptures – and as a result never mangle unveilings like that."

"I think you handled it well. I'm sure I would have strangled that idiot mayor if I were you," she said.

"I generally prefer to use weapons to extract revenge. They're more reliable," said Maxwell. "Especially when doing in such a big, round person."

The two of them chatted for a while. However, people began coming up to Maxwell, each wanting to share a word or seven with him. Some wanted to tell him how appalled they were by the dressing of his sculptures. Others suggested he sculpt other things such as cute animals or people with clothes on. Still others wished to demonstrate their self-presumed moral superiority by agreeing with the clothing, albeit not necessarily the chosen clothes.

Indeed, one older woman representing a major clothing brand suggested that there might be opportunities for sponsorship in this situation. But when Maxwell *accidentally* spilled his wine down the front of her elegant dress, she promptly disappeared. He felt badly about the waste of wine, but it was flung in a good cause, he reassured himself.

Amid the commotion, and much to Maxwell's disappointment, the brunette somehow disappeared. He had rather enjoyed talking with her, even though he had already not only forgotten her name, but also forgotten whether or not she had actually introduced herself. Nevertheless, he was determined to seek her out later.

6

Meanwhile, Wendy, who never enjoyed crowds, sat at a quiet table well away from the masses. She was reading the works of Aristotle when a couple of aliens from Zargon came up to her.

In order to visualise this scene properly in your mind, it is important to know that the average Zargonian looks like a heaping bale of hay balanced upon a pair of giant duck's feet. Atop the hay-pile body are several long stalks supporting globular eyes, and on opposite sides of the bale are two long spindly arms with long, spindlier fingers at the end of each.

However, it is usually their eyes that at best grab one's attention and at worst completely freak one out. Any Zargonian has between three and seven eyes, each upon a long, greenish stalk that extends from the top of the hay bale-body. Moreover, the eyes all move and look independently from each other. So, a five-eyed Zargnonian can actually be watching five different things simultaneously – making human multitaskers look like wimps in comparison.

Wendy was unperturbed by Zargonian biology and liked talking science with them, so when the aliens approached her, she looked up in enthusiasm – at least, as much enthusiasm as she could demonstrably muster, which to Zargonian eyes seemed precious little.

One of the Zargonians started speaking. It sounded remarkably like Joan Baez singing a medieval chant of made-up words, but as soon as he started speaking, a small box strapped to his chest began translating.

"I believe you are Wendy Penguin, are you not?"

"Yes, I am."

"It is an honour to meet you, Wendy. I am Lubidada and this is Snox. We are with the Zargonian representation office in Brussels."

"It is a pleasure to meet you," said Wendy.

"And you, Wendy Penguin. My colleagues have said good things about you."

"I am honoured," said Wendy, hoping Lubidada would get to the point soon.

Zargonians were the most advanced alien race known to humans, but they loved ceremony and could rabbit on with pleasantries for hours before coming to a point. Wendy, on the other hand, preferred to get to the point as quickly as possible; ceremony and small talk were an inefficient waste of time as far as she was concerned. Fortunately, she was usually astute enough to keep this opinion to herself.

Meanwhile, people nearby were watching. Denizens of Cape City liked to think they had seen everything and tended to take a nonchalant attitude towards events around them, but Zargonians were seldom seen in public and even less frequently engrossed in conversations with penguins.

Fortunately, Zargonians were held in sufficient awe by humans that said denizens kept their distance.

"We understand you and Maxwell van Mars have recently returned from a space journey to Gateway," said Lubidada, referring to a small black hole orbiting at the very edge of the solar system. Relatively recently discovered by humans – it was, after all, black and tiny by cosmic standards – Gateway was named thus because its gravity well provided a gateway into hyperspace which, in turn, made interstellar travel a piece of cake.

"Yes," said Wendy, wondering why this could be of interest to the Zargonians.

"Moreover, we understand that your spacecraft performed a swing-by of the black hole, in which you came within 6254.3 metres of its Schwarzchild radius."

"Yes, we did a swing-by manoeuvre, but I am not sure of the distance," said Wendy, recalling that one of the standard units of distance measurement for Zargonians was equal to 6254.3 metres.

"It was an incredible manoeuvre," continued Lubidada. "Any closer and your cruiser would have been twisted out of recognition by Gateway's gravity. Instead, you accelerated to a remarkable speed."

"Thank you," said Wendy. "I did the calculations for the swing-by."

"And are you aware that the stress you put on the fabric of spacetime as you performed this manoeuvre caused the fabric of the universe to tear?"

"It was Maxwell who performed the manoeuvre," explained Wendy, who was a stickler for accuracy.

"But tell me, what happened?" Wendy continued.

"As I am sure you know, the gravity well in which Gateway sits already stresses the surrounding space. Your swing-by increased the stress to the point where you tore the fabric of the universe."

Wendy considered this for a moment.

"What are the implications?"

"We are not sure," said Lubidada.

"I see," said Wendy.

"But possibly the end of the universe as we know it."

"What!?" exclaimed Wendy.

"Or possibly nothing at all. We're trying to answer this question now."

"I see," said Wendy, not knowing whether or not to feel relieved.

"You should also know that a few hours after your space cruiser caused the tear, a small object accelerated out of the tear at an incredible speed and is headed for Earth. By our calculations, it should land – or impact – somewhere in Southern Europa in about 18 hours," said Lubidada.

"Lord love a duck!" said Wendy, repeating one of Maxwell's favourite exclamations. "What is it?"

"We have no idea," said Lubidada.

7

Maxwell sat alone at a small table, drinking Valpolicella and looking forlornly at his sculpture. Earlier in the evening, sympathetic people started pulling clothes off the dancers. In response, the more puritanical ones put the removed clothing back on again or put completely different clothing on. A couple of religious freaks placed crosses and bibles on the exhibit – much to the delight of the biblical bookshop in the centre. A few minor scuffles broke out and, as a result, a handful of police officers were now guarding what had become a mockery of Maxwell's original sculpture.

On a more positive note, the dull pop band had been replaced by a jazz band and the music had become distinctly sexy in a saxophone-ish kind of way. The dancing figures on the sculpture had been programmed to dance to whatever background music played, and their sexy, jazzy dancing while half dressed with an absurd array of clothes seemed somehow obscene.

Maxwell took a deep sip and poured himself some more wine. The only positive point to the evening was that the friendly lad behind the bar kept Maxwell well stocked with Valpolicella, though he knew Wendy would not be amused; but she'd understand, he hoped.

While he mused upon this, someone put a soft hand on his shoulder and said with an equally soft voice, "you're looking forlorn there, handsome."

He turned around to face the brunette from earlier in the evening who, thanks to Maxwell's wine consumption, was looking even more attractive now.

"I thought you'd walked out of my life," he said to her.

"Well, I've walked right back in again, haven't I?" she said.

"Jolly decent of you," he said.

"I thought so," she said.

"But it was jolly indecent of you to walk out on me earlier."

"Walk out on you?!"

"Yes. Inconsiderate to say the least. I thought we had the beginnings of a beautiful relationship going there."

"I didn't walk out on you. You were mobbed by adoring fans and forgot about me!"

"Adoring fans and raving lunatics, with too many of the latter. But, I didn't forget about you, darling, I assure you."

"Then what's my name?" she asked.

"What, have you forgotten? That is worrying," he said.

"I haven't forgotten. I've used it all my life. I'm used to it. But you've forgotten it, haven't you?"

"I don't think you've ever told me your name."

"Now you are trying to pin the blame on me!"

"Precisely where it belongs. And don't think you can wriggle out of this one."

The brunette wriggled her body from head to foot and winked at Maxwell.

"Okay, perhaps you can," he acknowledged.

Just then, a couple of women in matching short, black dresses walked hand in hand up to the brunette and said, "hey, Lucy. We're going back to the hotel. Want to join us?"

Lucy looked at Maxwell and the girls.

"No, I think I'll stay here a bit longer. He's more entertaining than he looks," she said, pointing at him.

The women looked Maxwell over.

"Not bad, I suppose. Though I'd not have thought he was your type," said one of them. "Anyway, we'll probably have a drink in the hotel bar. Join us if you're not late." The women each kissed

Lucy and Maxwell on their respective cheeks before heading out of the centre and into the night.

"Lucy," said Maxwell.

"Yes," said Lucy.

"I knew it."

"No, you didn't."

"You are a very obstinate young woman, Lucy."

"No, I'm not!"

"And you've got beautiful lips."

"What?"

"I said, you've got beautiful lips."

"That's cute. I'll have to try that one day," said Lucy.

"I'm sure I don't know what you mean," said Maxwell.

"Oh, I think you know precisely what I mean. I should warn you: you're wasting your time. I swing the other way."

"What?"

"I'm a lesbian. I prefer girls over boys."

"Well, so do I! Clearly, we've got a great deal in common, Lucy."

"Um, maybe. But it doesn't really work from a mutual compatibility perspective, does it?" Lucy said.

"Don't be a nitpicker," said Maxwell.

"I am not nitpicking," said Lucy.

"It's no wonder you haven't got a partner if you are always fussing about trivial details," said Maxwell.

"Trivial details! I hardly think one's sexual preference is a trivial detail," said Lucy. "Anyway, who says I haven't got a partner?"

"It's obvious," said Maxwell.

"Why?"

"Because you are such a nitpicker."

"Now you are talking in circles."

"There you go. Nitpicking again. You've really got to drop this habit if you want to form a lasting, meaningful relationship."

"Is that what you have in mind, Maxwell? A lasting, meaningful relationship?"

"At the moment, I confess that I am thinking more about kissing and sex, but I don't want to rule anything out for the long term."

"You're funny."

"You are too, Lucy. See. There's something else we have in common. With so much in common, I think we have all the ingredients for a great relationship."

"Except that I am a lesbian and you are not a woman."

"Goodness! There you again. Now look, sweetheart: every relationship requires some compromise and sacrifice on each party's part. In our case, one of us is going to have to make a sacrifice in the sexual preference department. Under the circumstances, that person is going to have to be you. I wish it didn't have to be this way. Really. But I don't see how we can get around it."

Lucy laughed.

"Okay. Kiss me, then."

Maxwell kissed Lucy on the lips, where he was startlingly well received.

"No. Sorry. That wasn't good enough."

"Not good enough!?" Maxwell said in indignation.

"Girls kiss much better."

"I thought that was awfully good. You certainly tasted nice."

"Of course, but I'm a girl. Have you ever kissed a boy?"

"No, can't say that I've had the pleasure."

"It's no pleasure. Men just don't have such warm lips as women. Let's dance instead."

"Okay," said Maxwell, topping up their glasses again. His optimism about spending the night with Lucy had decreased significantly and he was now worried about his kissing skill, something he had – until very recently – taken pride in.

He had long held that every great seduction starts with a great kiss. Nevertheless, he couldn't deny that he enjoyed Lucy's company, which was more than he could say about everyone else at this bash. Under such circumstances, alcohol-fuelled dancing with an attractive woman seemed a decent alternative.

Lucy took Maxwell's hand and led him to the dance floor.

The night raged on.

The saxophonist was going wild with dirty, growling, sexy music and the band followed him with enthusiastic expertise. The interior lights had been dimmed. Shadowy people danced on the floor with wild abandon. Others sat at tables, drinking, talking, kissing, laughing.

Over time, the lights seemed to spin, the saxophone entered their heads and laughing, smiling, serious and crying faces appeared and disappeared into the crowd. The smell of human sweat mingled with perfume, wine, beer and fresh seafood. People came and went. The music played. People danced. It was crazy. Insane. Wild. As it can only be when the people of Cape City let loose on a glorious spring evening.

After much dancing, Valpolicella and dancing. Lucy made a decision. She took Maxwell by the hand and they stumbled, danced and walked back to his hotel. She had not slept with a man in years. She was curious. She hoped she was not making a mistake.

She was.

8

Long, long after midnight, Maxwell awoke with a raging headache, a queasiness that spoke of overindulgence and a great need to urinate. He opened his eyes and saw Lucy in bed next to him. Strewn across the floor were their clothes, two women who were either dead or unconscious,numerous empty wine bottles; two empty tequila bottles, a few hypodermic syringes, a smouldering something-or-other and some fresh fruit, presumably from the complimentary fruit bowl that had been on one of the tables.

"Fruit. It's always causing trouble," Maxwell mumbled to himself as he made his way carefully to the bathroom. Stepping over one of the bodies of dubious aliveness, Maxwell recognised it as belonging to one of the two the girls who had spoken to Lucy earlier. He hoped she was still alive. She seemed a nice enough lass during their 15-second encounter. Worse, if she had died in this room, the police would doubtless be around asking embarrassing questions. Well, it could wait till morning, thought Maxwell. If she was dead now, that wouldn't much change over the next few hours.

He found the bathroom door and stumbled in.

While peeing, he heard a muffled sound not unlike glass breaking.

"I hope that's not me," Maxwell said to himself with some worry as he checked his urinating penis. Fortunately, it seemed not to be emitting the sounds.

He flushed, washed his hands, opened the door and walked out to see an athletically slender woman in a black tracksuit topped off with a nun's habit. The woman was, of course, one of Phineas's ninja nuns. In a nano-instant, she reached behind her back and flung a metal disk with blades around its perimeter at Maxwell, who was so startled by the unexpected guest that he tripped and fell on top of one of the girls on the floor, causing her to scream at the same time as the disk shattered the bathroom mirror.

"Thank goodness you're still alive," said Maxwell, laying half on top of the screaming girl, with the bed between them and the ninja nun. "Though, I wouldn't be too sure about maintaining that status for long under the circumstances."

Maxwell struggled to right himself and debated whether Lucy was worth rescuing. Attempting to do so could very well cost him his life. Making matters worse, he couldn't remember whether the previous night would be worth dying for. Before he could make a decision, he heard a feminine "oh, poop!" as another disk bounced off the ceiling and the far wall. Hazarding a glimpse over the bed, he saw that the nun had slipped on a plum. Clearly, he had mis-judged the fruit, Maxwell thought.

"Cindy! Let's get the fuck out of here," said one of the girls to the other, as they scrambled to get up while remaining behind the bed.

"Do be careful," said Maxwell. "The lass in black has some an-ger management issues, it seems."

"I don't care about them," said the ninja nun. "They can go. It is you who must be expedited to Hell, Maxwell."

"Me?"

"Yes!"

"Have we met?" asked Maxwell, who crouched behind the bed while the two girls scrambled out of the room. He had pissed off more than a few women in his life, but he did not reckon the lass in black was one of them.

"No, but I know of your evil reputation," said the ninja nun.

"I'm touched that you know me, sweetheart, but I think I'd rather take my time going to Hell, if you don't mind," said Maxwell.

"That is not an option," said the ninja nun, hopping gracefully onto the bed that separated them. "God has willed that you must die," she continued as she stepped forward slowly.

For a ninja nun, she was not terribly observant. Not only had she failed to notice the plum a moment earlier, but she also didn't see Lucy, who was buried under the blankets.

However, Lucy was well aware of the nun and grabbed her leg as she moved across the bed. The nun tottered for a moment, then fell on top of Lucy.

"Holy Mother of God! There is another woman in here, and she is naked!" exclaimed the ninja nun on top of Lucy. "I have never seen such a vile den of iniquity!"

Meanwhile, Lucy stretched her head up and kissed the nun on the lips.

The nun, initially surprised by a tactic that she had not been taught to respond to at the convent, pulled her head away, but Lucy reached up, put her hands around the nun's head and pulled it gently towards her. She kissed the nun again. The nun pushed back half-heartedly, but only for a moment before she let herself fall onto Lucy and kiss her back with passion.

The ninja nun, you see, had never received much affection in her life. Moreover, she had been taught that men were evil and wo-men virtuous. So, when a woman kissed her with passion, the nun felt a flow of what she could only assume was love towards the woman in the bed. In fact, it was repressed lust combined with a lot of adrenaline.

Had a man kissed her, she would have known how to react. In-deed, any man trying such a stunt could at best have expected to see several important bits of his body sliced off within nano-seconds. Then the nun would have got nasty – very nasty.

But thanks to the naiveté of her trainer, this ninja nun had no preparation for dealing with a seductive lesbian. Moreover, following a life of being told that she was loved only by a rather cold, heartless Jesus – who seemed to spend most of his time either as a babe in Mother Mary's arms or hanging painfully from a cross to which he had been nailed, and who never personally acknowledged his love for her, let alone offered to hold hands – the nun felt a flow of loving passion towards the soft, warm woman who had kissed her. She returned the kiss with as much naïve passion as she could muster.

Maxwell thought briefly, very briefly, about suggesting a threesome, before deciding instead to disappear. He grabbed what clothes he saw on the floor and dashed out into the hall. As he did so, he saw a familiar moustache poorly decorating the face of an even more familiar preacher. Beside him was another nun in a black tracksuit who was in the disturbing process of throwing a spear in Maxwell's general direction. Fortunately, for Maxwell anyway, the nun had never seen a naked man before and the sight of one distracted her sufficiently to put off her aim by just enough arcseconds to ensure the spear missed Maxwell by a centimetre and a half.

"Lord love a duck, Phinny," Maxwell shouted. "Are you trying to kill me again?"

"Why yes, Maxwell, I am," said the preacher. "And, please: it's Phineas now."

"Surely you can find something more productive to do with your time," said Maxwell, dashing across the hall to the door opposite his, which, if memory served – and under the circumstances he desperately hoped that it did – was Wendy's.

"With you burning in Hell, I can be so much more productive, Maxwell." Then, looking at the nun, he said more quietly, "be sure to kill him this time, Sister."

"Yes, Father," she said, pulling another spear from the quiver strapped to her back.

Realising that this was not the sort of nun who would miss

twice in a row, Maxwell flattened himself into the doorway just as he heard a whizzing sound, which was followed by a stinging pain in his back and the clear thunk of a spear penetrating wood panelling with considerably more force than one might credit a slender nun being able to muster.

At the same time, the door opened and Maxwell somersaulted into the room, dropping the clothes along the way and coming to a halt at Wendy's feet.

"I say, Wendy, I think I'm in a spot of bother," he said to his avian friend.

"Let me see: naked, flesh wound across the back, clothes all over the floor and weapons being flung down the hall. I would say 'spot of bother' is an understatement, Maxwell."

"Yes, you could say that," said Maxwell, pulling himself up. "In fact, we may need to wing it with more than a little urgency."

"That's very inconvenient just now," said Wendy.

"I am sorry about that, but there seems to be a team of particularly twisted and violent nuns hell-bent on doing me in. And, as if that was not bad enough, Phinny Forge appears to be involved, too."

"You really need to plan these things better, Maxwell. You know I don't like sudden changes of plan."

"I didn't actually plan this."

"I know. That's the problem."

Maxwell started pulling the clothes on and was pleased to see that he had trousers, shirt and jacket, which was a good start. He was missing his socks and shoes, but seemed to have come out a bra ahead. While he was puzzling over the bra, wondering whether it was Lucy's or one of the other lasses who had been in the room, he heard an odd musical sound.

"Oh, my! Is that a new Joan Baez album? It sounds like she's doing medieval chanting."

"No. There are two Zargonians here. You've interrupted our

discussions."

"Oh, of course. They really do sound uncannily like Joan Baez."

This tangential bit of conversation was interrupted by a loud banging on the door, reminding Maxwell that he had not popped round Wendy's room in the middle of the night for idle chit-chat – and, indeed, if he was not careful, he'd never have an idle chit-chat opportunity again.

"You'll have to say your goodbyes. Wendy. We've got to leave before they kill me," said Maxwell.

"I can't do that, Maxwell. We're in the middle of a serious discussion about a tear in the fabric of the universe."

"A what?"

"The Zargonians tell me that we tore the fabric of the universe during our space journey."

"What? Really?"

"Yes. When we did that slingshot manoeuvre around Gateway, it stressed the fabric of spacetime in the gravity well and resulted in the tear."

"And is it serious?" asked Maxwell.

"We don't know. Potentially, it could destroy the universe as we know it, or it might not have any consequences."

"It's probably nothing. It's a big old universe. Surely it gets torn and battered on a regular basis. I wouldn't worry about it. So, let's go. Okay?"

"I don't think so, Maxwell. What's more important? The entire universe and every living being on it or your life?"

"I rather think my life," said Maxwell, without giving it much thought.

"That's not logical. If the entire universe as we know it is destroyed, you will be destroyed too. So, in either case, your life is limited, but in the second option, we can save everyone else."

Wham! The door shuddered at some impact from the other

side.

"Does the second option involve myself and everyone else perishing in the next very few minutes?" asked Maxwell.

Wendy thought for a moment. "Admittedly not."

"Then let us focus, briefly, on my preservation."

Wendy considered once again.

"Okay. I guess we can do that," she said.

"What is happening here, if I may ask, Wendy?" asked Lubidada, who had just walked over to the front hall where Wendy and Maxwell had been talking. "Oh, you must be the famous Maxwell van Mars."

"Pleased to meet you," said Maxwell, half dressed, bowing slightly.

"I, Lubidada of Zargon, am pleased to meet you also, Maxwell."

Wham!

"What is going on out there?" asked the Zargonian, reaching for the door handle.

"I really wouldn't recommend opening..." began Maxwell, but he was too late. The alien had already opened the door to find a ninja nun standing there and holding an axe behind her head with the intention of swinging it at the door again. Sadly, for her anyway, her training had focused on killing humans, and especially men, in numerous creative ways. She had been taught how to get out of just about any sticky situation a ninja nun might find herself facing – and there are a surprisingly large number of such situations.

However, neither her training nor her provincial upbringing had prepared her for coming face to face with a living and breathing Zargonian. Moreover, this being her first real mission, it had been a stressful day with insufficient sleep. So, no one could really blame the poor thing for promptly passing out in front of Lubidada.

Phineas, who had been standing behind the nun, looked down at her and drawled, "I need to find me a better class of nun. These girls aren't worth a hill of beans."

He then looked up at the alien standing before him. He had seen aliens before, albeit not often. In spite the Earth's having been visited by numerous alien races in recent years, not a single such race had expressed the slightest interest in becoming a Christian – or indeed a follower of any religion.

Shortly after the first aliens visited the Earth, the evangelicals had invested in heavy marketing in hopes of winning entire planets of converts. It was money wasted. More frustratingly, threats of burning in Hell for all eternity also failed to sway a single alien towards the church.

Initially, the more militant atheists embraced the aliens' complete lack of religious interest. Indeed, many attempts were made to include the aliens in anti-religious YouTube clips – but the aliens politely declined and showed no more interest in the atheists than in any religious group.

The reason that aliens as a whole had no interest in religion or lack thereof was that they simply and entirely failed to understand what the big deal was.

To give an example, on the planet Flitra, many members of its intelligent species are into *krufling*, a certain way of visualising geometric shapes in nature. Others are entirely against krufling, claiming that it corrupts the mind and leads to genetic issues that could affect the family line for future generations. Kruflers have been known to kill non-kruflers simply for their lack of krufling – and vice versa. However, to most humans, this all seems downright silly. This is how religion seems to most non-humans.

All of which is a long way to say that it took Phineas a few seconds to compose himself before the alien. Composure complete, he extended his hand and said, "I am pleased to meet you, sir. I am OOOF!"

The "ooof" was not the result of a curious name-change or alias on the reverend's part. Rather, it was the sound Phineas made as Wendy's head crashed into his abdomen, knocking him to the floor. The reverend downed, Wendy and Maxwell ran down the corridor towards the lift.

"Sorry, Lubidada, but we have to run. It is a life-and-death situation. I'll be in touch," shouted Wendy.

Lubidada watched them run away as his companion Snox came to the door and asked, in Zargonese, "what happened?"

"I am not sure. Perhaps we should have offered her a drink. Apparently it is something humans often do. Perhaps penguins are similar."

"Surely that would not have caused her to flee."

"What if she was dehydrated?"

"That could be. We must remember this for next time we meet with penguins – or humans."

Meanwhile, Phineas struggled to his feet and exclaimed, "Damn it to hell! They ran out on me. Did you all see which way they went?"

Lubidada started to answer, but Snox interrupted him before he could speak, to say, "no, Mr Ooof, we did not."

"Damn it," said Phineas again. "And what the hell happened to you, Sister?" he asked the nun at his feet, who was just now coming around.

The Zargonians gently shut the damaged door. Snox said, "I do not think it was a lack of drink that sent Wendy and Maxwell away. I think it was that strange man. He smelled funny."

"He did, indeed," said Lubidada.

In the corridor, Phineas shouted, "to the cars, Sisters! I believe he is attempting to flee."

9

Cape City is a place for wild partying late into the night, so at a few minutes before five on a Monday morning, the lobby of a hotel like the Splendouria was understandably quiet. A few groggy businesspeople in suits were checking out in order to catch early flights. Other groggy businesspeople in disgruntled suits and a few partying tourists were crawling back to their hotel rooms following a naughty night out on the town. Nevertheless, the staff of the Splendouria were sharply dressed, combed and smiling as if the hour – and their guests – were more civilised.

Amidst this typical hotel morningness, Maxwell dashed out of the lift and into the lobby. He, of course, looked curiously dishevelled, with long hair standing out in all directions and no shoes on his feet. Fortunately, society grants artists more latitude in dress than businesspeople, and Maxwell's reputation was well enough known that he suffered no more than a couple of jealously knowing smirks from men in suits and intrigued glances from women in more feminine suits.

Seeing an unoccupied clerk at the long, polished, wooden registration desk, Maxwell walked over to the young man in question.

"We need to check out in rather a hurry, lad," explained Maxwell, handing his key card over.

"Yes, sir," said the young man.

"Can you also put the penguin on my account?"

"Which penguin, sir?"

"This penguin," said Maxwell looking to his side, where he expected to see Wendy. Instead he saw only marble floor.

"What a lousy time to loose a penguin."

"Sir?"

Fortunately, Wendy waddled over to Maxwell before he had to explain fortuitous and non-fortuitous times for mislaying one's penguin, a discussion he did not relish, particularly in view of his current life-threatening circumstances.

"Is this the penguin you are referring to, sir?" asked the clerk.

"Yes, I trust it is," said Maxwell. "Put her bill on my card, please."

"Of course, sir."

"And there may be a few women in various states of undress in my room."

"Sir?"

"It's not what it seems," said Maxwell.

"Of course not, sir."

"It's far worse."

"I'm sorry to hear that, sir."

"No worries, lad. It's not your concern. But could you have room service send them up a breakfast feast? I feel badly about their near slaughter earlier."

"Sir?" asked the clerk, raising his left eyebrow some distance.

"Look, young man, I don't have time to go into the details. I've really got to run. Just put the breakfast and any damages on my credit card, tally it all up and email me the receipt so I can scare my accountant."

"Of course, sir."

"It's a good idea to scare one's accountant from time to time. Keeps them on their toes, you know."

"Of course, sir."

"Now, if we're all done here, I am going to skedaddle."

"Of course, sir. Thank you for staying at the Splendouria and have a good trip."

"Thank you." Maxwell started to walk to the stairway door

when he stopped and turned around. "Oh, by the way. There's a man upstairs with a monster moustache. I understand he is in the habit of stealing towels. You may want to check him out carefully before he leaves."

"Of course, sir."

"Toodle-oo, then."

"Good-bye, sir."

Walking more quickly to the door, Maxwell said to Wendy, "let's get out of here. I'm amazed that Phinny and his new girl-friends haven't burst into the lobby yet."

"Probably because I jammed the lifts," said Wendy. "I think they were inside a couple of them."

"So that's where you were," said Maxwell.

"Yes, that's where I was," said Wendy.

"You've jammed the lifts, you say?"

"Yes, I did. All of them."

"Remarkable! How did you do that?" asked Maxwell

"I accessed the lift software in the lift we took down. It was a simple matter of locking down the system."

"You are a wonder," said Maxwell.

"I know," said Wendy. The two of them dashed down four levels of stairs to the underground car park and found the Bentley waiting patiently. They hopped in, Maxwell put the key in the igni-tion and the massive old engine fired up with enthusiasm.

As Maxwell backed the car out, Mrs Miller lighted up.

"Hello, Maxwell. Where would you like to go today?"

"You're sounding rather sprightly for this hour, Mrs Miller," Maxwell said, putting the car into gear and steering his way through the car park and up the winding exit ramp.

"That does not sound like a destination," said the GPS.

"It's not. Take us home, please, Mrs Miller," said Maxwell.

"Calculating."

"Please do."

As the car exited the car park, Mrs Miller advised a left turn – advice Maxwell readily followed. At this hour of gently approaching dawn, the streets were quiet. Shops and restaurants were largely closed. Only the odd car disturbed the photo-like stillness. Maxwell accelerated the ancient Bentley up to a speed considerably, but not ridiculously, above the limit, and raced down the thoroughfare. The Waterfront quickly shrank in the rear-view mirror.

After a few moments, Mrs Miller announced, "take ramp right to North-South Highway." Maxwell acquiesced and steered the old Bentley down the spiralling ramp in question.

In his desire to put as much distance as possible between himself and Phineas's gang of nuns, Maxwell pressed the accelerator pedal flat to the floor. The engine roared in delight, the automatic gearbox down-shifted with enthusiasm and the wheels squealed with verve.

At least initially. As the entry ramp spiralled around to the highway and Maxwell accelerated above and beyond the call of sensibility, the wheels' squeals went from verve to panic as centrifugal force felt obliged to do its duty.

The rear wheels lost their grip, causing the back end of the car to drift away from the centre of the ramp. In response, Maxwell flung the steering wheel in the opposite direction and the huge car screeched around the ramp at an insane speed, its tail end flailing behind. Somehow, he managed to keep the car from spinning out and even brought it under control, but as soon as he had done so, he saw a battered old pickup truck puttering along at barely more than jogging pace in front of them. Right in front of them. Getting closer. Impact seemed imminent and Maxwell barely had control of the careening Bentley as it was.

Hoping that the ramp straightened out where he thought it would, Maxwell twisted the steering wheel further into the turn, sending the car skidding towards the concrete wall on the inside of the curve. Then, just before impact seemed imminent, he let the steering wheel recentre itself, manually downshifted and pressed the accelerator deeper into the plushly carpeted floor.

The car seemed as though it would slam sideways into the wall, but as good fortune would have it, the road straightened out and the wall disappeared. The Bentley hit the hard shoulder on the right side of the truck, shuddered as it did so, and fired forward, missing the truck by a few millimetres. A twitch of the steering wheel put the car back on the road and the tuck quickly disappeared in the rear-view mirror.

"Whew!" said Maxwell.

"Are you crazy!?" exclaimed Wendy. "You nearly got us killed!"

"I have heard rumours regarding my sanity – or lack of it – but I don't take them seriously," said Maxwell. "More importantly, we are still alive. Therefore, I have not got us killed!"

"And that's no way to drive an elegant old car like this," continued Wendy.

"What do you mean?"

"Racing around the entry ramp at such a speed. It's not dignified."

"Relax, old girl. It's a Bentley, not a Rolls Royce."

"Continue for 765 kilometres," said Mrs Miller.

Wendy sighed, then reached behind her seat and found the Nietzsche book she had been reading.

Once on the highway, the road was relatively straight and largely untrafficked. Maxwell continued to accelerate while selecting Bach's Brandenburg Concertos on the car's sound system.

On the smooth, gently winding road, the plush interior and sumptuous leather upholstery of the well-maintained Bentley made the car feel like a cosy sitting room – albeit one that was racing along at a steady 180 kilometres per hour.

Little traffic and long, clear roads meant that within a few hours they were able to put many, many kilometres between themselves and Cape City. As they did so, the landscape slowly evolved from urban to suburban to hilly countryside, and stayed like that for a long time, but it was not monotonous countryside by any means. The hills were rich in varied, multicoloured vegetation. Dotted along the road were massive stone statues. Clearly inspired by Salvador Dali, Yves Tanguy and René Magritte, the sculptures comprised a perverse mixture of human bodies, organic shapes, mysterious little creatures and animal heads that stared thoughtfully upon the road or into some mysterious point on distant horizon. From time to time, the scenery was disturbed by a town or village, some alive with dancing and festivals, some dead with empty shells of houses in near tears of lonely disrepair. Clouds racing overhead and the synchronised bending of trees were evidence of the strong wind, though it was neither heard nor felt inside the plush car.

Thinking about the incredible scenery, which he believed had become even more incredible since last he drove this route, Maxwell asked Wendy: "have you noticed that the world seems more surreal these days?"

"I can't say that I have," she said thoughtfully. "In fact, it could not be getting more surreal," she added after a moment's reflection.

"No?"

"No. Surreality must always be a reaction to realism or reality. If reality is changing, then what used to be surreal becomes real. Surrealism then needs to change to take the newer, stranger reality into account and respond to it with a new surrealism," said Wendy.

"So, you are saying that reality becomes more like what used to be surreality and surrealism just gets weirder?" asked Maxwell.

"That would be one way of putting it," Wendy agreed.

"And presumably, if it were the case that the nature of reality is changing, we conceivably might not notice this change as a result of being a part of that reality."

"Perhaps," said Wendy, trying to follow Maxwell's logic, always a dangerous pursuit.

They rode on in silence for a moment or two before Maxwell continued.

"Hmm. I wonder..."

"That's not unusual," said Wendy.

"That tear in the fabric of the universe you mentioned earlier..."

"Yes?"

"Is it possible that one consequence of the tear could have been a fundamental change in reality?" asked Maxwell.

Wendy considered this. "I suppose it's possible."

"And if that were the case, is it not likely that because we are an integral part of that reality, we would not notice the change even if it was a radical change?"

"How so?" asked Wendy.

"For instance, the entire world might have changed. The way people look. The landscape. Even the language we speak. Conceivably, all of these things could have changed, but because they are a part of our fundamental reality, our memories of these things would have changed along with our reality, and we would never notice."

Wendy contemplated this. "I suppose that's possible. But if it were not possible to detect this change, it effectively hasn't happened. This is our reality now, irrespective of what that reality might have been a few days ago."

"Good point. We might as well enjoy it, eh, Wendy?"

"Yes."

Wendy returned her attention to the book and Maxwell concentrated on driving up a winding mountain road. Having learned his lesson earlier, he reduced speed to a point where the tyres only occasionally squealed and, even then, not too loudly.

The road straightened out again and they continued in silence for some time. That was fine. They were comfortable with each other and neither was much into small talk.

As he drove, Maxwell thought back to the time when he and Wendy first met. It was in the bio-research dome in the Martian colony. He had recently returned home from Cape City University and, in theory anyway, was meant to be learning the family business which, legally speaking, was major shareholdings and directorships in the Martian Mining Company and several hundred associated companies registered on Mars, Earth and Titan (the moon of Saturn, which over the previous fifty years had become the Solar System's favourite off-planet tax haven). In practice, this meant that the family owned the Martian colony.

As eldest child, Maxwell was the family scion and one day, his father should have told him, this would all be his. But, in fact, Father was far too busy attending meetings and seducing administrative assistants to be bothered lecturing his son with clichés. He paid nannies and tutors to do that kind of thing.

On the day in question, Maxwell was supposed to receive a tour of the biological and genetic research facilities on the colony. However, an unfortunate incident involving carelessness with a hypodermic syringe had turned an otherwise quiet and studious young intern into an enraged flesh-eating zombie intent on having a couple of humans for lunch. Not surprisingly, the biological and genetic research facilities director, who should have been showing Maxwell around, had to deal with the intern-zombie before it caused more damage. To make matters worse, two of the researchers the intern-zombie had started to nibble on were showing signs of becoming zombies themselves.

As a result, Maxwell was tossed into the "Innovation Room", a casually fun room packed with beanbag chairs, low tables, lots of toys, a decent stereo system and an even-more-decent espresso maker. It was a room where lab employees were expected to relax, play and be innovative.

Of course, stubborn lab workers hated being told where to innovate and so the room had fallen into disuse for some time until it was discovered by Wendy, the reclusive, hyper-intelligent kairuku penguin who had been raised in the lab. She found it to be a comfortable and quiet place in which to read and reflect in peace, the sort of place that was difficult to find in the crowded, loud and claustrophobic environment of a hermetically sealed off-Earth colony.

When Maxwell was scuttled into the room, Wendy was reading *Bakunin on Anarchism*. She looked up at him briefly, then returned to the book.

"Lord love a duck!" he said. "Are you really reading Bakunin?"

"I am not a duck. I am a penguin," she replied matter-of-factly. "And yes, I am reading Bakunin's tome on anarchy."

"That's rather heavy going for a bird, isn't it?" said Maxwell rather tactlessly.

"It's not bad, though the translation is a bit stilted at times."

"That's what I thought. In fact, it was so stilted I don't think I finished it," said Maxwell.

Wendy said nothing and they sat quietly for a few moments.

"It's rather anarchic out there," said Maxwell pointing to the door, where muffled shouts and screams could be heard. "Reminds me of some of the more depraved parties I've been to."

Wendy looked at Maxwell politely and continued reading.

"Do you get out much?" Maxwell asked.

"No."

"And have you ever been to a depraved party?"

"No."

"Really? We can't have that. You're a full-grown penguin, are you not?"

"Yes, I am."

"Well, then you are overdue for a depraved party."

"I'm not sure I'd like that. We penguins prefer structure and order over depravity and," she glanced at her book, "anarchy. Anyway, I am not much of a people penguin."

Gun shots were heard outside the Innovation Room, followed by a brief cheer.

"You'll never know whether or not you like depravity unless you give it a try," said Maxwell.

"That's true, I guess," said Wendy uncertainly.

"Groovy. I'm off to a moderately depraved party this evening. It would make for a relatively safe introduction to the world of decadent fun for you. Why don't I come fetch you at eight?"

"Okay," said Wendy, returning her concentration to the book.

Outside a loud thwack, sounding remarkably like a fire axe chopping a zombie's head off, could be heard. A moment later, the director returned. There was a tiny bit of blood splatter on the left side of his suit.

"Sorry, Mr Maxwell," he said. "Are you ready to continue?"

"Yes, let's," said Maxwell. Then he turned to Wendy. "It's been a pleasure meeting you."

"You haven't met me. We haven't introduced ourselves," said the penguin, a stickler for details.

"I am sorry. How rude of me. My name's Maxwell."

"I know. Mine is Wendy."

Maxwell extended his hand. Wendy cautiously extended her wing. Maxwell took it gently and shook.

"See you tonight," he said.

"Okay," said Wendy.

The director led Maxwell out of the Innovation Room.

"The vaccination labs are a mess, I'm afraid. I hope you don't mind if we skip those today," he said.

"No worries," said Maxwell, who would have been quite happy to have skipped the entire tour. He had no interest in the family business, had already inherited enough money to live a life of lavish irresponsibility and was, in any event, already making a name for himself as a sculptor. Nevertheless, out of a sense of familial responsibility, he feigned interest in the labs and the work being done there before popping off for pre-party drinks.

Much to the distress of Wendy's sense of precision in promises, Maxwell arrived fashionably later than the promised eight o'clock. He took her to the party, which, as she anticipated, she did not much enjoy. However, Maxwell found that having a penguin in tow was an effective means of getting the attention of the opposite sex and exploited the situation by talking loudly with Wendy whenever he saw someone he wanted to impress, something that happened with increasing frequency as Maxwell drank more.

By the time they left the party, which was a couple of hours after Wendy would have preferred to leave, the labs were locked down for the night, so Maxwell brought Wendy to his suite, which happened to be in the same residential dome as the party venue. There, Wendy promptly fell in love with his substantial library and spent the night browsing books rather than sleeping.

She soon became a regular visitor to Maxwell's suite. The two of them quickly developed an intellectual affection and over time became inseparable. Indeed, had they been of the same species, it would doubtless have been remarked that they were like brother and sister.

It was while these thoughts rolled through Maxwell's head that a skunk darted into the road. Maxwell's mind promptly returned to the present as he swerved the car abruptly, avoiding the animal, but distracting Wendy from her reading for a moment.

"Sorry about that," said Maxwell.

Wendy blinked at Maxwell, her way of acknowledging the apology.

They drove on as the sun rose higher in the sky. The car raced past trees, unusual rock formations, various stone buildings and an angel hitch-hiking.

10

Lubidada and Snox were doing the Zargonian equivalent of gossiping when a flashing light appeared on what, to a human eye, would have looked like a sheet or laminated paper. Snox picked it up and looked at it with one eye while her other eyes remained attentive to Lubidada.

"Excuse me," she said, interrupting Lubidada's story involving a misunderstanding between the Zargonian ambassador to Europa and her human driver, which had resulted in an expensive escort coming to a dinner party in a nurse's costume.

Lubidada knew his companion would not interrupt him over a trivial matter and was not offended. "Yes?"

"The object that came out of the tear is approaching Earth and is decelerating quickly. It looks like it will land a couple hundred kilometres north of here. Take a look."

Snox showed Lubidada the sheet of paper, which displayed a topological map of Southern Europa and a dot representing the object.

"Interesting. Do we have a reading on it?"

"It seems to be a mixture of a carbon composite and organic material."

"I wonder..." said Lubidada thoughtfully.

"Yes?" asked Snox.

"I believe Wendy and Maxwell are headed north," said Lubidada.

"Do you think the object might be targeting them? Perhaps for tearing the fabric of the universe?" said Snox.

"It's possible, though it might also be a message, or maybe it's simply following them," said Lubidada.

"Or it could be a coincidence," said Snox

"Indeed. Oops! Where did it go?" asked Lubidada, for the object had disappeared from the screen.

Snox tried to find the object again without success.

"Curious. It was still 300 metres in the air when it disappeared."

"Could it have blown up?"

Snox queried the screen. "There's no evidence of that," she said. "It seems to have faded away."

"Curious," said Lubidada.

11

"I say, Wendy," said Maxwell, glancing in the Bentley's rear-view mirror.

"So it seems," said Wendy. "But what precisely do you say?"

"I believe we've just passed a hitch-hiking angel."

Wendy craned her head around and looked out the back window.

"I cannot make out what that was. Are you sure it was an angel? You had a wild night last night and have an hyperactive imagination at the best of times."

"I believe it was, but there's only one way to find out," said Maxwell as he slammed his foot on the brake and yanked the steering wheel around to full lock. The large car executed a perfect 180-degree turn leaving an arc of rubber on the road. For half an instant, the car was swayed, like a boat on a stormy lake, as it re-established its orientation with gravity. Then Maxwell accelerated more slowly back down the road.

"There you go again!" said Wendy.

"Where?" asked Maxwell.

"Driving the Bentley insanely," said Wendy.

"It's a tough old car. It likes it," said Maxwell.

"Recalculating," said Mrs Miller, who had been keeping to herself since they got on the highway, but apparently now wanted to get in on the conversation.

Maxwell slowed the car as they approached the hitch-hiker. On closer examination, she looked like a skinny teen with the face of a woman in her 20s and eyes of an incredible sky blue. She had high cheekbones and dirty blonde hair that was unkempt, yet clean.

However, it was the massive wings extending from her shoulder blades that gave her an edge of distinction over the typical hitch-hiking student. They were not the feathered bird wings of the typical angel one runs across on biblical paintings; rather, they were much more like bat wings, composed of soft angel skin stretched elegantly across long, graceful bones. They were oddly sensual.

The angel wore a white linen sack dress that billowed in the ever-present wind. It reached nearly to her feet, had three-quarter length sleeves and an open front that would have revealed her cleavage had she any to reveal.

"Where are you headed?" Maxwell asked her.

"To Hell," she replied in a soft, seductive French accent.

"I believe I am headed broadly in that direction as well," said Maxwell. "Hop in."

The angel climbed into the back seat of the Bentley. "Nice car," she said.

"But he drives it without respect," said Wendy.

12

Phineas was packed into a downward-inching lift with seven some-what sweaty, highly charged young ninja nuns. The sweet odour of the women threatened to arouse Phineas, a feeling that did not sit at all well with his vow of celibacy. The firm buttocks of one nun pressed against his leg, dangerously close to his manhood, made matters worse. Like many a prude, he channelled his growing sexual arousal into anger, something he found easier to deal with.

"In the name of God, why is this elevator so slow? Maxwell will be miles away by the time we get to our cars."

"Are you sure he's gone for his car, Father? Maybe he is hiding in the hotel or in Cape City," said one of the nuns in a voice Phineas was trying not to find attractive.

"I am certain that he is driving that old car of his to Erps-Kwerps, but we all will know for sure when we can check the GPS scanner," said Phineas.

Suddenly, the lift came to a halt. The sign on the control panel indicated they were on the ninth floor.

"Oh, for crying out loud!" said Phineas, expecting the door to open and some guests to find that the lift was too full for them. This would only slow them down. Four other nuns were in another lift, but even if they got to the underground car park before Phineas, they'd wait for him and the nuns in his lift.

That left young Judith, the most deadly nun. Phineas had assigned her to slip quietly into Maxwell's room and kill him. Unfortunately, she never came out of the room, although two partially clad women and the naked Maxwell raced out moments after

Judith had entered. Phineas could only assume the worst. Not only was Maxwell corrupting the souls of innocent women, but he was a nun-killer. He would roast in Hell all the more painfully for harming the nun.

In fact, while Phineas was assuming the worst, Judith was experiencing her first real orgasm at the hands (and tongue and toes) of Lucy. She was lost to Phineas and the church, but as far as she was concerned, she was reborn and totally in love with the older woman who gave her such pleasure.

When the lift doors failed to open after a moment's wait, Phineas snapped, "what is going on here? Can't you push a button to make this elevator get going again?"

The nun closest to the control panel pressed the basement button, the close door button and finally the open door button, but all to no avail. The lift refused to move.

"Sorry Father, I've tried. The lift – I mean elevator – won't budge."

"Lord grant me patience!" exclaimed Phineas as he pulled a phone out of his pocket. He fiddled with the touch screen then put it to his ear.

"Tomasa, our elevator is stuck. You and your girls go on ahead of us in one of the SUVs. Take the highway north towards Erps-Kwerps. We'll catch up with up with you as soon as we can."

"But Father, our elevator is stuck too."

"God is surely testing us this morning."

"Don't worry, Father. I have some explosives. I'm going to blow the door open."

"Good thinking, Sister."

"Just a second."

On his phone, Phineas heard the scuffling of someone at work. "Okay, hit the switch," said someone. This was followed by: "Oh, Jesus! I didn't mean to –" which was followed by an explosion, screaming, a rolling sound from just outside their lift and finally a distant thud from below.

"What the hell!?" exclaimed Phineas. "I thought you girls were trained in the use of explosives."

"We were, but I think Tomasa missed that class," said one of the nuns.

Phineas was about to ask why this was the case when a nun with a high-pitched voice shouted "Look!" and pointed to the message on the control panel: "Emergency System Override".

"Try the door," said another nun. The woman closest to the control panel did precisely that and the door opened, revealing that the lift had stopped about a metre above the ninth floor. Everyone scrambled out, with Phineas last. As they climbed out, each noticed the acrid smoke seeping out from between the doors of the lift adjacent to theirs, and each said a brief prayer for the sisters who had been in that lift.

"To the stairs," cried Phineas. "Quickly!"

The nuns and the preacher raced down the stairs, with the young women racing ahead of the middle-aged and less physically fit Phineas. Once they reached the car park, they found Ivan, the driver, waiting beside one of the massive SUVs. Phineas hopped into the back seat. Ivan hopped into the front and started the engine. The nuns climbed into two of the remaining three vehicles and started them up.

"Maxwell got away. Can you find him?"

Ivan pressed a button on a small device attached to the vehicle's computer. A map appeared on the screen, followed by a small cross in a rectangle icon, representing the SUV's location and a small devil's head in a rectangle representing the Bentley's location.

"Yes, Father," said Ivan.

"Excellent! Let's get him!" said Phineas.

Ivan led the small convoy out of the car park and on to the main road. The black SUVs with deeply tinted windows and growling engines seemed ominously loud in the quiet streets of Cape City at dawn.

As the SUVs drove out into Cape City and towards the mountains appearing out of the mist in the north, Phineas tried to calm himself. He had a long car ride ahead of him. He relaxed his breathing, let the tension out of his shoulders and sank his head back into the seat.

As he relaxed his body and mind, he reflected upon the early morning attack. He was flummoxed. How had Maxwell once again evaded punishment for his serial sinning, while Phineas – who devoted himself to Jesus, son of God – always came out second best or worse? Was God punishing him for past sins? Surely Phineas's past sins could not compete with Maxwell's ongoing accumulation of sin. Why, Maxwell did not even believe in God, or so Phineas had read somewhere; but to his mind, Maxwell's worst sin was his serial debauchery of innocent young virgins, corrupting them with his evil seed.

In particular, Phineas remembered Cathy – the beautiful, innocent young Cathy whom he had courted in Cape City University. She looked so young, with her thin, immature figure, her long, straight hair that gleamed in the sun, her childlike laughter that resounded in Phineas's heart. The girl was innocence in a picture.

In spite of her busy social schedule (was it surprising that such an attractive young lady was so popular?), she had eventually found the time to allow Phineas to take her to dinner. It was a surprisingly expensive dinner, as Cathy had ordered the most costly items on the menu, but it was worth it. Phineas was sure more dates and, in time, even a kiss, would be forthcoming.

More importantly, he was convinced that Cathy was destined to be his wife. Her innocent, modest appearance and soft-spoken demeanour would make her the ideal wife for the up-and-coming Phineas with his assumed great future with the church. Oh, how he dreamt of the day she would be his wife. Of course, he had not spoken to Cathy about their marriage, even though it was destined; it was too soon. Nevertheless, he was sure that she knew deep in her heart, as he did, that their destiny was to marry and start a family.

Until, of course, she was corrupted by Maxwell.

No! Phineas was not going to let his mind go there now. He had to stay calm and focused. Once he had sent Maxwell off to the gates of Hell, he would be avenged. Not that he was doing this for revenge, of course. He had no personal animosity towards Maxwell, he believed; he simply had a duty to rid the world of an evil demon who, anyone could see, threatened society with his evil thoughts, pornographic sculptures and serial molestation of pure virgins.

A sudden deceleration shook Phineas from his unpleasant memories. He saw that a slow-moving, dilapidated old pickup truck, stacked high with old trunks precariously tied to its bed, had forced Ivan to reduce the SUV's speed quickly. They trundled behind the small truck for some time while Ivan wove in and out of the lane in order to see past the load and determine whether or not he could overtake the slow-moving truck.

"Damn!" said Phineas. Surely Maxwell was getting ever farther ahead of them.

13

Lucy woke some hours later with a femininely muscular body wrapped around her and a hand resting on her left breast. She kissed the girl gently on the forehead as she reflected upon an evening of far more decadence than she had planned.

The good thing about lots of sex following lots of drinking is that the latter seemed generally to reduce the consequences of the former on the following morning. Considering all that she had drunk the night before, she reckoned she was feeling good. The lass next to her felt good too.

On the other hand, Lucy had not intended to get stinking drunk and have sex with interesting examples of each sex. Her original intention had been to have a drink with a few friends and check out the new Waterfront Centre, followed by a quiet dinner at home with the company of a good book.

In the end, she had allowed herself to be seduced by a man for the first time in 10 years and then herself had seduced the attractive young thing who apparently intended to kill the man.

Lucy didn't begrudge Maxwell his seduction and certainly did not want him killed. It had been fun; he knew better than most men, in her admittedly limited experience, how to give a woman pleasure. Even so, it was not the same as making love with a woman. Women knew instinctively. Maxwell, she rightly suspected, had been through a great deal of trial and error to learn his way around a body like hers – which, she was finally coming to acknowledge, was pretty damned good, even at 42.

As for the girl wrapped around her, she was awfully naïve. Indeed, Lucy not only had to seduce her, but also had to give her some rather explicit instructions on how to return the favour. In fact, she had never intended to seduce the girl. She merely wanted to prevent the girl from killing Maxwell and her friends who had camped out in the room the night before. Kissing the nun was an instinctive action designed to distract. And it worked. Then the nun started kissing back with surprising passion.

She also had a firm, youthful body, which she knew how to use in combat, if not in love-making; but Lucy could – and did – provide a few lessons there, which resulted a half-hour later in the young thing collapsing in a paroxysm of multiple orgasms as Lucy held her tightly.

"I love you!" the girl cried out as her body calmed itself into a post-climactic glow.

"You don't love me, sweetheart," said Lucy. "You've just had a great orgasm."

"Is that what that was? An orgasm?"

"Holy shit – was that your first orgasm?"

"Yes, it was my first time, ever."

"Your first time with a woman?"

"No, my first time ever."

Lucy kissed her gently. "How old are you, sweetie?"

"Twenty-three."

"And you've never had sex before?"

"Nope."

"Wow!"

"Yes, wow! That was so good. You gave me such pleasure. I can still feel my body tingling. Jesus never made me feel so good."

"Well, you've never fucked Jesus, have you?"

The nun stiffened.

"Oh, sorry. Don't get worked up about it. I can't imagine Jesus was much good in bed anyway."

"What?"

"By my understanding, he didn't do it a lot. And men who don't do it a lot don't do it well either, irrespective of parentage. Actually, even a lot of men who do it a lot do it poorly. They focus too much on their performance and insufficiently on how they make their partner feel."

"I don't think I'd want a man. Aside from Father Phineas, the ones I've met have been smelly, evil creatures," said the nun.

"Oh, there are a lot of decent men out there, sweetie," said Lucy, feeling an unfamiliar need to defend a sex she sometimes thought the planet would be better off without.

"But I don't care. I love you!" said the nun.

"I think you are deluded by post-orgasmic pheromones," said Lucy.

"What?" asked the nun.

"Don't worry about it," said Lucy with a yawn. "Let's get some sleep."

"Okay," said the nun, kissing Lucy and wrapping herself in the older woman's arms. It had been a long night for both women and exhaustion took its toll before either could reflect upon the unusual chain of events that had put them in bed together.

But Lucy was reflecting upon it in the morning when she woke up. Presumably, or at least hopefully, the girl would no longer be in love with her; but Lucy was concerned that the girl – what was her name, anyway? – might also freak when she realised what had happened. After all, she was apparently a member of the American evangelical religious screw-balls that seemed largely driven by their envy of how much fun the people of Cape City enjoyed on a daily basis. She was also apparently trained in the use of deadly weapons.

"Hey there, sweetie," said Lucy, kissing the girl on the head again. At this, the girl jumped up and landed in a combat stance on top of the bed. For a moment, Lucy thought last night might have been the last fuck of her life.

Then the girl smiled and let herself fall on Lucy, straddling the older woman and kissing her with remarkable passion on the lips.

"Oh, I love you so much!" she exclaimed.

"You cannot fall in love with someone so much after a single night together, no matter how spectacular the sex, sweetie," said Lucy.

"I can," said the girl.

"Now look, um, sweetie. Actually, what is your name?"

"Judith. And yours?"

"Lucy. Pleased to meet you."

"Oh, and I am pleased to meet you, Lucy!"

"Now, Judith," began Lucy.

"Yes, Lucy?"

"Judith, you cannot fall in love with someone when you don't even know her name."

"I can. I've fallen in love with Lucy!"

"You think you've fallen in love with me, and you're cute, but let's deal with that later. First, why don't you tell me what was going on last night. You nearly killed a man."

"Yes. I failed."

"If you ask me, that's a good thing. Tell me what happened. I am a quiet woman who likes an occasional night out with a drink or two and maybe some good sex, but I don't like people being slaughtered around me. I normally sleep with women closer to my own age and I don't believe I've ever slept with a nun."

"A ninja nun!" Judith said proudly.

"Definitely no ninja nuns," said Lucy, "but you are evading the subject. What happened last night?"

"The Evangelical Church of America has decreed that Maxwell is a demon operating under the auspices of Satan and so must be killed and sent to Hell."

"That's a bit extreme, don't you think? He seemed a nice enough chap to me, albeit a bit eccentric."

"That's what is so evil about him. He charms innocent women and then does terrible things to them."

"Really?! Like what?"

"Like seducing them."

Lucy looked at Judith for a moment. "Seducing women?"

"Seducing innocent women – unmarried women – and corrupting their souls."

"If that were the only criteria for being a demon, a substantial portion of the male population of Cape City is destined for Hell," said Lucy. "And quite a lot of women as well, come to think of it."

"And he makes filthy pornographic sculptures that corrupt young minds and lead otherwise good men to think impure thoughts and do impure things," said Judith.

"Actually, I kind of like his sculptures."

"Oh, Lucy, how could you? They are so depraved and sick!"

"Um, have you ever actually looked at his work?"

"Never. It is too impure for me."

"How can you possibly judge his work if you've never seen it?" The nun was puzzled.

"In any event, seducing women and making naughty sculptures may not lead to VIP treatment at the gates of Heaven," Lucy conceded, "but surely there are far more evil people walking the earth– my ex-wife, for instance. On the other hand, he did leave me alone with a woman who gave every impression of being a homicidal maniac. That's hardly gentlemanly behaviour."

"He did!?" asked Judith.

At that moment, there was a knock on the door. Lucy wrapped herself in a towel and answered. It was room service.

"Breakfast, madam," said the lad in a hotel uniform.

"But I haven't ordered anything," said Lucy.

"It's compliments of Maxwell van Mars, according to the ticket," said the lad, checking said ticket.

Lucy thanked the lad, who rolled the trolley brimming with

food into the room.

"Now, can a man who orders us a breakfast feast be so bad?" asked Lucy. Judith did not reply, but looked at the food with large, hungry eyes. Post-midnight ambushes and one's first sexual adventure depleted an awful lot of calories. Now was the time to replace them.

"Come on. Dig in, kiddo," said Lucy.

The women enjoyed their morning meal, then showered and dressed. Judith pointedly did not don her coif, and Lucy had to go braless as she could not find hers anywhere. While getting dressed, Judith found on her phone a text message from Father Phineas ordering all the nuns to meet by the lifts and then to proceed to the cars to pursue Maxwell, who had fled. After a moment's thought regarding loyalties, she shared this information with Lucy.

"Well, it seems Maxwell got away. Have there been any more messages?" asked Lucy.

"No, that's all," said Judith. "I wonder why no one came looking for me."

"Good question," said Lucy.

"They're my sisters – sisters under Jesus. Why did no one come looking for me?"

"Honey, I don't know, but you're with me now. Okay?"

As soon as she said these words Lucy regretted them. What on Earth was she doing hooking up with a battle-trained, naïve nun whom she had only known for a few hours? Surely, she should leave the girl to her own devices and get on with her own life. A girl like this, who falls in love at the drop of a hat – or panties – would surely be a clinger. Probably the jealous type as well. Most clingy girls were, in her experience. And this one was trained to kill!

Did Lucy really want a clingy, jealous and dangerous girl in her life? And how would she introduce Judith to her friends? How would those friends respond when they asked Judith what she did

for a living and she answered that she was a ninja nun who specialised in assassination? Friends would suspect that Lucy had cracked
and was going through some kind of weird lesbian mid-life crisis.
Perhaps, she thought, this was precisely what she was doing –
mind you, she was a bit young for a mid-life crisis, wasn't she?

"Do you have any place to go?" Lucy asked.

Judith had not thought about that. Now that she had left the
nuns and had premarital sex with a woman, she could hardly return to Escher Abbey.

"When I was a teenager, I stayed for a year in a convent in
Tours," she said.

"Were there ninja nuns there?" asked Lucy.

"Oh, no. It was the opposite. Lots of meditation and reflection. No combat training." Judith smiled, knowing this was what
Lucy wanted to hear.

"It sounds perfect."

Judith's smile faded as she realised that the downside to this
scenario is that she would be without Lucy.

"But," she started.

"I tell you what," said Lucy. "You can come stay with me for a
couple of days. You can call the convent in Tours, make arrange-
ments to stay there and then I'll see that you get there."

Okay," said Judith. At least she would have more time with this
incredible woman. Maybe she could figure out how to extend their
time together.

Although it seemed a viable plan, Lucy was worried about Judith's belief that she loved Lucy and that the girl might try and stay
on rather than go to Tours. Worse, a part of Lucy rather hoped
this would happen. For a beginner, Judith was damned good in
bed. Lucy also liked – really liked – being adored. Who doesn't?
No, thought Lucy; she would ensure the girl went to Tours. Or
somewhere.

They collected their things and walked down the long, plushly carpeted and handsomely wallpapered corridor to the lifts, which they found roped off with police tape and a sign leading them to an alternative lift at the back of the building.

Not surprisingly, with three lifts out of operation, the remaining lift, a glass one running outside the building, was kept busy. It was while riding a crowded lift down to the ground floor that the women overheard talk about an explosion in one of the main lifts that had killed several heavily armed nuns and that this was why all of the central lifts were shut down. Lucy and Judith eyed each other knowingly, but said nothing.

Once they arrived on the ground floor and their fellow life occupants scattered, Judith said, "oh, my God. Some of my sisters must have been killed. Do you think Maxwell could have done that?"

"I doubt it. He didn't actually seem the type," said Lucy.

"No. I thought he was kind of cowardly, actually," said Judith.

"Indeed," said Lucy, reflecting on the speed at which he had fled the night before.

They walked across the lobby and down the stairs to the underground car park. As they walked towards Lucy's car, they passed the lone SUV remaining from the convoy.

"That's one of our cars," said Judith, pointing.

They stopped and looked at it for a moment: a massive black vehicle with black windows and wheels. It emanated a sinister, dark energy even when sitting still. It inspired a certain irresponsibility in Lucy – further evidence, perhaps of a feminine mid-life crisis, she would think years later.

"Fuck it," she said. "I have an idea."

14

The ancient Bentley raced along the two-lane highway that wended around, over and under the mountains of southern Europa. Multicoloured and multi-textured vegetation lined the roads, dotted the mountainsides and had been nibbled upon by the odd animal. Here and there, massive ancient Roman walls, arches and columns sprouted from the vegetation, and an occasional disintegrating roadside sculpture cast its shadow upon the car as it raced past.

Wendy bent round her seat to look at the hitch-hiker.

"Are you an angel?"

The hitch-hiker thought for a moment and replied in her curious and slightly girlish French accent.

"I am not sure. What is an angel?"

"*Une ange*," said Maxwell.

"I am still not sure, but I might be," said the angel.

Wendy contemplated this for a moment.

"Where are you from?"

"I think, maybe Angiers."

"Angers?" asked Maxwell.

"Maybe," said the angel.

"From this world – from Earth?" asked Maxwell. He noticed out of the corner of his eye that Wendy was puzzling over this conversation.

"No and yes," said the angel after a moment's pause.

"Sorry?" asked Maxwell. "Are you from this world or not?"

"No, I think not. You do not look like me," said the angel.

Maxwell thought about this. He wondered whether the angel

might be a new kind of alien. He'd never seen or heard of a such a human-looking alien. Certainly, she was more pleasing to look at than the Zargonians or Gronks. He wondered if there would be any reward for finding a new alien race. That would be cool.

"So, you are not from Earth?" he said, just to confirm.

"But I am," said the angel.

"Either you are or you are not," said Maxwell. "You cannot be an Earthling and not be an Earthling at the same time."

"But you asked me two different questions," said the angel.

"What?" asked Maxwell.

"She's right," said Wendy. "You asked if she is from this world, and she said she was not, but when you asked if she is from Earth, she said she was."

"Is it not the same thing?" asked Maxwell.

"I come from Earth. Surely. But maybe not this one," said the angel.

Now it was Maxwell's turn to puzzle.

"Do you understand?" he asked Wendy.

"I might. Let me think about it," said Wendy.

"If you are not from this world, do you know how you got here?" asked Maxwell.

"Yes. You stopped your car and picked me up," said the angel.

"Yes, that's true. But before that. How did you get to the side of the road on the North-South Highway?"

"I believe I was sent," said the angel. Then she added, "but I am tired. I wish to sleep for a short time." And she did so.

The old car progressed rapidly, eating up kilometre after kilometre of scenic road. In the early afternoon, their impressive progress was slowed by roadworks. First came warning signs; soon, threatening signs implied that any driver racing though the roadworks at an excessive speed would be hung upside down from one of the trees by the side of the road. Finally, they came to a red traffic light in the middle of a long, straight stretch of the highway.

It was manned by a single, bored-looking chap in a hard hat. Beyond the traffic light, one lane of the road was torn up, restricting traffic to a single lane. In the distance, some roadworks vehicles sat motionless in the afternoon sun while groups of men stood around seemingly doing very little which, in fact, was the case.

Just in front of the Bentley, a pickup truck had also come to a stop at the traffic light. In the back of the truck were at least eight kroaches drinking beer, flinging the tins to the side of the road as soon as they finished each one and laughing amongst themselves. From time to time, they also tossed candy wrappers, empty crisp bags and other rubbish onto the roadside, seemingly oblivious to the aesthetic – not to mention environmental – damage they were doing to this beautiful stretch of highway.

Kroaches, it should be understood, are the unfortunate result of a genetic engineering experiment gone horribly wrong. Several decades ago, while working on a genetic therapy for impotence, a less-than-meticulous team of scientists at the University of Pisa inadvertently allowed a human gene culture to become contaminated by cockroaches. Somehow, a mixture of the genes spliced themselves together, creating a cell that was half-human and half-cockroach.

Had it stopped there, it would have been a fascinating scientific curiosity. Sadly, it didn't stop. Thanks to a chain of incompetent events, unprecedented at the ancient university, the cells in question were injected into the eggs of two dozen healthy women who ought to have been participating in another experiment altogether.

The resulting human-cockroach offspring – or 'kroaches', as they became known – were of low intelligence, perpetually horny and had extremely bad attitudes. This last characteristic is hardly surprising; if you were half-cockroach, ugly as sin and insatiably horny, you would doubtless have a bad attitude as well.

For a couple of decades, a legal argument as to whether or not the kroaches were human raged on. The anti-kroach contingent wanted to eradicate kroaches and forget they ever existed. At the very least, this contingent felt kroaches should be sterilised so that their artificial breed would come to an end within a generation. The caring contingent, on the other hand, felt that kroaches had rights too, and to eradicate or even sterilise them would be inhumane.

Most people verbally sided with the caring contingent, but did little about it. Over a couple of drinks, the same people would privately admit that while kroaches were jolly decent demi-humans, they wouldn't actually want any of them living in their neighbourhood, and they would cite disturbing rumours of violent crime, child molestation and unbearably loud parties to back up their feelings.

While this debate raged on, the kroaches fucked like crazy, resulting in a population of inbred kroaches that were even uglier and less intelligent than the first generation. Not surprisingly, this led to an even worse attitude among young kroaches. That little in the way of education was provided to kroaches only further distanced them from human society and encouraged ever-worsening attitude problems.

Although short on intelligence and, by human standards, as ugly as reheated sin, the kroaches were physically strong, physically comfortable in almost any environment and had an amazing ability to climb up things. Hence, they were largely employed in the construction industry, where they could earn a living wage while making construction industry executives and shareholders filthy rich.

As it happened, the pickup truck in question was taking the kroaches home from an early morning shift of work on a nearby construction site. The tired kroaches were guzzling cheap beer with the aim of cheering themselves up. They were not succeeding.

Finishing a chapter in her book, Wendy looked up to see the

kroaches flinging their rubbish into the countryside. She flinched with each fling.

"That's terrible!" she exclaimed.

"What's terrible?" asked Maxwell, who was lost in abstract thought while waiting for the light to change.

"The kroaches throwing their rubbish onto the roadside like that. It really makes me angry," said Wendy.

"Oh, yes, indeed," said Maxwell

"Let's talk to them!" said Wendy.

"Let's not and say we did," said Maxwell. "Kroaches can be disagreeable things at the best of times and violent when full of beer, a state they are clearly pursuing with enthusiasm. Telling them we don't like their behaviour could result in really, really bad consequences for us."

"But if no one talks to them, they'll continue to litter the countryside with their rubbish," said Wendy.

"True, but if we don't scold them, you and I will live to be outraged by it," said Maxwell.

"What is happening?" asked the angel groggily from the back seat.

"The kroaches are throwing their rubbish out onto the countryside," said Wendy.

"What are these kroaches?" asked the angel.

"They are these kroaches," said Maxwell, pointing.

"Oh. They are vile," said the angel with an almost childlike expression of disgust on her face.

"I would have thought an angel would be more loving of all creatures," said Maxwell.

"Only beautiful creatures. These kroaches, they are ugly creatures. I can feel very comfortable about despising them," said the angel.

"I think we should talk to them about littering," said Wendy loudly.

"Yes, that is a good idea," agreed the angel.

"No, it's not! The kroaches might get violent. I am not in a position to protect you two if they do," said Maxwell.

"Chicken shit," said the angel.

"What?!" exclaimed Maxwell.

"The light is green," said the angel.

Maxwell drove forward, somewhat annoyed by the turn the conversation had taken, but largely relieved that the light had changed before Wendy could do something rash like scold the kroaches. She had a strong sense of what was right and what was wrong. Wrong things, at least as so perceived by her, really got under her feathers, and she often felt compelled to try and put those wrong things right.

Maxwell hoped to be able to overtake the kroaches' pickup truck and get well ahead of them, but the roadworks meant that one lane of the highway was impassable for several kilometres. After that, oncoming traffic and the winding road prevented overtaking. Before long, they were again stopped behind the kroach pickup truck at a red light while oncoming traffic drove through.

Meanwhile, the kroaches were getting drunker and flinging their empty tins as far as they could onto the roadside fields.

"Look, they are still littering all over the place," complained Wendy. "I am going to talk to them!"

"I really do not think that's a good idea," said Maxwell.

"Then you should talk to them," said the angel.

"Good gods, no!" said Maxwell.

"Why not?" asked the angel.

"Because I don't fancy being beaten to a bloody pulp on the roadside," explained Maxwell.

"So, you are a coward then," said the angel.

"No!" said Maxwell, with manly instinct. But after a moment's thought changed his mind. "Yes, actually. I am. And proud of it."

"This is silly. I am talking to them," said Wendy as she opened the door and jumped out of the Bentley.

"Oh, shit," said Maxwell.

"Cool!" said the angel.

"What do you think you are doing, throwing your rubbish onto the fields like that?" demanded Wendy of the kroaches.

The kroaches became completely silent for a second; then an elderly kroach looked at Wendy thoughtfully and said, "you are quite right, my avian friend. What we are doing is not only wrong, but it is damaging to the environment and reflects badly upon all of us kroaches. On behalf of my species, I hereby vow to stop littering immediately and devote my life to encouraging my fellow kroaches to behave more responsibly towards our environment and the planet. In recognition of your kind indication of our poor behaviour, I shall see that a statue is erected in your honour in this very spot."

Actually, that's not what happened at all. Although the kroaches did indeed go quiet when Wendy shouted at them, the quiet lasted for about three seconds before a particularly dim kroach pointed at Wendy and said: "Chicken!"

Several other kroaches contemplated this insight and agreed, proclaiming: "Uhn, chicken".

"I am not a chicken. I am a penguin, a kairuku penguin. There are many obvious differences," said Wendy.

Taken aback, the first kroach thought for a moment before deciding, outspokenly, "talking chicken."

"Uhn, talking chicken," was the consensus of his buddies.

Having come to a prompt agreement in this intellectual debate, the kroaches sipped beer thoughtfully in the back of the pickup truck. Maxwell breathed a sigh of relief. It seemed the kroaches were not going to get violent with Wendy. He rolled down the window of the car to call his friend back in when an inspired kroach suddenly got creative.

"Roast talking chicken," he said with a proud laugh. This was quite an intellectual jump for the other kroaches, who had to stop and think. However, once they got their tiny heads around the concept, it appealed to them and they agreed.

"Roast talking chicken," they all said, completely out of unison.

"Bloody hell on a stick," said Maxwell. "This has taken a distinct turn for the worse."

"Wendy, get back in the car now!" he shouted out the window; but it was too late. A kroach jumped out of the pickup, grabbed Wendy and threw her to his friends while giggling delightedly. At the same time, the light turned green. The kroach jumped back into the pickup truck and it lurched forward.

"Holy shit!" exclaimed the angel.

Maxwell jumped out of the car and ran towards the pickup truck, but it was already accelerating too fast. He ran back to the Bentley, put the key in the engine and started the old car up.

"Don't worry, old friend, I'll save you," he said softly.

"Why the hell did she do that?" asked the angel.

"She barely understands human nature and fails utterly to comprehend kroach nature. What's more: you encouraged her!" said Maxwell, pressing the accelerator to the floor.

"No, I did not," said the angel.

"Yes, you did. You prodded her," said Maxwell.

"Really?"

"Yes!"

"Funny, I don't remember."

"Lovely. An amnesiac angel."

"You may be right. I think someone else has said that about me."

Maxwell followed the pickup carefully, but was unsure what to do. Trying to ram it or run it off the road could hurt Wendy, especially as the truck was picking up speed. Suddenly, it braked and veered hard to the left onto a dirt road leading into a dense forest, which had not been visible a moment ago. Maxwell followed the truck.

The big old Bentley was not made to drive over rough and muddy dirt roads, so Maxwell proceeded as carefully as he could. He wanted to maintain speed in order to keep up with the pickup, which merrily bounced up and down as it drove along the road, exploiting a high clearance and four-wheel drive. He dared not drive too fast. He knew the road could damage the Bentley or simply trap it. If that happened, saving Wendy would become even more complicated, at least from a logistical perspective.

The pickup truck was putting distance between itself and the Bentley. Maxwell could see the sad, frightened face of his old friend getting smaller and smaller.

"Recalculating," said Mrs Miller.

15

"Do you have a key for that thing?" asked Lucy, gesturing towards the sinister SUV.

"No," said Judith.

"Damn."

"I don't need one."

"What?"

"I just enter a code on my telephone and it should start. Father Phineas wants to be sure any of us ninja nuns can use the vehicles in an emergency."

"Cool," said Lucy. "Now, can you find out where they are going?"

"Yes. I can call one of the sisters," said Judith. "But I thought we were not going to help send Maxwell to Hell."

"We're not. We're going to try to prevent that from happening," said Lucy.

"We're going to convert him?" Judith asked in astonishment.

"Convert him?"

"To Jesus!"

"What on earth does that have to do with anything, honey?"

"If Maxwell becomes a Christian and accepts Jesus into his life, he won't go to Hell. He'll go to Heaven."

"Actually, I was rather thinking of postponing God from having to make that decision for a while."

"Huh?"

"Let's try and stop your group from killing Maxwell," said Lucy. "It seems to me your reverend is a bit obsessed with the

whole thing and could lead your sisters to make a horrendous mistake that you would all regret."

"Uh, okay," said Judith, a bit doubtfully.

"Does your Bible not say something about 'thou shalt not
kill'?" asked Lucy.

"Yes, of course. It's the sixth commandment!" said Judith, with
the pride of a young girl having answered a question correctly in
school.

"Isn't that precisely what Reverend Fudge –"

"Forge."

"Sorry. Isn't that precisely what your Reverend Forge intends
to do with Maxwell? Kill him?"

"Oh, yes!"

"Well, it seems to me that Forge is in danger of reserving a
place in Hell for himself if he succeeds."

"I'm sorry?"

"If Forge kills Maxwell, then surely he will have broken the
sixth commandment."

"I guess so."

"And the consequence of breaking a commandment is severe,
is it not?"

"But..."

"But what? Is there a bit in the Bible after the 'thou shalt not
kill' commandment that makes exceptions for Phineas Forge? A
footnote perhaps?"

"Of course not! But..."

"But what, dear?"

"Oh, I don't know! I'm confused!"

Lucy took both of Judith's hands in hers.

"Don't worry, sweetheart. You went to church school, didn't
you?"

"Yes."

"You probably didn't get much of an introduction to logical

thinking, did you? I understand the evangelicals abhor that."

"I don't know."

"It's all about faith, isn't it?"

"Yes, of course. You must have faith in God!"

"And never question that faith of God?"

"Never!"

"Pity. I sense that deep beneath your indoctrination there lurks in your skull an enquiring mind begging to be let free."

"Are you making fun of me?" Judith asked with wide eyes, one of which threatened to expel a tear or two.

"Oh, I'm sorry, honey," said Lucy, hugging Judith. "You see, I'm a scientist – an astrophysicist – so for me, life, the world, the universe: it's all about questioning and trying to understand. I have faith in the scientific process, but little else."

"But you believe in God, don't you?"

"To be honest, no. Not the Judeo-Christian God, anyway."

The threatened tear decided it had had quite enough and made its way down Judith's cheek. To say she was suffering from con-flicting emotions was an understatement. She was in love with this woman, this older woman who held her and kissed her and cared for her in a way she had never been cared for before. But the same woman was forcing her to question beliefs that she had been taught never, ever to question. Worse still, the woman was an athe-ist.

But worst of all, Lucy's observation was correct: beneath the indoctrination, the religious teaching, the force-feeding of obeying church leaders, there lurked within Judith an intelligent, enquiring mind.

And this intelligent mind was being seduced by Lucy every bit as thoroughly as Judith's body had been seduced by Lucy the night before. While Judith's church-programmed mind wanted her to make the sign of the cross and send Lucy away, Judith's deeply buried enquiring and intelligent mind wanted to embrace Lucy's mind and learn how to be free like hers. The conflict was a bit much for Judith, who found herself incapable of action.

Lucy sensed the situation was overwhelming for Judith and suspected, correctly, that she had not been taught to make decisions for herself. Lucy would have to make the decisions for both of them.

"Trust me, Judith. I may not be much of a Christian, but 'thou shalt not kill' is pretty straightforward. If Forge and your sisters kill Maxwell, they may well expedite his way to Hell. But they may condemn themselves to Hell as well, and we do not want that, do we?"

Judith shook her head.

"So, let us see if we can prevent this killing."

"Okay," said Judith reluctantly.

"Good girl! And it's summer break. I've got a couple of weeks to kill that would otherwise be spent writing a research paper I don't really want to write. So, let's chase after them, try and stop the killing and get to know each other better, okay?"

"Okay," said Judith with more enthusiasm. Lucy kissed her.

"Why don't you make that call, find out where the sisters are headed and we'll follow in this thing," said Lucy, patting the SUV. "Oh, and don't mention that we are going to try and stop them, okay?"

"Okay," said Judith, tapping a number into her telephone.

16

The three SUVs roared up the North-South Highway as the sun rose in the sky. Phineas, riding in the back of the first SUV, sat looking out the window at the horizon as it raced past. In the distance, he saw the abandoned and partially deteriorated SpaceElevator towers thrusting impotently into the heavens. Hundreds of metres high, the three towers were once the Earth stations of the SpaceElevator, which lifted massive platforms into orbit.

The SpaceElevators had, of course, been the human race's means of putting people, spacecraft and equipment in to space and, as a result, had been a primary driver of the local economy — until, that is, the Zargonians visited Earth and introduced their dark-energy-powered space vehicles. Because dark energy is essentially free, non-polluting and available in abundance if you know how to tap into it, as the Zargonians did, the dark-energy space drive pretty much fucked over the SpaceElevator business.

Now, of course, the towers had become obsolete and unused. Their once-gleaming glass and concrete surfaces were slowly fading into the environment as vegetation, animals and dust reclaimed the massive buildings. Although invisible from the road, from each tower cables, made of incredibly strong carbon nanotubes, extended 35,000 kilometres through the sky and into geostationary orbit, where they connected to the Interplanetary Trade Station, the largest orbiting space station humans ever made. Sadly, big was no competition for progress, and the station was largely abandoned, except for a few squatters and an artists' colony.

This morning, the great towers sat forlornly on the eastern horizon with a rising sun behind them, casting them into shadow. In spite of their ruin, they retained an air of dignity and once-greatness not unlike that of a ruined medieval cathedral.

However, none of this whatsoever was on Phineas's mind as he stared out the window. Rather, he was thinking back to the day at Cape City University when he first met Maxwell, who was defiling his bride to be.

It was not long after his first and last dinner date with Cathy. Phineas had heard from one of Cathy's friends that she was going to model that afternoon for an up-and-coming young sculptor in the art faculty. At the time, Phineas did not know Maxwell, his work or his reputation. He had only heard that Maxwell had a remarkable talent, so he felt delighted that his sweetheart had been chosen to model for the star sculptor. Doubtless, Phineas reckoned, Maxwell recognised Cathy's classic beauty and presumably intended to carve a marble sculpture of her in a sort of young Virgin Mary kind of way.

He devised a plan to visit the art studio in the afternoon and *accidentally* come across Cathy while posing. He would off-handedly compliment the sculpture in progress, but point out how much more beautiful the real Cathy looked in whatever long, flowing robes she would surely be dressed in.

He would claim that he was visiting in order to find a sculpture to decorate the new evangelical studies building associated with the university's religious studies faculty. Why, he might even suggest Maxwell donate the sculpture of Cathy! That would surely impress his wife to be.

He was walking down the corridor of the arts building, trying to work out where Cathy might be, when he heard a woman shouting "Oh, my God! Oh, my God!" in a voice that sounded like Cathy's. It was coming from Studio 7, just ahead of him on the left. Worried that it might indeed be the voice of his darling and that she might be in danger, Phineas raced to the door and flung it open.

The room was a mess. There was clay and plaster everywhere. On a stand was a half-completed clay figure of a nude woman that he knew must be Cathy. It stood there, frozen with a gleeful smile on the verge of becoming a laugh. In normal circumstances, the smile would have been delightful, but Phineas could not escape the feeling the sculpture was laughing at him.

The nude figure of Cathy, while shocking and inappropriate, was bad enough, but it was the sight on the table across from the work that tore apart Phineas's heart as thoroughly as if it had been dropped into a paper shredder. Sprawled out on her back, naked and splotched with clay, was his darling Cathy, squirming and moaning like she was possessed by the devil. Kneeling on the floor and equally naked was a skinny demon with long curly hair, who had his mouth around Cathy's private parts and appeared to be chewing on them. What satanic ritual might this be, wondered Phineas apprehensively.

Just as he stepped forward to pull Cathy away and save her from the demon, she saw him, pulled herself up to sitting position and demanded, "what the fuck are you doing here, Phinny?"

At the same time, the demon, whom Phineas would later learn was Maxwell, started and turned to look at Phineas.

"Lord love a duck! What kind of caring mother names her son 'Phinny'?"

Phineas froze for a moment. He had never seen a naked wo-man before, but he was pretty sure most did not have silver rings in their nipples. Had the curly-haired demon done this to her? Had he somehow used dark power to enslave her through her breasts? Phineas was not sure. He was confused. He shook his head. He needed to act fast if he was going to save poor Cathy, but he was not sure how to act. This visit was not going at all to plan.

"I'm going to save you from this demon, Cathy. Don't worry!"

he announced after a moment.

"Save me? Those were the best three orgasms I've had in my life!" exclaimed the presumed sweetheart.

"Orgasms?" asked Phineas, confused.

"Yes, and there might well have been a fourth if you hadn't come barging in!"

"I wouldn't give up hope yet, darling," said the demon.

"I do not understand. Now, why don't you get dressed and come with me to the church? I'm sure Father Benedict can help you find –"

"I don't want to go to church, you fool! I want you to get the fuck out of here now!"

"You are rather spoiling the mood in here, old sport," the demon added unhelpfully.

"But..." said Phineas.

"Now! Get out or I'll call campus security!" said Cathy.

"I expect she'll do it, ace," said the demon. "She's done it to me before."

"That's because you and that crazy Vietnamese girl sneaked into my bed at three in the morning, baby," said Cathy with a laugh.

Confused and heartbroken, Phineas left the room, walked to a nearby church and began a prayer marathon session that became legendary at Cape City University, even among the evangelicals who thought nothing of devoting an entire afternoon to prayer.

Seven days later and four kilogrammes lighter, he walked back to his rooms. On his way, he saw a poster for an upcoming art show. On the poster was the same young demon with long curly hair and mocking smile, albeit clothed: Maxwell, of course.

Phineas knew then that Maxwell was a demon sent to Earth to test him by performing unspeakable acts, such as deflowering young virgins, putting rings on their breasts, deceiving them with orgasms and corrupting their precious souls. At the same time,

Phineas knew, or at least believed, that God had great things in store for him.

Doubtless, ridding the Earth of a particularly evil demon was one of God's tasks for him –though why God had chosen his beloved Cathy to be the demon's star victim was a mystery to Phineas. He knew well that God worked in mysterious ways, and normally respected God's decision to act as He pleased. After all, if God gave man free will, then man must surely give as much back to God. But this time he rather wished God had been more transparent about His motives.

Phineas also knew, or at least suspected, that Cathy was no longer a virgin. In his hazy understanding of sex, a man had to put his *Thing* into his wife's *Thing* in order to have sex. He was not entirely sure how mouths fit into this picture and did not want to think about it much anyway. Nevertheless, Cathy and Maxwell had lain naked together and, as far as Phineas was concerned, Cathy had lost her virginity to the demon, and perhaps his mouth had something to do with it. Of course, this meant that he could no longer marry her. As a man of God, Phineas could only marry a virgin.

It was during this thoughtful walk that Phineas vowed two things: firstly, that one day he would destroy the demon Maxwell, and secondly, that if he could not have his sweet, but now corrupted, Cathy – he would have no one.

And he had kept those vows for many years now, he thought, as he looked out the window of the SUV. Destroying Maxwell had thus far proven more challenging than he had expected. A task that he thought he could accomplish in short time had taken years, but he was close to eradicating Maxwell; by the end of this day, he was sure. Indeed, tonight, maybe God Himself would come to Phineas in a dream and thank him for it.

There had never been another woman in Phineas's life. Indeed, he had never even kissed a woman, except in a couple of shocking dreams in which he finally discovered what an orgasm was. Nevertheless, he remained confused. Orgasms were messy things that left his pyjamas sticky and his heart dirty. How could having three of them be so great, he wondered.

Surely, it was the work of the devil.

His telephone rang, shaking him from these unwanted thoughts and bringing him back to the present.

"Judith has called me. She's okay and is coming after us in the remaining vehicle, Father," said the nun calling him.

"Why, that's marvellous," said Phineas. "Praise be to God for his mercy. I was so afraid that the demon Maxwell had destroyed her as well. Too many innocent women have been ruined by him."

"Amen," said the nun.

"Amen, and thank you, Sister," said Phineas, ringing off.

It was a small victory, but a victory nonetheless. Phineas was becoming optimistic that they would capture and destroy Maxwell before the day was out.

"Roadworks ahead, Father," said Ivan. "It looks like they are down to one lane for long stretches of the road."

"Tarnation!" exclaimed Phineas. "Just when I thought things were looking good."

"I don't know, Father." said Ivan. "The roadworks will slow Maxwell down, too. On the open road, that car of his is faster than ours. With these roadworks, we have a chance."

"Why, yes, son. I hadn't thought of it that way. Thank you."

"You're welcome, Father. I'm..."

"Yes, Ivan? Is something wrong?"

"It looks like Maxwell has turned off the highway and into the forest about four and a half kilometres from here."

"Why, that's strange," said Phineas. "I wonder where he's going."

"We'll know soon," said Ivan.

"And we'll take care of him soon, too," added Phineas.

17

Maxwell followed the pickup truck along the dirt road, which soon became more of a mud road decorated with large stones, bits of tree and puddles of water. All of the Bentley's power did it no good here. Meanwhile, the battered pickup truck overloaded with kroaches bounced slowly but steadily down the road, getting further ahead of the Bentley all the time. Eventually, on a narrow path bordered by tall reeds, the Bentley decided that it had had quite enough and came to a standstill. Attempts to reverse only made the situation worse.

"Damn it all to hell and back again!" said Maxwell, before adding, "twice!" for good measure.

He started to open the door when the angel said, "go on, leave her. You need to get to Erps-Kwerps. There's nothing you can do to help her. Why risk your own life?"

"Because she's my best friend, you fool!" said Maxwell, jumping out of the car and running down the path after the pickup truck – or at least trying to run. 'Stumbling in a consistently forward direction' might better sum up Maxwell's progress. After a moment and a scant few metres, he suddenly wondered how the angel knew he was going to Erps-Kwerps. He was sure he'd not shared this information with her.

Unfortunately, attempting to run on a muddy path and think about something unrelated to the path in question was not a viable combination. Maxwell stumbled and fell in the mud. He picked himself up and looked around to see the angel floating about a half-metre off the ground, just behind him.

He stumbled forward again, concentrating on running this time. In a few minutes he came upon a clearing and stopped to checked it out. The now empty pickup truck was parked near the centre of the clearing. The kroaches were busy and Wendy was tied by a noose to a two-metre stake in the ground. Still drinking from their seemingly unending supply of beer, the kroaches were stumbling about trying to gather wood for a fire.

"Good gods! They do multiply fast!" said Maxwell, noting that there somehow seemed to be about three times as many kroaches now as there had been in the pickup truck a few minutes ago. "We'd better act fast before there are even more of them."

"We?" said the angel.

"Okay. *I*, then."

"Actually, I do not think they have reproduced. I think this is a small settlement," said the angel.

Maxwell looked again, more closely, and saw that indeed, there was something settlmentish about the clearing. It was littered with rusted-out cars, dilapidated farm machinery, old garden furniture, mangy animals and naked, running kid kroaches.

"By golly, I do believe you are correct. At least we – or I – don't need to worry about them multiplying at the speed of light while trying to fight my way through them," said Maxwell.

"'By golly' – is this a trendy English phrase?" asked the Angel. "I do not know it, but you have used it several times."

"What? No! Lord love a duck, angel! Let's save Wendy first, then worry about English lessons."

"'Lord love a duck' – that is another phrase you use very much. Is it also trendy English?"

Maxwell ignored the angel, who seemed to have a peculiar set of priorities, even to his mind – and his priorities could hardly be considered standard-issue. Instead, he looked at the settlement more carefully.

Wendy had been tied to a pole, while several male kroaches

were drunkenly attempting to get a fire going in a massive brick barbecue. Fortunately, from Maxwell's point of view, if not the kroaches', their growing inebriation combined with their limited intellectual capacity ensured that getting the fire started would be slow going. This would be to Maxwell's advantage. He reckoned his only option would be to run in, cut Wendy free and flee back to the car as quickly as possible. The car might be stuck, but they could lock themselves inside it. As nasty as the kroaches were, they would be unlikely to kill a human over a presumed chicken dinner. They would probably scratch the hell out of the Bentley, though. Maybe he should just give up, then, and...No, he had to save Wendy!

Then Maxwell saw one of the kroaches pick up a large meat clever, beckon crudely to another kroach and start walking towards Wendy.

18

The convoy carrying Phineas and the nuns was luckier than Maxwell. They were received by green lights at each of the traffic control points and raced along the under-construction portion of the highway. As they approached the point where, according to the computer, Maxwell turned off the highway, they slowed to a snail's pace as they looked for a road.

"There it is," said Ivan, braking hard. The two SUVs behind him also slammed on their brakes and only just avoided an accident.

"Excellent," said Phineas. "But I still wonder why on Earth Maxwell went down this road."

The big four-wheel-drive SUVs were made for dirt roads such as this, and bounced along the winding dirt path, up and down a series of hills and into a patch of reeds.

As the first SUV burst through the reeds, Ivan saw the Bentley and hit the breaks. However, he was not sudden enough and the big vehicle skidded the back of the Bentley with a bang. Fortunately, neither vehicle suffered more than minor damage, though the Bentley was knocked forward a metre and a half.

Ivan turned around.

"Are you okay, Father?" he asked, but Phineas was already climbing out of the car. "I'll take that to mean 'yes'," said Ivan to himself as he followed the preacher.

The two men and a couple of nuns checked out the Bentley.

"There's no one here. The demon Maxwell must have gone forward on foot," said Phineas.

"Indeed. He appears to have walked from here," said a nun, pointing at foot prints leading from the Bentley.

"What do you think we should do, Sister Ingrid?" asked Phineas.

She thought for a few seconds.

"I suggest we follow slowly in the cars. He has a head start. If footprints go off the path or the path becomes impassible, we can leave the cars and go forward on foot."

"Very good, Sister. You all go first, now. You are better at following tracks."

"Yes, Father."

They returned to their SUVs. Sister Ingrid carefully drove hers around Phineas's and the Bentley. The others followed behind her.

19

Wendy saw two kroaches, one carrying a massive meat cleaver, walking towards her. The cleaver-wielder said something to the other, which resulted in laughter. Her eyes grew big and her mind prepared to go into a state of panic. She had been hoping that Maxwell would somehow save her, but she was beginning to realise that was less than realistic. Maxwell was a coward at the best of times and the kroaches were strong, stupid and had weapons. Maxwell did not stand a chance against them. It suddenly seemed that her life would end here and now, amidst these loud, smelly, awful creatures. She did not want that – but what could she do?

Oddly, one thought that did not pass through her mind was that she should not have scolded the kroaches for littering. Littering was wrong. Someone had to tell the kroaches. Their intention to kill her and eat her was unreasonable and unfair. If anyone should be rethinking their actions, she would have thought (had her thoughts gone this way, which they did not), it was the kroaches.

Meanwhile, Maxwell realised that he no longer had any time to size up the situation and plan. He had to act, and the only action his normally creative mind could devise at the moment was to run, grab Wendy and flee to his car. So he started running.

As he ran closer to the clearing, the kroaches looked in his direction. So much for the element of surprise, he thought; but he also noticed that they seemed frightened, which surprised him. They outnumbered him, were much stronger than him and probably had weapons. Nevertheless, he hoped their apparent fear would work in his favour. When a shadow passed over him, he realised that the kroaches were not looking at him, but at something flying above him.

He stumbled to a halt when he saw a massive bat swoop down, grab the kroach with the cleaver and then fly up into the air. A moment later, sticky liquid splattered down from the sky and left dark splotches on the muddy field. Chunks of flesh also hit the ground, making the sound of meat being thrown onto a grill, albeit without the sizzle. The cleaver, now blood-stained, fell within a metre of where he had come to a stop.

He looked up and saw that the bat was not actually a bat. It was the angel. With elegantly flapping wings, she hovered in the sky. In her hands was about a half of the kroach she had nabbed. With remarkable ease, she was tearing bits of its body off and flinging them to the ground. When there was nothing left in her hands, she swooped down towards another kroach.

"Maxwell!" Wendy shouted, pulling his attention away from the angel's killing spree.

"Wendy!" replied Maxwell, picking up the fallen cleaver and running towards her. He chopped the rope that had bound her to the tree, pulled her free and gave her a hug, which she returned awkwardly. Penguins are not used to hugging, though Wendy had learned to appreciate the emotions behind them.

There was another splatter of flesh and blood.

"You will fuck with my friends, will you, you filthy kroaches?" shouted the angel in a deep and throaty – yet still French-accented – voice as she swooped down again and grabbed another kroach.

"She's not very angelic, now is she?" said Maxwell, watching the angel rise into the sky with a petrified kroach in her hands.

"I don't like it here. Could we go to the car, please?" said Wendy.

"Oh! Yes. Of course, poor girl. The car's just up there." He pointed to the path down which he had run. "Come on!"

Kroaches may be slow-witted, but even the dimmest of this tribe could see that their barbecue party had taken a decidedly nasty and potentially fatal turn, so they did as their cockroach forebears had done for millions of years whenever the going got rough: they scrambled in all directions at once, most of them disappearing into the forest.

Maxwell and Wendy ran to the edge of the clearing just as the first of the ninja nuns' SUVs roared down the path and out of the forest. It was followed by two more. The SUVs came to a halt in the clearing. Doors opened. Ninja nuns hopped out and crouched in attack position. Phineas also stepped out, smirking, into the swirling dust kicked up by the vehicles.

"Lord love a duck and its aunt!" said Maxwell. "This day is just going from bad to worse to dismal, and it's not even lunchtime!"

"Maxwell! It is time to meet your maker!" thundered Phineas, who always appreciated an opportunity to be dramatic. However, a sudden splatter of blood on his head and shoulders spoiled the moment. He looked up to see the blood-stained angel hovering above with a kroach head in her hand.

"Holy mother of Jesus!" Phineas cried in near ecstasy. "It is an angel of God come to witness the death of Maxwell. Oh, yes! I knew the Lord God was at my side during this mission!" A kroach head hit the ground in front of him and burst, sending blood and bits of brain in all directions.

The nuns looked up and saw the angel. She swooped down, grabbed another kroach and tore it apart, flinging bits of its body left and right. The nuns stared in awe and confusion. On one hand, they did not recall angels in the Bible performing such massacres single-handedly like this. On the other hand, as trained killers, they could not help but appreciate the angel's technique.

The angel soared down and landed in front of Phineas and the nuns. She was an impressive sight: standing before them, hands on hips, wings spread partially and her blood-spattered dress dancing madly in the wind. Blood was smeared across the parts of her face, chest and arms, and it glistened in the sun.

"How dare you look upon me like that, you vile and filthy sinners? God, She knows what you have done and She is very, very disappointed in you! Get down on your knees now and pray! Pray that God forgives you!" the angel thundered in an unrecognisably deep voice.

The nuns, used to taking orders, promptly fell to their knees. Phineas continued staring at the angel.

"She?" he said to himself.

"Get down on your knees now, you fucking sinner, or God will smite you dead and send you to the gates of Hell immediately!" the angel screamed at Phineas.

He dropped to his knees, but continued to stare at her. Something was not right about this angel, he thought, but he wasn't confident enough of his assumption to question her. If he was wrong, he reckoned the consequences could be more than a little nasty. Maxwell and Wendy also stood watching the angel, albeit upon their feet rather than their knees. They were seeing a side of their hitch-hiker's character they had neither seen nor expected based on their brief acquaintance with her.

While all were staring, the angel looked down at her bloody dress.

"Merde" she said. She pulled it up over her head, revealing a lack of underwear on a stunning winged body. Although she was short on curves, her body was perfectly proportioned. Small, symmetrical breasts and hips joined by gracefully subtle curves and unblemished skin combined in feminine perfection. Phineas, who had not seen a live woman's naked body since he discovered Maxwell defiling Cathy years ago, was transfixed. He even felt a disturbing tingling and movement in his trousers.

Sensing this, the angel walked over to Phineas, crouched down in front of him, kissed him on the lips and caressed his trouser-covered penis for a few seconds, leading to further tingling and stiffening.

She stood up and stepped back. "You filthy, fucking perverted excuse for a preacher. How dare you get a fucking hard-on for me?! I am the angel of God and not some fucking sex toy for a pervert like you!"

With this outburst, Phineas's penis decided that this was not a good time for an erection and promptly shrank as much as it could, hoping to hide in his scrotum. Phineas himself was mortified. How could she know what he was thinking, he wondered. Perhaps she was sent by God. He was so ashamed. He promptly began praying.

The angel walked to a nearby water pipe with a tap and hose attached to it. She turned on the water, hosed herself down and rinsed off her dress. As she was finishing up, she sensed Phineas sneaking a peek at her.

"Pray, you dirty old man. Pray!" she shouted in the deep voice. The nuns, worried by their leader's confusion, started praying twice as hard.

The angel turned off the tap, wrung out the dress and walked back towards the path. "Come on. They will be busy for a while," she said softly in her normal voice to Maxwell and Wendy. To Maxwell, she added, "don't even think about it."

"With a body like yours, you leave me no choice with respect to thinking about it, but don't worry, I won't act upon it. You've made it clear that you do consequences in a big way."

Seeing that Wendy was slowing them down with her short legs, the angel picked her up and flew towards the car. As she did so, she felt the already-tense bird stiffen in fear.

"Do not worry, my dear friend," she said in an almost motherly tone – if, that is, one's mother spoke English in a French accent. "I am not going to hurt you. I am here to help you and Maxwell."

They landed beside the car. Maxwell arrived a moment later.

"Damn," he said, looking at the Bentley. "That fool Phinny must have hit the ancient Bentley." He looked at the dent in back.

"But I think that he has knocked your car out of the mud hole," said the angel

"Well, that's something," said Maxwell. "I don't suppose I can get his insurance to pay for the damage."

"Could we please get going?" said Wendy.

"Oh, yes! An excellent idea, and one to put into practice immediately," said Maxwell approvingly. "Let's go."

They climbed into the car. Maxwell started it up and discovered that the angel was right. The car had been knocked clear of the mud hole and was no longer stuck. He reversed the car for several hundred metres before he came to a place were he could execute a 180-degree turn. He did so and drove out of the forest and back onto the highway. Seeing that the light ahead was green, he floored he accelerator. The old car crouched and then raced forwards with a hint of skidding wheels – and a curious clunking sound coming from the rear.

"Damn," said Maxwell.

"What?!" shrieked Wendy, twisting round to look behind her."

"Calm down, Wendy. It's not that bad."

"How bad is it?" she asked in an uneven voice.

"There's a funny sound coming from the back of the car – the differential, I'd guess. The old Bentley was not made for off-road driving or being smashed into by religious lunatics."

"Are we going to be okay?" asked Wendy.

"Maybe the wheels will fall off," suggested the angel unhelpfully.

Maxwell glared at her.

"We should be fine. But I'll need to get it fixed before long."

He hoped that the car would hold out until he could put some distance between them and Phinny's gang. But it was an old car. He could only hope.

20

To say the atmosphere in the Bentley was one of relief and joyous laughter would be so far from the truth that to get there one could acquire a great many frequent-flyer miles. Maxwell was firmly gripping the steering wheel of the car while racing along the road and checking the rear-view mirror from time to time to ensure they were not being followed by Phineas and crew, or kroaches. So far, the only thing he had seen in the mirror were the vehicles he had overtaken while racing away from the slaughter at twice the speed limit.

Meanwhile, Wendy had her head wrapped in her wings and was rocking back and forth in her seat, moaning quietly. Maxwell knew it was how she would withdraw from the world around her when she felt she unable to cope. He wanted to stop and comfort her, but felt that putting distance between them, the kroaches and Phineas's ninja nuns was a better strategy for the time being.

The angel was shivering in the back seat. Whether from fear or a chill, Maxwell was not sure, but she was obviously a tough cookie and possibly a dangerous one, so he wasn't worried about her.

He was, however, worried about the clunking sound coming from the back of the car. He thought it might be getting worse. It seemed to be getting louder. If the differential failed, they would be stranded on the road. Nevertheless, he felt that continued fast driving was the best option for the moment. If the differential did give out, they would at least have put as much distance between themselves and Phineas as possible.

After another 15 minutes of driving and no sign of anyone following them, they passed a bright-orange concrete building with thatched roof and a sign out front indicating that within the building in question one could purchase coffee, ice cream and local handicrafts. Maxwell braked the Bentley surprisingly gently, backed up and entered the drive. He drove behind the building and pulled in beside a dilapidated delivery van where he reckoned the car would be out of sight from the highway.

He turned off the engine and put his hand on Wendy's back. He wanted to hold her, but knew that she could be sensitive about being held when she was upset.

"It's okay, Wendy. We're far away from the kroaches now. You don't have to worry any more."

She wrapped her wings around Maxwell and held him tightly for a minute and Maxwell held her just as tightly in return.

"I thought I was going to be plucked and eaten!" she exclaimed with tears in her eyes.

"Don't be silly, old girl. I would never let anyone do that to you!"

"But, there were so many of them..."

"It doesn't matter. Allowing Wendy to be plucked and eaten by kroaches or indeed any other species is expressly prohibited according to paragraph something or other, item something else, of our friendship agreement."

"We don't have a friendship agreement," said Wendy, loosening he grip and pulling back to look at Maxwell.

"It's an implied agreement, silly bird."

"Okay."

He looked at the angel in the rear-view mirror. She was shivering and staring forward. He was not quite sure how to deal with her. She did, of course, save Wendy's life. However, her methods were on the extreme side and suggested one would not want to get on the wrong side of this particular angel.

He looked at Wendy again.

"Are you going to be okay?" he asked.

"Yes, I just need a little time."

"Good girl. Now let me check on our hitch-hiker," he said softly.

Maxwell turned to look at the angel. "Are you cold, freaking out or having some kind of attack?" he asked, and then added for good measure, "or a combination of the above?"

"C-c-c-c-cold, I th-th-think," she said.

"Hang on a second, then," he said. He got out of the car, walked round back and rummaged in the boot for a moment.

"Aha!" he shouted, closing he boot. He opened the rear door of the car and handed the angel a large, soft towel. "Here you go."

"Merci," she said.

"Now, why don't you step out of the car and dry yourself off?" he said, offering his hand.

She climbed out, dried herself off and wrapped the towel around her.

"Let us go inside the shop here, see if we can find a new dress for, um, angel, have a drink and work out what to do," suggested Maxwell.

Checking first to ensure that the road was empty of traffic, the three walked round to the front of the orange building and went inside, where they found a sleepy shop, dimly lit and slightly dusty. There were a few tables in front. A well-chalked chalk board on the wall described a limited selection of refreshments. Scattered behind the tables were a dozen wooden shelves haphazardly occupied by half-hearted handicrafts. One got the impression that the responsible artisans had turned to alcohol or some such and were no longer putting their hearts into their artwork.

Behind the counter, an obese woman in her twenties sat reading a book that clearly interested her rather more than the customers.

"Coffee? Tea?" Maxwell asked.

"Tea, please," said Wendy.

"Excuse me, have you some cognac?" the angel asked the woman.

Looking up from her book, she raised her eyebrow slightly at the sight of the angel. Her wings were hidden under the towel, but one assumes not many wet, towel-draped customers visited the place.

"No, just beer," she said.

"Yes, okay," said the angel.

"And a coffee, please," said Maxwell.

While the woman prepared the drinks, Maxwell and Wendy sat at a table away from the window, but with a view of the road, while the angel looked around the shop. She found a long skirt with a flowery pattern on it and a white sleeveless top that was cut low enough on the back to allow room for her wings. She put them on in the women's toilet, came out and drank the beer in a couple of quick guzzles.

"Another beer, please!" she called out to the woman behind the counter.

"You know, um...What should I call you? Angel?" Maxwell said.

"'Angel' will do perfectly," she said.

"You know, Angel, that was a rather extreme thing to do to the kroaches – tearing them apart like that," said Maxwell.

"But they are filthy, dirty, horrible creatures!" said the angel.

"Yes, but they are half human, you know," said Maxwell.

"Yes. That is the part that is filthy, dirty and horrible," said the angel.

"You may be on to something there, young, um, Angel. But it was a rather extreme action to take, wasn't it?" said Maxwell.

"I had to save the penguin," said the angel.

"Yes, that is important," agreed Wendy who was calming down, though she was still rocking gently.

"That is a noble deed, indeed," agreed Maxwell. "But should we find ourselves in a similar situation, perhaps you could just..."

"Yes?" asked the angel.

"I'm not sure, actually. Let's try and avoid another such scenario."

"That's a good idea," agreed Wendy. "I didn't like that scenario at all."

"Okay," said the angel.

"Well, what's done is done," said Maxwell. "The kroaches are doubtless pissed off in a big way. But they are more likely to drink away their anger than seek revenge."

"Do you think so?" asked Wendy.

"Yes. They are dim creatures without much of a memory."

"And do you think they might contact the authorities?" asked Wendy.

"Drinking themselves silly and poor memory will probably prevent such an action. Mind you, if the authorities visit that camp anytime soon, they will see some disturbing evidence. But frankly, our greater concern is Phinny and those ninja groupies he's got in tow. He really seems intent on doing me in this time," said Maxwell.

"He has tried to do you in like this in the past?" asked the angel, signalling for another beer.

"Yes. Every now and again he destroys a sculpture, organises a protest about my work, or threatens violence. Oh, and a Subaru of mine mysteriously exploded a few years ago, though I don't know if that was his doing. There was a particularly pissed off ex-girlfriend in my life at that time..." Maxwell became thoughtful for a moment, then continued.

"But before now, it seems he's never really put his heart into killing me. Anyway, you put the fear of Jesus into him."

"Jesus?" asked the angel.

"Jesus Christ," said Maxwell

"Who?" asked the angel.

"You don't know Jesus?" asked Maxwell in surprise.

"No. Should I?" asked the angel.

"Probably not," said Maxwell, "but you are a curious angel, I must say."

"Yes, I think I am," agreed the angel.

"Meanwhile, I would like to avoid giving Phinny and his groupies another opportunity to kill me," said Maxwell.

"A good plan," commented the angel

"Do you think he intends to kill Angel and me too?" asked Wendy.

"No, I expect it's just me he's got a grudge against. But those nuns seem kind of clumsy. I am worried about collateral damage."

"Why does he intend to kill you?" asked the angel.

"I am not entirely sure, but I suspect it goes back to my university days," said Maxwell. "We both were at Cape City University together, although he was a graduate student in the seminary and I was in the art school. I first met – perhaps I should say 'encountered' – him when he walked in on me while I was, um, performing cunnilingus – and good cunnilingus at that – on a girl he apparently fancied, though she didn't have a very high opinion of him! Had he not barged in on me back then, I doubt I would have known who he was."

"Perhaps that is why he hates you," said the angel.

"Perhaps, but I doubt it. The girl in question was awfully promiscuous. If Phinny is feeling homicidal thoughts towards me for having had sex with her, he'd have to be a serial killer in order to deal with all of the boys and girls she slept with in university alone."

"Was she a good fuck?" asked the angel.

"You know, I really cannot...Hang on! That's hardly relevant," said Maxwell.

He sipped his coffee thoughtfully, the angel ordered another beer and Wendy looked out the window.

"Changing the subject, I assume he's guessing correctly that we are headed towards Erps-Kwerps," said Maxwell.

"Yes, I assume so, too," said Wendy, who had finally stopped rocking and seemed to be calming down. Making plans and creating structure soothed her.

"I expect he's also assuming we'll take the North-South Highway to Brussels and then go on home," said Maxwell

"Yes," said Wendy.

"And he and those ninja nuns will doubtless again try to kill me along the way," said Maxwell.

"Yes," said Wendy.

"And as much as I admire a chap with a vision, when that vision involves my violent death, I feel a compelling need to thwart that vision and stay alive and violence-free," said Maxwell.

"Yes," said Wendy, hoping Maxwell would get to the point. He had an irritating tendency to talk in circles.

"So, I reckon there are two things we can do to make his goal less attainable," said Maxwell. "First, I need to make a phone call."

He rummaged through his pockets until he found his telephone, clicked a few buttons to reroute the call across multiple towers – a function Wendy programmed in at his behest not long ago – and punched in the number for the national police.

When he got through, he explained that he and his friends had stopped for a picnic in a lovely forest off the North-South highway. However, their luncheon plans and appetites were utterly spoiled by a gang of religious freaks who seemed to be slaughtering small children. There were screaming kids and was blood everywhere, Maxwell explained dramatically. He made a noise that sounded remarkably like stifled tears. He then answered a few questions, said they were on the road somewhere far south of where they actually were and rang off.

"But Maxwell," said Wendy. "There were no small children being slaughtered, just kroaches!"

"I know, but if I tell the police that kroaches were being slaughtered, they will hardly rush to the scene of the crime. We'd be lucky if they found time to deal with it today. But slaughtering children? Why, there is probably a convey of police cars, lights blazing and sirens screaming, dashing there right now."

"And they didn't kill anyone. We did. Well, she did." Wendy nodded towards the angel.

"Thank you," said the angel modestly.

"Goodness, your grip on reality is even more fragile than mine, young lady," said Maxwell to the angel. He turned to Wendy. "Don't worry about it. I am hoping and expecting that the police will haul in Phinny and crew and toss them into prison, but when the police realise that the only victims were drunken kroaches and that Phinny is a prominent religious loony, he'll be able to bribe his and the nuns' way out easily enough. By then, I hope we'll be safe in Erps-Kwerps."

Erps-Kwerps was the Flemish village where Maxwell's family's Earth-based estate had been located for generations. It was a quiet village in a prosperous region where his family held considerable sway. He did not think Phineas would be daft enough to try and kill Maxwell in Erps-Kwerps and probably not even in Flanders. The police there were less tolerant of religious nuts and less easily bribed, particularly as Maxwell's family made regular generous donations to various police-related causes.

Wendy thought about the phone call for a moment. Like most penguins, she was very honest and uncomfortable about lying. However, she could see these lies might save Maxwell's life – or at least prolong it. Moreover, it was Maxwell doing the lying, not her. Over their years of friendship, she had learned to tolerate an awful lot of unpenguinish behaviour in Maxwell – particularly when that behaviour made her life easier.

"You said there were two things we could do," Wendy said.

"Yes. The second thing we need to do is to get off this road," said Maxwell.

"Why?" asked Wendy.

"Phinny expects us to take the North-South highway. If he does not get hauled into jail, he'll charge up this way looking for me."

"But any other route would slow us down. Would it not be better just to go as quickly as we can?" asked Wendy.

"Normally, yes. But I reckon we need to have the Bentley seen to. That clunking noise makes me uneasy."

"I could sing along with this noise," suggested the angel.

Maxwell raised an eyebrow. "Well, that might be an option. But unless your singing has magical properties, we'll still need to have the car fixed."

On his telephone, Maxwell called up a local map. He thought for a moment. "I believe our best option will be to turn off the highway at the Daliville exit and drive into the Valley of Dreams. I'm sure we can find a garage and a decent hotel there and camp out until the car is fixed."

"And then?" asked Wendy.

"We can follow the valley northeast to Route 103 and take that to Erps-Kwerps." said Maxwell.

Wendy looked at the telephone's screen and thought a moment. "That may take days," she said, worriedly.

"Yes, but in the event the police don't arrest Phinny and the nuns, or they get out quickly, they'll be looking for us on the wrong road. So, it should provide us with an additional safety net," said Maxwell, adding, "mind you, the thing about the Valley of Dreams is not so much that it will take longer. Rather, it can get awfully weird in there. Nevertheless, I reckon it's our best bet."

The angel ordered another beer.

21

"The more I think about it," said Phineas, still on his knees long after the angel left, "the less I think that angel was an angel of God."

"But she looked like an angel and flew like an angel, Father," said the nun nearest to him.

"Maxwell works in mysterious ways and is surely in a pact with the devil. I believe that angel was no angel, but a demon."

"Oh my God!"

"Yes, Sister, 'oh my God'. But do not worry yourself. He will guide us to Maxwell. It is surely His will that Maxwell and that satanic demon be destroyed as soon as possible." Phineas stood up. One by one, the nuns followed suit.

As the last of them stood up, the forest in front of them exploded with flashing red light. Three nuns promptly returned to their knees and began praying anew.

A dozen white SUVs with flashing lights burst into the clearing. Two of them hit Phineas's and the nuns' SUVs. One of them hit a nun, knocking her across the bonnet and on to the ground, but hurting only her dignity.

Police officers exploded out of the vehicles and mostly jumped into raid position, crouched, weapons drawn and ready for action. A few rookies tripped over themselves as they rolled out of their SUVs, but quickly righted themselves.

"Throw down your weapons and put your hands on your head," announced a megaphone in front of a police officer's mouth.

The nuns looked to Phineas for leadership.

"I said, put down your weapons and put your hands on you head. Now!" repeated the megaphone.

"I think we should do what the officer says, sisters. God will guide us through this," said Phineas, putting his hands on his head. One by one, the sisters followed suit.

"Weapons down now!" screamed the megaphone.

"We do not have any weapons, officer. We are but agents of the Lord God,"

"Okay, then. I want everyone down on their knees and we are going to check," said the megaphone. The officer gestured to a male and two female officers to frisk their suspects.

"Now, do you have any more children held hostage?" asked the megaphone in a stern voice.

"Children? Did you say children?" asked Phineas.

"We know you religious nut-cases have been slaughtering children for some sick ritual," said the megaphone. "But it looks like we are too late," it added as the officer looked at the blood stains on Phineas's and the nuns' clothes, the spatter across the ground and the bloody bits of flesh scattered about. Although kroaches are unmistakably kroaches when viewed in their entirety – their exoskeletons being a give-away – their bits and pieces, when torn off their bodies, look remarkably human.

"Children!?" exclaimed one of the nuns, a one-time teacher, appalled. "We have not been slaughtering children, just trying to slaughter a full-grown man."

"Sister!" scolded Phineas to the outspoken nun before turning to the police officer. "Sir, we are not slaughtering children. We are agents of the Lord God and representatives of the Evangelical Church of America on a mission."

"I don't care what you nut-cases do in your own country. Here in Europa, we do not slaughter children for any god!" said the megaphone indignantly. "Take them away before I puke!" the megaphone added, presumably to the police and not Phineas.

"Do not worry, sisters. The Church will take care of us," said Phineas just before a policeman hit him on the head.

"Shut the fuck up!" he said, yanking Phineas by the arm and dragging him to one of the police SUVs.

"God, please forgive him. He does not know what he is doing," said Phineas, only to be hit again.

The police SUVs turned around, again hitting Phineas's team's SUV at least three times while manoeuvring, and drove back out of the forest, sirens blaring.

By this time, the kroaches had scattered far and wide. It would be more than a week before they dared come back to their settlement.

22

It is human nature, when one is a member of neither the slaughtering party nor the party to be slaughtered, to be slow to intervene in the slaughter in question. Intervention in order to prevent unnecessary death is a noble act, but it is also a risky act that, if performed less than skilfully, could readily lead to one becoming an involuntary member of the slaughtered party. If one cares passionately about the party to be slaughtered, one might understandably be willing to take the risk. But when the party to be slaughtered consists solely of a promiscuous and hedonistic – if charming – artist of dubious sanity, there is little motivation to hurry.

Had Judith and Lucy discussed the matter, they doubtless would have said as much between themselves. But women, being women, tend to understand such things instinctively and find more important matters to talk about. Nevertheless, this was the unspoken reason that Judith was driving the SUV at a more leisurely pace than the other two parties in this insane journey. Meanwhile, the two women used their time to get to know each other better.

Judith told Lucy about her own upbringing in a small evangelical community in Eastern Europa. Her parents were devout Christians who did not believe in birth control. Judith did not know, but would not have been surprised to know, that in their 30-odd years of marriage, her parents had had sex precisely nine times – seven of which produced offspring. Judith was the sixth child and, like her brothers and sisters, was raised in a devout, Jesus-loving and fun-hating household.

At the St. Catherine School for Young Christian Women, where she received an evangelical Christian education of dubious value outside the religion, Judith had shown a propensity for athletics that had her captaining the school team at a young age. It was during a match against a visiting American team that Judith's talents were spotted by a member of the Christian Olympics management team. She was recruited for the Europa team and showed great promise.

However, after a game against a Catholic team from the Italian provinces, a boy squeezed her left breast and made a lewd comment in Italian. It was the last time he spoke for six months. Judith, outraged, beat the boy to a pulp within 30 seconds. Indeed, it took four people to pry her off the lad, and even then she somehow managed to retain bits of his body in her clenched fists and mouth. Needless to say, slaughtering other athletes is considered by the Christian Olympics committee to be less than acceptable behaviour. Judith was asked to apologise to what remained of the boy and bow out of the Olympic team.

Doubtless, the matter would have ended there – in humiliation – except that on this particular day, two senior members of the evangelical church's intelligence arm happened to be at the game, watching for girls with potential to become ninja nuns. Although the agents only saw the last few moments of Judith's attack, it was clear to them that potential was an understatement in this girl's case. She was promptly recruited.

Able to focus her aggression in an environment that encouraged it, Judith did well in her training and was soon a full-fledged ninja nun. Not long after this dubious graduation, she was selected by the prominent preacher in the Cape City region, the Reverend Phineas Forge, to join his team.

It was while talking about basic ninja nun training that Judith suddenly exclaimed: "Whoops, what's that?" in response to a police SUV parked across the highway and an officer signalling for her to stop, which she did.

"Road block?" asked Lucy.

Before Judith could reply, a dozen SUVs with police lights flashing and sirens blaring roared out of the woods, turned onto the highway and drove past the two women.

"Looks like a big bust," said Lucy, watching the vehicles race past.

"Holy Mother of God!" exclaimed Judith, pointing at an SUV going past. "There were some of my sisters in that one!"

"What?" asked Lucy.

"And there's Father Forge!" said Judith, pointing at another vehicle.

"Holy shit! It looks like they are covered in blood!" said Lucy.

"Oh my God, you're right! What do you think has happened?" asked Judith.

"I don't know, but I am afraid we might be too late," said Lucy. "It looks like someone was brutally slaughtered, judging from all the blood on your friends."

"That is an awful lot of blood," agreed Judith, who, although younger than Lucy, had considerably more experience with violence. "Do you think they succeeded in killing Maxwell?"

"Let's see what we can find out," said Lucy, opening the door.

She walked over to the police officer blocking traffic. Judith paused for a moment, then ran after Lucy.

"Excuse me, officer," said Lucy. "Could you tell me what's happened here?"

"I'm not sure, ma'am," he said. "We got a report that some religious nut-jobs were slaughtering kids in some kind of devilish ritual."

"Slaughtering children?" exclaimed Lucy in surprise.

"What?" said Judith in equal surprise.

"That's what we heard, ladies. And there was a shit-load of blood in there. Pardon my language. I don't like to think about what happened in that wood, ladies."

"Thanks, officer," said Lucy who took Judith's arm and led her away from the policeman.

"Is your gang killing children?" Lucy demanded of Judith.

"Oh my God, no! Of course not!" exclaimed Judith. "My team takes care of people who cause trouble with the church, people that God wishes us to send to Hell, but..."

"'God wishes you to send people to Hell'?" asked Lucy.

"Yes, God sometimes tells us to expedite bad people to Hell."

"You personally?"

"I would never go to Hell! I serve God!" said Judith indignantly.

"No, I mean does God tell you personally to expedite bad people to Hell?"

"Oh. No, of course not. He talks to more important people, like Father Forge."

"I see. And does God tell you, or Father Forge, to send bad children to Hell?"

"As far as I know, that has never happened. And I don't think it would. Children are innocent."

"Indeed."

"Why don't I call Sister Agatha and ask her?"

"No, I don't think that would be a good idea just now, Judith."

Judith thought a moment, laughed uneasily and agreed. "What should we do then?"

"Let's drive on, find some place to have a coffee and work out what to do next," said Lucy.

Half an hour later, they pulled up at a combination petrol station and café.

As soon as she stopped the big SUV, Judith turned and hugged her lover.

"Oh, Lucy! What's happened to my sisters? I don't understand!"

"It's okay, sweetheart," Lucy said. "I don't know what happened. But you are here with me now." She kissed the younger woman on the forehead.

As sometimes happens in situations like this, particularly among recent lovers, Judith looked up and Lucy kissed her cheeks and her lips. And then there was a fair bit of kissing and comforting, some of which involved the removal of clothes behind the tinted windows of the SUV. It was another half hour before the two women headed to the café.

Inside was a television mounted on a wall. They caught the tail end of a news report confirming what the policeman had said: members of an American extreme fundamental religious group had been arrested for allegedly slaughtering children in some kind of ritual.

Judith looked as though she would cry again, so Lucy took her hand and led her to a table where they ordered cappuccinos and cakes.

"I don't know what happened in that forest, Judith, but your Father Forge seems hell-bent on killing Maxwell. And you and your sisters are lethal," said Lucy.

"Yes," said Judith quietly.

"Maybe some kids got in the way of something. Maybe someone made a mistake. I guess we'll have to wait until we hear more."

"Yes."

"Anyway, my dear," Lucy took Judith's hands in hers, "I'm glad you are with me now and not them."

"Yes, me too," said Judith, smiling wanly. A lot of emotions were stirring inside her mind, which had never been prepared to deal with conflicting emotions. Judith had decided, only half consciously, to put her trust in this older woman whom she had so suddenly come to love.

They nibbled at the cakes and sipped their coffees in silence for a couple of moments.

"I'm in no hurry to get back to Cape City. Are you?" asked Lucy.

"No. No, I don't know what I'd do there," said Judith.

"Let's not worry about that now. I suggest we camp out in a hotel for a couple of days and enjoy ourselves. We can also keep an eye on the news. How does that sound to you?"

"Oh, that would be great!" said Judith.

"I know a really beautiful hotel in the Valley of Dreams. It's a three- or four-hour drive from here. I can help with the driving if you want a break."

"No, I'm fine."

"First, let's do a little shopping. We both need some clothes."

"Oh, yes," said Judith, who was feeling a bit dirty in her ninja sweat-suit.

"And I need a bra. I don't know if you've noticed, but guys keep looking at my boobs," said Lucy.

"That's because you have beautiful boobs," said Judith, with her first real smile since she had seen Father Forge and her sisters being taken away.

"Thanks, sweetie," said Lucy with a smile. "Still, I prefer to wear a bra. Now, let me see if I have the number of the hotel in my telephone...Yes, I do!"

Lucy booked a room. They finished the coffee and cakes, paid up and went out to the SUV, which, to Lucy's eyes seemed to have grown while they were away. The climbed in, started the engine and drove off in the direction of the Valley of Dreams.

23

Sitting in an interrogation cell in the Zamora police station, Sister Henrietta was tired, confused and just wanted to go back to the convent. The life of a ninja nun should have been about glorious, heroic actions in the name of Jesus Christ. It should not have been about running around in posh hotels, chasing after a scrawny guy who seemed stronger on cuteness than threat and driving cross-country in an SUV. Ninja nunnery should not have involved watching some kind of angel tear apart kroaches and, above all, it most certainly should not have included being interrogated in a dirty police station cell while feeling tired, sweaty and hungry.

She had spent what seemed like hours answering the questions of the police officers, accompanied by a local lawyer who seemed more interested in her chest than in her situation. After the interrogation finished, he popped out to find some coffee and a snack for her. At least that was something, but he was taking his time about it.

The cell door opened. Three men came in. They wore navy blue unisex suits comprising trousers and jackets over white, collarless shirts. Two of the men had close-cropped hair and firm mouths that gave the impression they had not smiled in the past decade or two. They had dark glasses propped upon their heads and appeared to have earpieces in their ears.

The third man, who walked in behind the other two, was, upon closer inspection, not a man; he was a humanoid alien whose proportions ensured the human-shaped suit was a poor fit. On his face he wore a mask of an average caucasian man, and a blonde wig. The mask was tied around his head like a cheap children's costume. The wig was too big, and flopped about oddly as he walked. Had Henrietta seen him walking down the street, it would have been funny. In this hellish interrogation room, it was ominous.

They took seats across from the ninja nun.

"You are Henrietta Maria Saldez?" asked one of the human men.

"Yes, I am," said Henrietta, wondering where her lawyer was and whether she really needed him anyway.

"My name is Dan, this is Sam and this is Frank." Frank was the alien in disguise.

"Um, hello," said Henrietta.

"We are from the IIA – the Interplanetary Intelligence Agency. We understand there was something very unusual about your, ah, incident in the woods earlier today. Something involving a non-human."

Henrietta looked at them quietly.

"Don't worry, Henrietta," said Dan. "We are not here to incriminate you. Crimes between humans and, in this case, near-human kroaches, are not our jurisdiction. However, if non-humans are involved in a serious crime, that is our concern. We believe that may have happened this morning."

"Where is my lawyer?" asked Henrietta.

"Unconscious in the men's toilet," said Sam.

"What?!" exclaimed Henrietta.

"He doesn't need to know about this, Henrietta. We need to keep it confidential," said Dan.

"And let's face it: he was a shit lawyer," said Sam.

Henrietta thought for a moment.

"True. He kept looking at my breasts."

"They are very nice," said Frank.

"Frank," said Dan. "That's not appropriate."

"Sorry, Ms Saldez. I am taking a human social interaction

course, but I have a lot to learn. In truth, to my race, your breasts are not at all interesting and you have too few."

Henrietta was not sure how to take the alien's apology and decided to let it pass for now.

"Okay, folks, can we get back to the subject at hand?" asked Dan. The room went quiet. He continued. "Good. Now, Ms Saldez, did you see an unusual non-human sentient being in the woods this morning?"

"Is...Is an angel a non-human sentient being?" asked Henrietta. Like most ninja nuns, she was fearless in the face of nasty foes and meek in the face of authority.

"Could be. Tell us about this angel."

Henrietta told the story from her perspective, omitting the bit about intending to kill Maxwell. As she had been instructed in training, she was to say simply that the nuns wished to confront Maxwell regarding crimes against God. This claim, the Church's legal experts assured, was less likely to land the responsible nuns in jail for the rest of their lives.

From time to time, Dan or Sam interrupted with a question. They were particularly keen to get a detailed description of the angel. Once Henrietta had finished her story, Dan thanked her and the IIA agents left the room.

The agents found a set of chairs in a corner and sat down.

"Did you recognise the description?" Dan asked Frank.

"No. But I have passed the information on to headquarters. They will check the database," said the alien.

"It would be very unusual for a new race to visit Earth, or any of the planets in the populated zone, in the manner she described," said Sam. "Surely any aliens would follow protocols."

"You'd think so," said Dan. "But what if it's a new race that doesn't know about the protocols?"

"That would be something, wouldn't it?" said Sam.

"You bet," said Dan.

Frank cocked his head for a moment as if listening to a speaker in his ear, which was precisely what he was doing.

"No, there is nothing similar to this angel in the database. The closest match is you humans. But that did not seem like a human to me. Did you think so?"

"Well, humans cannot fly..." said Dan.

"And that means?" asked Frank.

"Sorry. That means no, this angel is definitely not human," said Dan. "So maybe we're onto a new alien race."

"I am doubtful," said Frank.

"You never know," said Dan. "Let's talk to that preacher and some more nuns and see what they have to say," suggested Dan.

Sam and Frank agreed. Over the next couple of hours, they spoke to three nuns and Phineas. The nuns largely corroborated Henrietta's story. Phineas, however, was delusional, and while parts of what he said fit the nuns' stories, other bits were confused religious observations. The agents reckoned it was best to discount the priest's account for the time being.

Two hours later, they reconvened in the same chairs.

"Well, what have we got?" asked Dan.

"The cumulative description of the being in question is of a highly humanoid, apparently female being with fleshy wings, great strength for her size and the ability to fly," said Frank.

"So it's gotta be an alien," said Dan.

"I am concerned about the high level of human description," said Frank. "We have no record of two distinct races from different planets sharing so many characteristics."

"You need to keep in mind that these descriptions are coming from religious nuts," said Sam. "And they were highly agitated. I think they saw something that reminded them of an angel and they convinced themselves they saw an angel. Religious weirdos are called 'weirdos' for a reason."

"That makes sense to me. What do you think, Frank?" asked

Dan.

"Human psychology is not one of my strengths. If you believe this is likely, I accept your judgement," said the alien. "That means that the actual alien might look different to what they have described, does it not?"

"Yes," said Sam. "I think we need to assume this might be the case."

"Agreed?" asked Dan. When the others nodded, he added, "it seems this unregistered alien is travelling with Maxwell van Mars, the artist, in a vintage, burgundy-coloured car, probably a Rolls Royce or Bentley."

"With that information, can we find and follow the car on the road?" Dan asked Frank.

Frank thought for a moment, then cocked his head as he did when he was in remote communication.

"I've requested a scan across Southwest Europa," he said.

"Good," said Dan.

Frank cocked his head again.

"Interesting. It seems that two days ago, Maxwell came back from a space trip outside the solar system."

"Really? Where did he go?" asked Sam.

"That's the strange thing. He simply skimmed Gateway and returned to Earth," said Frank. "What's more, it seems he took one of his family's company's cruisers without asking permission."

"That is strange! Do you think he could have brought the alien to Earth?" asked Sam.

"It could be, though there is no evidence of him doing so. He never stopped, nor does he seem to have made contact with any other spacecraft."

"So, maybe not," said Sam.

"But Gateway's gravity well is Earth's portal into hyperspace," said Frank, "so it is conceivable that he somehow collected the alien as he skimmed Gateway."

"Skimmed Gateway?" asked Dan, who was more a man of action than a man of intellect and so was having trouble following the exchange.

"Yes," explained Frank. "Maxwell's cruiser came into extremely close contact with Gateway's Schwarzchild radius."

"And that means?" asked Dan, who was no clearer.

"Because Gateway is a black hole," explained Frank, "it has a very intense gravitational field, which creates a well in the fabric of the universe. This also allows the area to function as a doorway into hyperspace, which effectively allows faster-than-light travel. Although it is not clear how it could have happened, it is possible that the alien came through hyperspace as Maxwell's cruiser came into near contact with Gateway."

"So, you're saying Maxwell picked up the alien a couple of days ago?" said Dan.

"We don't know this. It may just be a coincidence. But it seems possible, and would explain why the alien is still travelling with Maxwell," said Frank.

"Or maybe the alien somehow caught a lift with Maxwell," he added.

"Okay. Then we need to be careful here," said Dan.

"Ah ha! We've found a burgundy Bentley S1 driving north," said Frank.

"That was fast!" said Dan. "Okay. This alien is apparently dangerous. Sam, call HQ and have them send an armed response unit."

"Okay," said Sam.

"And gents, make sure you're armed."

"Yes," said Frank. Sam, who was on the telephone to HQ, nodded.

"Let's meet at the hovercar in five minutes," said Dan, "and chase this so-called angel down."

24

The angel lay sprawled across the back seat of the ancient Bentley, singing "Ne Me Quitte Pas".

"She's rather good, isn't she?" Maxwell asked Wendy, who had calmed down considerably over the past couple of hours.

"Yes, she is," said Wendy.

"And it does rather cover up the sound of the clunking," said Maxwell, referring to the noise coming from the car's damaged differential. "Mind you, one would expect an angel to sing nicely."

"Why is that?" asked Wendy.

"In art, angels are often depicted playing harps. I reckon if you know your way around a harp, you can probably sing a decent tune as well."

"Why is that? I see no connection," said Wendy after a moment's thought.

"Well, both require musical skill and awareness," said Maxwell.

"Yes, but playing a harp is a skill of dexterity, timing and ability to translate written music to strings, whereas singing is about vocal dexterity. Surely one could be an excellent harpist and sing like a seal."

" I've never heard a seal sing," said Maxwell.

"They sing terribly," said Wendy.

"Ah, there's the Daliville exit," said Maxwell, slowing the car and veering onto the exit ramp with amazing restraint. The car sedately followed the winding ramp as it exited onto a tree-lined but somewhat worn-looking dual carriageway that twisted its way between the mountains ahead.

The waving branches of the trees and the speed at which the clouds travelled across the sky indicated that the wind had picked up. A scarecrow did a wild dance in a field on the right.

"Recalculating," announced Mrs Miller.

"You forgot to reprogram her for the new destination," said Wendy.

"Well, the destination is the same, but the roads to get there have changed. That's kind of deep for Mrs Miller," said Maxwell, adding , "sorry, Mrs Miller. Change of plans. Please cancel the destination and enjoy the trip."

"Destination cancelled," said Mrs Miller.

"Good woman," said Maxwell.

"Though I do wish you would tell me these things in advance. I feel like a fool now," said Mrs Miller.

"She's taking on a curious attitude, don't you think? Have you reprogrammed her again, Wendy?" asked Maxwell.

"I do not like being talked about like that when I am right here on your dashboard," said Mrs Miller sternly. Though, to be fair, everything she said sounded stern. Navigation unit voices are not noted for their wide range, nor should they be; their purpose is to get you to your destination; not to get emotional about it.

"Sorry, Mrs Miller," said Maxwell.

"Apology accepted," said Mrs Miller.

"No, I haven't," said Wendy.

The Bentley wended along the winding road between the mountains. On either side of the road, multicoloured plants climbed up the mountainside. Here and there a stone farmhouse could be spotted and occasionally a sculpture commemorating someone long forgotten stood by the roadside in lonely hopes of recognition. A sign announced that it was 18 kilometres to Crashsite.

Crashsite, as you doubtless know, is the area where a spacecraft from the planet Fynsha crashed into the Valley of Dreams. Until that time, no other aliens had visited Earth, so when a bright light flashed across the sky and slammed into the side of a valley, hurting no one, the incident was understandably assumed to be a meteor crash rather than a spaceship crash.

Of course, the European Space Incident Investigation Office (ESIIO) sent out a team to investigate, as they did with all significant meteor collisions, but the resulting report described an ordinary, if relatively large, meteor impact of no scientific interest.

Some years later, when the Zargonians became the second alien race to visit the Earth, but the first to survive landing, and were taken to meet leaders and eventually establish a diplomatic and trade presence, they asked about the Fynshan crash. Initially, the ESIIO had to admit, much to its embarrassment, that it knew of no such crash. However, the Zargonians insisted, a search was done, and it was discovered that the Valley of Dreams meteor impact was in fact a spacecraft accident.

ESIIO embarrassment continued when the government asked how it was possible that the office had sent out a team to investigate the crash and yet the resulting 48-page report detailed a typical meteor strike. Initial accusations of professional incompetence soon gave way to charges of dishonesty and horniness when it was discovered that the male investigators spent their "investigation" time in the notorious whorehouses that line the North-South highway near Santander airport, the nearest airport to the Valley of Dreams. Instead of actually investigating, which they apparently found less fulfilling than paid-for sex, they used a standard meteor impact report template, which they filled in while drinking gin and tonics in a whorehouse bar. In truth, the investigators never even visited the Valley of Dreams.

Upon learning this, the ESIIO sent out another team of investigators, this time all female, to examine the site. They found that the spacecraft in question had crashed into the ruins of a long-abandoned and forgotten castle, creating a rather spectacular site of mingled medieval and alien ruins upon a ridge halfway up the mountainside. Not surprisingly, this surreally beautiful spot soon became a tourist destination, and the town of Crashsite was born.

The Valley of Dreams has always been an oddly picturesque area with an inherent strangeness that gives it character. Many feel that the crash and multidimensional disintegration of the space-craft's dark energy drives in the valley made it even stranger. Yet for all the valley's natural beauty, it had been a largely unknown place until the establishment of Crashsite. Since then, it has become more popular among tourists and travellers keen on the unusual.

However, none of these things were on Maxwell's mind when he switched on the car radio and sought a news station. It took some time before he found the story he was hoping to hear.

Earlier today in a forest near Vega de Tera in Zamora, police arrested several members of an extremist wing of the Evangelical Church of America who are alleged to have slaughtered several children in an apparent religious ritual in the forest. Onlookers near the site say they saw members of the order, covered in blood and what appeared to be bits of flesh, being arrested by the police.

[voice of female onlooker] "It was the most horrifying thing I have seen in my life! I saw the police lead a bunch of woman, all dressed in black and all of them with glistening red splotches all over them. Oh, those poor children..." [sobbing can be heard]

[Voice of male onlooker]. "It was disgusting, I tell you. Disgusting! We should never have let those American religious freaks into our country. Imagine, killing poor, innocent children."

At this time, we have no information about the victims of this heinous crime.

"Well, that gets them out of our hair, at least for a while," said Maxwell, "but it won't do anything to improve Phinny's attitude."

Wendy nodded. She continued to have mixed feelings about Maxwell's lying about Phineas and the nuns. Nevertheless, she also had to admit to herself that she felt relieved that no one would be trying to kill them for the time being. Being nearly killed once that day was one time too many as far as she was concerned.

"Let's find a hotel and relax for a day or two," suggested Maxwell. "It's been a very stressful return to Earth."

"It has indeed," agreed Wendy.

The angel started singing "The Rose of Allendale", an Irish folk song, albeit in a French rather than Irish accent, which gave the song a curious sound.

"Have you ever considered a career in singing?" Maxwell asked the angel.

The angel shook her head but continued to sing.

"You've got style, a unique style," Maxwell added.

The angel continued to sing.

At the next intersection, a sign indicated that by turning left and driving two kilometres, one would find the Hotel de Memorias Desvanecidas.

"Let's see what this place looks like," said Maxwell, slowing and turning left.

Two kilometres later, as promised, they came to the hotel, a massive stone building that had clearly been around for a fair few centuries and was beginning to meld with the environment around it. The building was a large rectangle with an orange roof and several smaller wings jutting out here and there. At the ground floor level, a series of Gothic arches surrounded the building. Above, large rectangular windows looked out across the valley. The building looked faded, but somehow reliable and very beautiful.

Their rooms were every bit as attractive as the exterior. Stone walls painted pale orange and dark green, large cast-iron beds with canopies, mosaic tiling on the floors and plush armchairs made the rooms cool and comfy. Massive windows, overlooking a lake behind the hotel and the valley wall beyond the lake, opened wide, allowing the fresh, clean air to billow in and make itself at home in each room.

Once they were settled in, Maxwell announced that he was going to seek out a mechanic worthy of the Bentley. He advised Wendy to take it easy – and to consider one of the small cognacs in her room's mini-bar. She declined in favour of an herbal tea and a good book. He asked the angel to keep out of trouble. She simply smiled in what Maxwell hoped was a gesture of acquiescence.

A seemingly competent mechanic was soon found and he promised Maxwell that he'd fix the old vehicle up in no time. The time-consuming problem, the mechanic explained, would be in waiting for the specialised parts necessary to repair the differential. Maxwell begged the chap to press forward with due speed, which the mechanic promised he would do.

Maxwell explored the town and tried a local beer or three before returning to the hotel in the evening.

Dinner was a quiet affair, with each lost in his or her own thoughts. Maxwell was surprised to see that the angel matched him in wine consumption yet she ate very little food. In spite of that and her small size, she seemed little affected by the alcohol.

As angels go, thought Maxwell later, while drinking a glass of cognac in the hotel lobby bar, she was an odd one. He promptly amended his observation when he recalled that she was the first angel he had ever met. The angel was odd by any measure, but he would need to meet a few more angels in order to set a standard for angel normalcy.

The angel and Wendy had long since retired to their rooms. Maxwell was trying to read a book, but the insane day – even by his standards – and alcohol were together conspiring to spoil his concentration. He decided to step outside for a splash of fresh air.

"Young man!" he called to a passing waiter.

"Yes, sir!"

"I am going to step outside for a few minutes in order to find some fresh air. Then I will come back and give the remainder of this fine cognac the attention it deserves."

"Of course, sir."

"So, guard it with your life, please."

"Sir?" the waiter smiled, unsure whether Maxwell was being amusing or dangerous.

"Are you armed?"

"Of course not, sir!" said the waiter, beginning to suspect the dangerous option.

"Then you'll have to use martial arts should it be necessary to defend my cognac."

"But, sir..."

"Yes, lad?"

"I don't know martial arts."

"No worries, son. It looks like you've got a Jackie Chan film on the telly there." Maxwell pointed at the large screen in one corner of the room. "Just watch him in action."

"Yes, sir," said the waiter, veering back towards amusing.

"Jackie always comes out ahead and wins the girl, doesn't he?"

"I guess so, sir."

"I assure you he does. And you cannot ask for much more in life than coming out ahead and winning the girl, can you?"

"No, sir."

"Very good then. Study Mr Chan's moves carefully while I am gone. They will put you in good stead should you need to use violence to save my drink."

"Yes, sir."

"Excellent. I am sure my cognac is in safe hands. I'll see you soon."

"Of course, sir."

As he made his way outside, Maxwell reflected on his own life. He had never had to fight to get ahead; he had started out ahead thanks to the hard work and business sense of his grandfather and father and the business empire they had built across much of the solar system. Moreover, his sister had demonstrated the business sense that he completely lacked. Her continued hard work running the Martian Mining Company would doubtless provide dividends that would keep his various bank accounts and other financial instruments flush with money for the rest of his life.

But, when you have a substantial head start in life, it's hard to come out even further ahead, particularly if one wants to experience life's manifold pleasures along the way, as was the case with Maxwell.

At least, he reckoned, he had won quite a few women. Of course, he had also lost just about all of them and had fled from the rest, so he'd not done well in that department either.

That said, he had made a name for himself as a sculptor, in spite of his family rather than because of them; though, even then, his family name and their network of business contacts had given him a substantial head start over the other art students with whom he had been to school. Still, he was now regarded as the world's best robotics sculptor, so perhaps he had come out ahead in his own way.

With these thoughts of his past on his mind as he stepped outside, Maxwell walked away from the lights at the front of the hotel and looked up into the sky for Mars. In this, he had an advantage over other roamers. No matter where on Earth he was, it was often possible to look up into the sky at night and see the planet on which he had been born and spent the first part of his life. He had no great desire to return to the closed colony domes and restricted space of the red planet, but it was always nice when he was able to see his place of birth floating in the night sky. Over the years, it had also proved a useful excuse to bring women out of parties and into the dark night, he mused.

It took a moment for his eyes to adjust to the darkness. He sought and quickly found the ecliptic. He knew that Mars was in Libra, and indeed it was, the tiny orange dot of reflected light that had been his home for the first part of his life.

In his youth, he used occasionally to go to the observation dome, with its massive transparent roof, and look at Earth, which from Mars was a somewhat brighter blue dot. It had seemed strange that nearly all of the history he had learned in school – the rise of the human race, wars, technological progress and more – had all occurred on that tiny blue dot, the tiny blue dot upon which he was now standing.

It was as these thoughts danced about slightly drunkenly in Maxwell's mind that he caught in the corner of his eye a curious flickering. He scanned the sky. There it was, between Scorpius and Sagittarius: a glimmering, flickering spot of light. Strange, he thought; he had never seen anything like that before in space or on a planet.

As he watched and his eyes became increasingly adjusted to the dark, he could make out that it was not a spot, but a tiny doughnut shape. He would have to ask Wendy about it in the morning. He suspected that she would know what it was and could probably cite a paper or two about the phenomenon. She was impressive that way.

Meanwhile, he felt that it was time to relieve the waiter of his onerous cognac-guarding duties, and so returned to the bar, where he found his drink unharmed and waiting. He also noticed that the bar was no longer empty. Across from his armchair were two very young women, students by the look of them, who were stealing glances at him and chatting.

Maxwell was well enough known in the art world that this kind of thing happened from time to time. The girls were attractive enough, but a bit young, he thought. Youthful beauty was nice, he reckoned, but women in their 30s and 40s, with more experience, were more fun. He returned to his novel and hoped he might now be able to concentrate.

"Excuse me," said one of the girls, coming over to Maxwell's chair. She was a brunette, barely past 20 by the looks of her, with bright blue eyes. She was dressed in torn jeans and a sleeveless shirt, which showed off her youthful figure in a way Maxwell really wished it would not this evening. He wanted an early night in bed.

"Yes?" asked Maxwell.

"Are you Maxwell van Mars?" she asked.

"Indeed, I am," he said.

"The sculptor?" she asked.

"The very one," he said. "And who might you be?"

"Oh, my name is Sandra. That's Teresa over there," she said, waving towards her friend at the other table. "We love your work!"

"Why, thank you," said Maxwell.

"So, what you are doing in this little town? Are you doing a sculpture here?"

"Oh, no." Maxwell thought about the train of events that had brought him to the hotel where he was sitting. He surely did not want to go into detail with this lass. "Just escaping the excitement of the big city."

"Oh, I know what you mean! My friend and I are taking a break from university. It's so stressful there right now!"

"Speaking of your friend, she looks lonely over there, don't you think? Why don't you invite her over and the three of us can have a drink before I retire for the night? I've had a long day," said Maxwell.

Sandra waved Teresa over and Maxwell bought a round of drinks: gin and tonics for the women and another cognac for himself. Although he really and truly intended to limit himself to that one last cognac – he was exhausted inside out following insufficient sleep and excessive adventures – he also had a weakness for attractive women. Both Sandra and Teresa fit that category nicely. Not surprisingly, then, the first round of drinks led to a second and third.

Sandra explained in some detail, which might have been a bit dull in a less-attractive person, that she and Teresa were third-year economics students at the University of Lisbon and that during midterm break, they were doing a motorcycle tour in the area. Teresa occasionally added details and entertaining anecdotes to the background story.

"My goodness, you really have beautiful lips," said Maxwell after she had finished.

"Oh, um, thank you," said Sandra, blushing.

"What about me?" asked Teresa with mock indignity that hid true indignity. "Have I got beautiful lips?"

"Let me see," he said as he looked at her lips studiously for a moment. "Yes, they are very nice lips."

"But are they beautiful lips?" she asked.

"Yes, very beautiful," said Maxwell.

"Are they more beautiful than Sandra's?" she asked, winking at her friend mischievously.

"Well, your lips are very, very beautiful," said Maxwell. "But

Sandra's might be just a wee bit more beautiful."

"Ha!" said Sandra.

"Surely not!" said Teresa. "Take a closer look at my lips."

"Are you questioning my judgement, young lady?" asked Maxwell with mock seriousness.

"No, of course...Actually, yes, I am. You are wrong. I have the nicest lips," said Teresa.

"Sorry, Teresa, but you will just have to accept that you have the second-best lips," said Sandra. "That is nothing to be ashamed of. Not everyone can be number one!"

"I would not be ashamed if I had the second-best lips, but it is not true. I have the most beautiful lips. Now, Maxwell, I want you to look more carefully at our lips. I am sure you will see that mine are more beautiful," said Teresa.

"The thing with lips," said Maxwell, "is that their beauty is not merely in their appearance, but also in how they taste. To be absolutely sure who has the most beautiful lips, I must kiss those of each of you. I am doing this, of course, purely in the interests of science. But, if either of you are uncomfortable being kissed by me, you are welcome to forfeit."

"Forfeit? No way!" said Teresa.

"Me neither," said Sandra.

Maxwell kissed them both on the lips.

"Oh my, this is a difficult decision. I believe I will have to try again, if you don't mind."

Neither of the women minded.

"I'm sorry, Teresa," said Maxwell. "It is really very close. You have marvellous, moist, full lips and they are very kissable. But Sandra's are just a little softer and glisten in a certain way. I still have to award the best lips prize to her."

Teresa took Maxwell's hand.

"No, you are wrong. The differences in quality can be very subtle. In order to fully appreciate great lips, it is sometimes a good idea to put your hand on a woman's breast while kissing her lips. Like this." She put his hand on her breast, which was not encased in a bra.

"Teresa!" said Sandra laughing.

"Oh my, that does make a difference!" said Maxwell, feeling a firming nipple pressing into the palm of his hand. Noticing that the barkeep was watching them with some surprise, Maxwell added, "but I think we had best take this competition upstairs, don't you think?"

25

By the time Lucy and Judith had bought the clothes they needed, had a coffee, made a wrong turn, decided to have some dinner, and finally found their way to the Hotel de Memorias Desvaneci-das, it was nearing midnight. They were exhausted yet happy as they stumbled out of the big SUV and onto the hotel car park.

The unique, slightly damp, slightly rocky landscape and very green smell of the air reminded Lucy of her childhood visits to the valley and this hotel. Her mother used to bring her and her brother here for a week every year or two. Sometimes, mother's latest boyfriend would come along, but mostly it was just the three of them. Her mother, from whom Lucy liked to think she inherited her scientific intelligence, was a brilliant virologist distinctly on the high-functioning side of the autism spectrum. As a result, Mother was passionate about her work and less passionate about people – especially her lovers, who never lasted long. After a year or two at most, the typical lover came to realise that he could not compete with infectious diseases in terms of her love and so left her for someone less intellectually interesting but more obviously affectionate.

Children, however, understand their parents on a level sexual partners often fail to do. And while her mother seldom displayed any physical affection towards her children, Lucy and her brother – each from a different father – never doubted her love.

Fortunately, Lucy seemed to have inherited her artist father's emotional maturity and robust affection. Indeed, in terms of affection and emotional support, Lucy was more of a mother to her brother than their mother was. When her brother went to Vancouver to complete a master's degree, it was Lucy who called regularly to ask how things were going. Their mother seldom called, but she watched the news, weather and other information for Vancouver online, satisfying herself that her son was okay. It never dawned on her that her son might prefer that she call and ask him. Checking online was simply more time-effective as far as she was concerned.

Lucy remembered her mother showing her the night sky here in the valley, where it was darker and richer than in the Cape City suburb where they had lived. Although a virologist, Mother (it was always "Mother", never "Mum" or even the popular Americanised "Mom", which had been trendy when Lucy was a child) knew well the constellations and what lay within them. She happily pointed the same things out to Lucy every time they visited.

Though Lucy soon came to know the constellations and their features even better than her mother, she always looked forward to this tradition,perhaps because it was one of the few times her mother demonstrated physical intimacy, putting her arm around Lucy and holding her head close to her daughter's as she recited the features of the night sky. Lucy could still smell her mother's ever-so-slightly-perfumed scent mixing with the smell of the valley and wafting into her nose.

Lucy felt Judith take her arm, bringing her gently back to the present.

"It looks exactly as I remember it," said Lucy. "I used to come here with my mother and brother when I was a kid."

"It's beautiful!" said Judith.

"Wait till you see the...Holy Fuck!"

"The what?"

While reminiscing, Lucy was scanning the night sky, looking for the constellations her mother used to show her. On the ecliptic between Scorpius and Sagittarius, she saw a tiny, shimmering doughnut shape. She had never seen anything like it – and she knew the sky better than most humans.

She put her head against Judith's to ensure they were looking in the same direction, pointed and said, "do you see that tiny shimmering spot over there?"

"What? Oh, yes – the little doughnut next to Scorpius?"

"Oh, you know your constellations!"

"Yes. I've always loved the night sky."

Lucy kissed Judith. "Me too, as you know. But I've never seen anything like that."

"Neither have I," said Judith.

"It must be huge, or very nearby. It looks like..." Lucy thought for a moment and was startled to hear singing.

"Judith, that's a beautiful chant. You have a wonderful voice, like that old folk singer," said Lucy, still looking at the shimmering doughnut.

"It...It wasn't me," stuttered Judith, staring in awe at the newcomer in their conversation.

There was some more chanting followed by a few clicks and a not-quite-human voice.

"It was me. Allow me to introduce myself: I am Lubidada and this is Snox."

Surprised, Lucy finally tore her attention away from the sky and looked to her right to see two Zargonians standing beside her, nearly lost in the darkness. Lucy had encountered aliens at numerous conferences and workshops, but this was the first time she had come face to face with one.

"'Informational Wave Movements in Dark Energy'," said Lucy.

"You know my paper, Lucy Heisenberg," said the translation box on the alien's chest.

"Of course I do! I've read it, too. It had a profound effect on me," said Lucy. "And you know my name."

"Of course we do, Dr Heisenberg. Your work is well known,

and not just on Earth."

"Oh, thank you," said Lucy with pride.

"Would you like some water?" asked Lubidada, holding up a one-litre bottle of spring water.

"No, thank you," said Lucy.

"You have seen the tear," said the alien.

"What tear?"

"That tear," said Lubidada, holding what looked like a translucent sheet of plastic in front of the shimmering doughnut. Suddenly, a much-enlarged image of the doughnut shape appeared on the sheet.

"Fuck me with a spoon," said Lucy.

The translation box on the Zargonian's chest emitted a burst of what sounded like confused medieval chanting by Joan Baez.

"I am sorry, my translator does not understand what you have just said. Could you please repeat yourself?"

"Oh, sorry. No, it's better I do not. It was an expletive, and a very rude one at that. I am sorry, but I was stunned. I am stunned. What is that?"

"It is a tear in the fabric of the universe."

"Can that happen?"

"It seems it can. It has."

"Lucy, what's going on?" asked Judith, out of her depth. Her scientific education was sadly limited to the idea of God creating the heavens and earth – which was fine and good if one preferred simplicity over fact and certainly made for easy term-paper composition. But such simplistic notions left people, even intelligent people like Judith, sadly incapable of interpreting the world around them in any meaningful way.

"Give me a minute, sweetheart. I'm trying to understand it myself."

Lucy's mind raced.

"That must have happened in the sixth dimension," she said.

"But how?"

"That seems to be the case. We believe it happened when a space cruiser raced around Gateway, nearly touching the Schwarzchild radius," said Lubidada. He tapped the screen and line showed the path of the cruiser. "See?"

"Wow! That would stress local space, but would it create sufficient stress to tear the universe?"

"Apparently, it did. As far as we can tell, that is what happened."

"I would have thought the universe would have been made of stronger fabric," said Lucy.

"Me too," added Judith, finally understanding several words being spoken between her lover and the alien.

"What are the implications?" asked Lucy.

"We are not entirely sure. This has never happened before. But we are seeing three things. Firstly, the tear seems to be getting bigger."

"Okay. That cannot be good. And?"

"And the tear opens into an alternative universe that seems to be very different from ours. Possibly dangerous."

"That's worse. And there's a third thing?"

"Yes. An object flew out of the tear and towards Earth at great speed."

"How long before it arrives?"

"We are not sure. It disappeared about 300 metres above the Earth's surface, not far from here."

"Holy..." Lucy swallowed the word 'shit' when she looked at Lubidada and the translation box on his chest. She didn't want to have to explain that concept.

"Yes, it is disturbing. We are searching for the object or its remains."

"And what about the tear? Can it be fixed?"

"We hope so. We need to find something that can bind the fabric of the universe."

"Can you do that? Does such a binding agent exist?"

"Theoretically. We have a conceptual design of what might bind the tear across all dimensions, but we have not found a, um, substance that fits the design."

"Can you elaborate on that?"

"Take a look at this," said Lubidada, handing Lucy the sheet he had held up against the tear; in fact, it was an incredibly thin tablet computer.

Lucy looked at the screen, puzzled. Before she could speak, the Zargonian reached over and tapped the tablet. Suddenly the strange markings were replaced with English text.

"Thank you," said Lucy, studying the diagram. "I'd need to study this. Chemistry is not a strength."

"It's not entirely chemistry. There's a biological component as well, we think," said Lubidada.

"That's even worse," said Lucy.

"Worse?"

"I understand biology less than chemistry. Can I study this for a while? Can you give me a printout or something?"

"You can have the device. Just touch this for user information."

"Thank you."

"It is not a gift. We hope you can help us."

"Don't get your hopes up too high."

"Do not underestimate yourself, Lucy."

Lucy smiled.

"And if you need insight, talk to the penguin."

"The penguin?"

"Yes, of course. The penguin. Now we must go. As you will see, there is a way you can contact me or one of my team using the tablet. Now, we bid you good night. You smell very tired."

"Good night," said Lucy.

"Good night," said Judith.

"Oh God, that was so cool!" exclaimed Judith once the aliens had disappeared.

"It was. Let's check in and go to bed," said Lucy. "I can barely stand."

As it turns out, she had sufficient energy to be seduced by her new lover who, she noted, was learning remarkably quickly. But as they lay in each other's arms afterwards, caressing each other, she soon fell asleep, only to dream of the tear growing and an army of demons coming out.

26

Maxwell woke up at around seven in the morning in a large double bed with two young woman asleep on either side of him. All concerned were naked and decorated with body paint. Maxwell recognised his style on the two women's bodies and was pleased. He'd painted a stylised dragon on each. Sculpture was his speciality. Painting was not. He was always happy when a painting came out well.

Glancing around the darkened room, he saw see a couple of gin bottles, several tonic bottles and tubes of paint scattered on the floor. Although this suggested he had drunk a considerable amount the night before, he was not feeling too badly. His only real concern for the moment was: who were these women and why was he in bed with them?

This was not the first time Maxwell had found himself in such a situation. Far from it. There was no need to panic. It was not difficult to work out why he was in bed with the lasses, at least in general terms. They were very attractive. It was only the details of how they got there that puzzled him. Actually, he thought as he glanced around the room again, it was how he got here and not the other way around; this was not his room.

He simply needed to do a little mental backtracking in order to remember the circumstances that brought him to the room, any unfortunate promises he might have made and who the lasses were. As he was backtracking in his mind, his fingers stroked the back of one of the women. She moaned softly. Maxwell stroked more thoroughly. She moaned a bit more. Maxwell's stroking lingered on her erogenous bits. She pulled him back down to the bed. He was beginning to remember the details. When the other woman joined them, Maxwell stopped caring about the details.

At half-past eight, an enlightened and sexually over-satiated Maxwell kissed the women goodbye and made his way back to his own room. He showered off the paint job, as charming as it was, put on some fresh clothes and knocked on the doors of Wendy's and the angel's rooms to suggest breakfast.

At the buffet, Maxwell filled his tray with food – like most skinny chaps, he could eat a tremendous amount and usually did so. Wendy helped herself to a generous portion of pickled herring, which she was delighted to find at the buffet, and the angel took a croissant. At the table, they all ordered cappuccinos. As soon as the angel received hers, she guzzled it down and ordered another. Knowing the angel's habits, Maxwell suggested that the waitress bring three over in order to keep his winged companion happy and not tire the waitress unnecessarily.

As they were eating, Lucy and Judith came down to breakfast.

"You!" the former exclaimed upon seeing Maxwell.

Maxwell looked around.

"There are three of us at this table for whom that form of address would be accurate, if less than polite, um, Lucy. Which of us are you exclaiming towards?"

"You, of course, Maxwell," said Lucy.

"Well, 'Maxwell' would be a nicer form of addressing me, but I've been called a lot worse over the years, so I suppose 'you' will suffice if it pleases you. Now, why don't the two of you pull up a couple of chairs and plates of breakfast and join us? Wendy is doubtless bored to tears having to listen to me so much."

"I am not," said Wendy.

"Wendy?" said Lucy.

"Sorry, have you not met?" asked Maxwell. "This is my friend Wendy. Wendy, this is my..."

"New friend?" suggested Lucy.

"...new friend, Lucy," said Maxwell.

"And you are?" Maxwell asked Judith. As he looked at her, he felt a stirring of recognition. "Lord love a duck! Are you the young lady who tried desperately to kill me a couple of nights ago?"

Judith blushed, not knowing how to reply.

"I trust you've had a change of heart about killing me. I'm not sure I'd like to share breakfast with my assassin. Or if you really must do me in, at least wait until after breakfast and, ideally, my toilet. I'd truly hate to leave an embarrassing mess when I've died."

"No, no...I'm..." stuttered Judith.

"No, you won't let me finish breakfast? Or, no, you are not my assassin? You lack clarity, young lady. You will never get far in life without clarity, believe me," said Maxwell.

Lucy stepped in.

"Goodness, I forget how much you can talk with so little meaning."

"What? I am full of meaning. Some of it is very deep, my dear. It is your own fault if you fail to grasp it."

"Sure. I'll take your word for it. This is Judith."

"Hi," said Judith waving timidly to everyone. She felt very much out of her element here and, as a result, was feeling increasingly awkward. She was pleased that Lucy was handling things, but she also felt a twinge of discomfort at the easy banter between her love and Maxwell.

"And Judith..." began Maxwell.

"Yes, Judith was a part of the Reverend Forge's team, who are out to kill you," said Lucy. "But we've had some talks and she realises that killing you would not be a wise thing to do."

"Good for you, Judith!" said Maxwell approvingly. "Now, why don't the both of you load up your plates and come join us."

They did precisely that and sat down. At the same time, the angel ordered her fifth cappuccino.

Judith caught sight of the angel's wings.

"Oh my God! Are you an angel?" she asked.

"Yes, I think so," said the angel in her soft French accent.

"Her behaviour falls well short of angelic from time to time," said Maxwell, "but it's not clear what else she might be. So, until someone comes up with a better hypothesis, we'll work on the operating assumption that she is an angel."

"Wow," said Judith.

"Wendy?" asked Lucy.

"Yes?"

"Last night, I met a Zargonian who asked for my thoughts about a tear in the fabric of the universe. He said that if I got confused, I should ask the penguin. Might you be the penguin?"

"I am not sure. But I do not know of any other penguins who are knowledgeable about astrophysics."

"No, I don't imagine there are many," laughed Lucy. "I haven't had any time to review the information he gave me or even think much about it, but it's nice to know you. May I contact you if I have questions?"

"It is nice to know you too, Lucy. Of course you may contact me." Wendy reached into her satchel, which was hung over the back of a chair, and pulled out a phone. "Let me give you my details."

Lucy pulled her telephone out of her bag and they exchanged information.

"There is one more thing you should know about the tear," said Wendy.

"Yes?" asked Lucy.

"We probably caused it. Did the Zargonian tell you that?" said Wendy.

"No, he didn't. That is interesting."

Wendy told Lucy about their voyage in the space-cruiser, the sling-shot manoeuvre around Gateway and the equation she had worked out for the manoeuvre. Lucy asked a number of technical questions, which Wendy answered with clarity and depth. The two females soon gained intellectual respect for each other.

Meanwhile, Judith was attempting to converse with the angel, but finding, as did everyone who spoke to the angel, that she was awfully vague about who she was, where she was from and what she was doing. Later, Judith would tell Lucy, "it's almost as if she is a newborn baby in a grown-up's body and with a grown-up's brain. She has the coordination and vocabulary of an adult, but hardly seems to know what most of those words mean."

As they were finishing their breakfasts, and the angel her eighth cappuccino, Lucy remarked to Maxwell, "you've got an interesting entourage there."

"Thank you," said Maxwell. "Mind you, your entourage is interesting, if a little disheartening."

"What do you mean by that?" asked Lucy.

"While I appreciated your distracting my attacker and saving my life, it is curious, if not a touch disrespectful, to be in love with her."

"I'm not in love with her, but I do like her a lot. And she's fucking good in bed," said Lucy with a wink. "Anyway, you are a fine one to talk, running away and leaving me with a potential killer."

"You seemed to be doing jolly well without my help," said Maxwell. "Indeed, I felt rejected. I thought we had a beautiful thing going."

"You thought nothing of the kind!" said Lucy. "You just wanted to get laid, and I did too. Let's not pretend it was anything more than that."

"You misjudge me, young lady," said Maxwell.

"Do I?" asked Lucy.

Sandra and Teresa, decked out in rucksacks and motorcycle leathers, waved at Maxwell and walked over. He stood up and they each kissed him on the lips.

"You were wonderful," said Teresa. "I haven't showered your painting off yet!"

"Oh. Thanks. You were jolly good yourself," said Maxwell.

"And me?" asked Sandra.

"Brilliant, just brilliant," said Maxwell.

"Thanks," said Sandra, kissing Maxwell again and patting him on the bottom.

"Would you like to join us for breakfast?" asked Maxwell.

"No, thanks," said Sandra. "We've got to get going. We slept in far later than we intended this morning, thanks to you."

"Me?"

Sandra winked at him. "Yep! Bye!"

"Bye-bye," said Teresa.

"Toodle-oo. Travel safely!" said Maxwell.

"You were saying?" Lucy said as he sat down.

"They're just good friends."

"Oh, really?"

"Yes, really. Are you questioning my integrity?"

"If I could find it, I might indeed want to question it, but at present it seems non-existent."

"Lord love a duck, you are difficult. What did I ever see in you?"

"My tits?"

Maxwell looked at Lucy's chest. "Well, yes, they may have been a contributing factor."

"Thought so."

"Changing the subject, as this one is on its last legs," said Maxwell, "We're planning on investigating the lake behind the hotel after breakfast. Would you and Judith like to join us?"

"Perhaps," said Lucy. "If we do, we'll look for you on the beach."

As Lucy turned her head towards Judith, she noticed the angel was gone. Odd, she thought, she hadn't seen her leave. But when she blinked her eyes, the angel was there again, smiling at Lucy.

Curious, thought Lucy. Very curious. She took Judith's hand. "Let's go, kiddo."

"Okay," said Judith, glad to be her lover's focus of attention again.

"We should get going as well," said Maxwell. "Finished?" he asked Wendy and the angel.

As the five of them passed through the lobby to the lifts, Judith suddenly exclaimed "Father Forge!" and pointed at a large-screen television in one corner of the lobby. Indeed, the reverend was being displayed on a local news show. All except the angel walked over to watch.

...rumours are that the forensic team has found no evidence of human victims in the bloody slaughter. However, there has been no official confirmation of this from the Vega de Tera police.

Meanwhile, at a press conference this morning, a spokesman for the Evangelical Church of America announced that the church was launching its own investigation into the Vega de Tera baby slaughter.

[Cut to press conference; handsome priest in his mid 30s, with impeccably groomed hair and a strong chin, is speaking] The Evangelical Church of America is appalled by the apparent recent slaughter of small children in southern Europa yesterday. Although it is alleged that members of the church may have been involved with this terrible incident, such an action is certainly something the church absolutely and unquestionably condemns.

We have launched our own investigative unit and will co-operate completely with the police in Europa.

"I'm glad you left them," said Lucy.

"Me too. But I'm worried about my sisters," said Judith. "And I really can't believe they would have killed little children."

"That does seem extreme," said Lucy. "But they did intend to kill Maxwell and, presumably, still do."

27

The angel did not want to visit the lake and became noticeably un-comfortable when Maxwell pressed her. Instead, she opted to explore the nearby town on foot and wing. Maxwell and Wendy packed a couple of rucksacks with beach towels, some food and drink and walked down a dirt path that wended its way through a colourful chaos of plants capped with yellow, red and purple flowers that danced madly in the ever-present wind. Within a few moments, they walked out onto a smallish sandy beach peppered with a handful of chairs, each decorated with the hotel's logo, and a bar hut that was closed.

The wind rolled across the lake, flung Maxwell's hair about playfully and set the plants behind them into their rustling dance that created a soothing, unending background noise interspersed with the chatter of birds. Tiny waves gently licked the beach with equally tiny splashing sounds.

The lake was named, with a certain lack of creativity, the "Lake of Dreams". Like much of this curious valley, the lake had a repu-tation for strangeness. Over the centuries, a number of swimmers and a handful of boats had mysteriously disappeared from the lake. Those who favour supernatural explanations over scientific ones claimed that aliens had been abducting humans from the lake for reasons unclear.

Not long after the Zargonians established themselves on Earth, one of them explained in an interview that no aliens of the federation had previously visited Earth, that there were no known aliens outside the federation, and that abducting sentient beings was expressly prohibited according to the Galactic Charter on the Exploration of Inhabited Planets.

Not surprisingly, conspiracy lovers promptly decided that the Zargonian explanation was a clever conspiracy to hide top-secret visitations by secret alien races with devious intentions towards the human race, though when pressed to explain why the Zargonians would want to do this, conspiracists were unable to give a convincing answer.

Those who favour science over conspiracy, on the other hand, noted that strong and frequently changing winds that blew across the valley likely led to sudden undercurrents, which surely toppled the boats of novice sailors and pulled down swimmers.

More intriguingly, perhaps, during the late 1800s, water from the lake was believed to cause madness, loss of memory and sexual depravity. This belief was problematic to say the least. The lake was the primary source of water for the region. As a result of this belief, many people moved away from the villages near the lake and for some time, the area was a virtual ghost town. Even today, a rumour taken half seriously by the locals, persists that drinking the water can cause madness or, at least, cause people to behave oddly. Not surprisingly, the local bottled water providers enthusiastically promote the rumour.

All this information and more was in a booklet that Wendy had bought at the hotel. The booklet stressed that these rumours were unfounded, though swimmers should indeed be careful about undercurrents and sailors should be alert to changing winds. Maxwell glanced at the booklet over Wendy's shoulder, as much as Wendy had a shoulder.

"What do you think, Wendy?" he asked. "Do you reckon it's safe to dive in?"

"Probably. You're already mad," said Wendy.

"Nonsense. I am a shining example of sanity in an insane world," said Maxwell. "How about you? Are you prepared to risk your sanity in this lovely lake?"

"No, thank you. It's too warm. I'll sit here and read instead."

"You're probably right," said Maxwell scanning the lake. "I rather fancy swimming to that island. If you get bored reading, there's no need to wait here. I can meet you back at the hotel."

"No worries," said Wendy. "Take your time. I'm happy relaxing and reading here. These past couple of days have been far more hectic than I like, you know."

"I know indeed. I am hoping we can both take it a little easier now that Phinny and his nuts..."

"Nuns."

"Oh yes, nuns. Now that Phinny and his nuns are locked up."

"I hope so too."

Maxwell took off his shirt, waded into the water and, as soon as it was sufficiently deep, breast-stroked his way to the little island.

Wendy flipped through the booklet until she found a map of the lake. She could see that the island was one of a small handful near this side of the lake where the water was presumably relatively shallow. Maxwell was going to the biggest island; it looked to be about 30 metres wide by 100 or so long.

"That's a strange image of the tear," said Lucy, who had walked up behind Wendy and was looking down at the map. Lucy was wearing a one-piece, modest red swimsuit with a loose, unbuttoned blouse that billowed in the wind, as did her hair. Her eyes were covered by oversized sunglasses.

Wendy looked at Lucy for a moment. "Where?" she asked.

"There," said Lucy, pointing at the map of the lake.

"It's not the tear. It's the Lake of Dreams," Wendy said.

Lucy looked more closely at the map.

"Silly me. Of course it is. I've been reading about the tear all morning. I guess it's too much on my mind. Still..."

"Yes?"

"The shape does look similar to this radio map of the tear," said Lucy, pulling the Zargonian tablet out of her bag and sliding her fingers across it. "Yes, here. Look." She handed the tablet to Wendy.

"Yes, it does look similar. Very similar. But there could be no connection. This lake has been here for hundreds of years," said Wendy.

"Of course. I suppose both the tear and the lake were formed by stress in the fabric around them, so it's not that surprising that their shapes are broadly similar. Anyway, the tear exists in more than three dimensions..." said Lucy.

"While we are only seeing the top of the river in two dimensions," said Wendy.

"Exactly. Tell me, when did the tear happen?"

"Friday morning GMT."

"Okay, assuming the 'doughnut' appeared yesterday, it must be a couple of light-days from here at the most."

"Doughnut?" asked Wendy.

"Oh, sorry. Have you not seen it?" asked Lucy.

"Until I know what it is, I have to assume I haven't," said Wendy.

Lucy described the doughnut and her meeting with the Zargonians.

"Hey, are you going to come into the water, my love?" called Judith, who wore a matching red swimsuit and was wading in the water.

"Give me a few minutes with Wendy first, honey, then I'll join you."

Then to Wendy, she said, "the Zargonian said the tear was in the sixth dimension."

"Yes. That also corresponds with what I saw on the cruiser's computer," said the penguin.

"Okay, but when I model it, it only makes sense in at least

eight, if not ten, dimensions. Look." Lucy showed Wendy the tablet.

Wendy looked at it. "May I?"

"Of course."

Wendy took the tablet and moved the line model around and examined the human's numbers. "Lord love a duck!" she said.

"What?!" said Lucy, smiling.

"Oh, sorry. Maxwell likes to say that. I guess it's contagious, but I'm not sure I say it as well as he does."

"You say it perfectly, dear," said Lucy, smiling. "It's just an unusual exclamation in this day and age, especially,well..."

"When said by a bird?"

"Yes," said Lucy, laughing. "I'm sorry."

"Don't be," said Wendy, crinkling her eyes in a smile. "I know I am a bird and I'm proud of it. But you seem to be right. This tear looks like it runs all the way into the tenth dimension. I wonder what that implies..."

"I'm not sure, but I am trying to work it out," said Lucy.

"Interesting." Wendy puzzled for a moment, then continued. "How could a hyperspace craft cause such a tear? It always remains in parallel time-space to the universe, but surely such a tear could only come from stress in tangential time-space."

"Good question, and I'm afraid I haven't got a good answer just now. Let me think about it," said Lucy.

"Tell me, does this tablet allow you to see the tear in real time?" Wendy asked.

"Yes, if I understand correctly – and to be honest, the Zargonians have not done a great job translating the operating system on this tablet – this is a direct hyperspace feed from a Zargonian cruiser orbiting a few million klicks from the tear."

"Klicks?"

"Sorry. Kilometres."

As Maxwell approached the island, he stood up and looked around. The island was sandy with a few rocky outcroppings and some sparse, wind-blown grass growing here and there. On Maxwell's left, as he walked onto the island, were the remains of a circular structure and two partial walls at a 90 degree angle to each other. The ruins were no more than a couple metres tall at the highest point.

It looked like the ruins of a medieval tower which, as history would have it, was precisely the case. Numerous chunks of decorative stonework, bits of gargoyle and bricks littered the area around the ruin. Nearby were two lounge chairs with Hotel de Memorias Desvanecidas logos on them; presumably previous guests had brought them to the island.

Finding little else of interest, Maxwell decided to sit and rest for five minutes before heading back. He had not had a decent night's sleep since returning to Earth and the swim had tired him more than he thought it would. He missed his youthful days when he could spend all night out drinking, taking drugs, dancing and more, get a couple of hours' sleep and be up and ready to sculpt entirely hangover-free in the morning. Other men might have seen this as a solid argument for growing up and acting their age. Not Maxwell. He reckoned it was best to keep trying.

"Whoops, did you see that?" asked Lucy.

"I think so. That, um, ripple?" asked Wendy.

"Yes. Maybe we can rewind it," said Lucy.

"Oh, poop!" exclaimed Judith.

Lucy looked up to see that her sweetheart had fallen on her bottom.

"Are you okay?" Lucy asked.

"Yes. I must have slipped on the sand or something. It felt like the ground shook."

"Be careful, Judith. Apparently there are strong under-currents in the lake," said Wendy.

"It must have been one of those," said Judith.

"Ah, here we go," said Lucy, who had taken back the tablet.

"It does indeed look like a ripple," said Wendy. "Can we see it again? Maybe it's an issue with filming or image transmission."

"I think it's real. See how the ripple is limited to the boundaries of the tear?" said Lucy.

"Indeed," said Wendy. "Curious."

Maxwell was half dozing off when he saw the black bikini walking out of the water towards him. He refocused his eyes and saw the bikini was being worn by an extraordinarily attractive woman, dripping water and with what appeared to be a diamond stud in her navel. The diamond sparkled brightly in the sun.

"Why does the opposite sex continually insist on spoiling my sleep?" asked Maxwell to himself.

"What have you said?" asked the bikini-wearer in a French accent that reminded Maxwell of the angel. Indeed, as he looked at the woman, he believed he saw a physical resemblance as well, as if they were sisters. The bikini-wearer had a more mature, more womanly body than his angel. Her hair was also darker, almost brown, compared to the dirty blonde hair of the angel, but the high cheekbones and exceptionally large, penetrating blue eyes were similar.

"I said, why do you women insist on spoiling my sleep?" repeated Maxwell.

"We women?"

"Yes, you women. I've not had a decent night's sleep – or midday nap – in days, thanks to you women."

"You are seriously mistaken," said the woman, walking over and sitting upright on the chair next to Maxwell's "Those other woman may be causing trouble to you. But when you miss out on sleep because of me, it is sleep worth missing."

"Is that so?" asked Maxwell.

"Very much so," said the woman.

"And can you back this up with fact, or is it just your opinion? Because, my dear, if it is just your opinion, then we have to bear in mind that you are likely to be biased in the matter."

"I am not biased!"

"Then prove it!"

"Okay," said the woman. She sat on the edge of Maxwell's chair, bent over and kissed him full on the lips. "Well, what do you think? Is that not worth losing sleep over?"

"Very possibly," admitted Maxwell, vaguely concerned by the speed at which flirtation had turned into action. In his experience, a considerable amount of verbal jousting and drinking were necessary to get to this stage. That said, if both parties were drinking heavily, less verbal jousting was necessary. However, he had not had any alcohol since the night before and the woman seemed sober. She certainly neither tasted nor smelled of alcohol.

"I will prove it beyond doubt, then," she said, leaning over and kissing Maxwell again. This time, Maxwell kissed her back with some passion.

"Ooh là là! You are worth losing sleep over yourself, Maxwell." she said, getting up and straddling him. Something vaguely worried him about her remark, though he was enjoying himself too much to worry about it at the time. With her weight supported on her legs on either side of the reclining Maxwell, she was able to take Maxwell's head in her hands as she kissed him. He kissed back. There was no further need to analyse quality.

In remarkably little time, swim suits were pulled off and tossed to either side of the recliner. Maxwell was deep inside the now bikiniless woman, and they moved together with surprising harmony, considering they hadn't known each other 10 minutes ago.

They climaxed simultaneously and Maxwell could feel the woman's body clenching in delight. At the same time, he felt an unusual release of tension throughout his body and even in his head.

The woman bent down and rested her head on Maxwell chest for a moment. As they lay together on the chair, Maxwell reflected that the experience was one of the most enjoyable quick ones he had experienced in a long time. Indeed, Maxwell generally avoided quick ones in favour of long, slow ones. He preferred to invest time and energy in creative foreplay.

To his mind, a gentleman should ensure a woman has had two orgasms before he has had his first, which ideally should coincide with her third. Most of his partners liked the results of this philosophy, though they might have questioned the necessity of ascribing such a depth of philosophical thought to sex.

However, none of this would have interested the bikiniless woman, who seemed to be in a hurry.

"You were marvellous," she whispered in his ear, kissing his earlobe. "I needed that so much."

"Gosh, thanks. You were more than a little fantastic yourself, young lady."

"Unfortunately, I cannot stay with you," she said, kissing him on the lips one last time. Then she stood up, replaced her bikini, waded into the lake and then began swimming.

"That is a pity," said Maxwell, still in the hotel chair. Alone again on the island, he felt exhausted and unable to stay awake. Just as he was nodding off, he realised what was troubling him: how had the bikini clad woman known his name? Perhaps she had recognised him. But, in his experience, recognition was typically preceded by a "are you Maxwell van Mars?"

Lucy had joined Judith in the water and they were both swimming when they felt a curious shudder in the water.

"That's what happened before," said Judith. "Is that how an undertow feels?"

"I don't think so," said Lucy thoughtfully. "It was strange. If it happens again, we should probably get out of the water."

"I think so too," said Judith. They continued swimming for a while longer, then dried off and lay in the sun near Wendy, who was now reading Aristotle. A short while later, Maxwell swam up to the shore and waded out of the water.

"What took you so long?" asked Wendy. "I was afraid you had disappeared."

"No such luck, old bird," said Maxwell, drying off. "But I do apologise for being away so long. There were a couple of lounge chairs on the island. I sat down on one for a moment and inadvertently fell asleep for a while."

"You came back just in time," said Lucy. "We were about to call the Coast Guard."

"I doubt they'd look for me. There was a misunderstanding a couple of years ago involving several members of the Viennese Young Women's Choir and me on a yacht. Apparently, someone complained that we were dumping rubbish on a protected coral reef – and the Coast Guard were called out.

"In fact, I had simply thrown our swim suits overboard. I had no idea they landed on a coral a reef, let alone a protected one. It's not like there was a sign or anything."

"And to make matters worse, the captain's daughter and a sailor's fiancée were part of the choir on the yacht, Maxwell," added Wendy. "You know that upset them."

"Yes, it seems petty jealousy runs rampant in the Coast Guard. It's not like I..."

"I really do not want to hear more of this story, Maxwell," interrupted Lucy.

"Changing the subject, then: did you see a woman in a black bikini swim out of the water here?" asked Maxwell.

"Holy shit, another girl?!" exclaimed Lucy.

"Probably," said Wendy. "He's like that. I don't understand why he doesn't settle down with a nice woman."

"That is the business of neither of you. The thing is, the woman in question swam from the island about 10 or 15 minutes before I did. I thought she swam in this direction," said Maxwell.

"No one but us has been here for the past hour," said Judith, wanting to get in on the conversation and still a bit uncomfortable about the easy banter between Lucy and Maxwell.

Maxwell subconsciously sensed this discomfort and the equally subconscious predator within him sensed opportunity. He sat down next to Judith – albeit not to closely. After all, this is the woman who had tried to kill him a couple of days ago.

"So, I gather you're in the assassination business," said Maxwell.

"What? Um, no. Not any more, anyway," stuttered Judith.

"Well, you certainly gave me the impression you intended to assassinate me back in Cape City," said Maxwell.

"That's because I am...Or was...An agent for the American Evangelical Church's European arm. There's a holy order to dispatch you to Hell," explained Judith.

"Presumably I would need to be dead in order to go to Hell, would I not?" asked Maxwell

"Yes, of course," said Judith.

"And that would require assassinating me, would it not?" said Maxwell.

"Well, yes, that was the plan," admitted Judith.

"A plan that I thoroughly frown upon," said Maxwell. "Surely an attractive young woman like you could find a less dangerous profession: pickpocketing, bank robbery or the kind of thing that does not involve my dying at your hands."

"But Father Forge said that you corrupt the souls of innocent woman, and that the only way to make the world a safer place for innocent women would be to speed your departure to Hell, and since you were going there eventually, it wouldn't be a sin to speed up your descent. In fact, God would reward us," explained Judith.

"Corrupt the souls of innocent women!?" exclaimed Maxwell. "For a chap lacking both an imagination and a sense of humour, Phinny can come up with some awfully wild ideas!"

"Phinny?"

"Your Father Forge."

"Oh."

"I've probably pissed off a few lasses over the years," admitted Maxwell. "But I don't believe I've corrupted anyone – at least not anyone who did not wish to be corrupted. I wonder what on Earth lodged this curious notion in Phinny's addled brain?"

"Maybe it's because you have had sex with so many women," interjected Wendy, who had listened in on the last bit of conversation. "You know the Evangelical Church doesn't believe in sex before marriage."

"But I've been married," said Maxwell. "Three times."

"I believe you are only supposed to have sex with your current wife," added Wendy.

"That would be awfully boring," said Maxwell. "Mind you, I guess that's why the marriages ended."

"You have had sex with lots of women?" asked Judith, appalled but also curious. She had heard about such people, but never knowingly met such a sinner.

"Depends on how you define 'lots'," said Maxwell to Judith. To Wendy he asked, "why on Earth do you insist on discussing my sex life with everyone you see?"

"I don't discuss it with everyone I see," said Wendy. "But why are you so concerned? Are you ashamed of it? If so, you could easily stop."

Lucy looked up from the tablet over at the discussion taking place and smiled.

"You just keep your wicked thoughts to yourself, young lady," Maxwell said to her, seeing the smile.

Lucy winked at Maxwell, then looked back at the tablet.

"Is that why Phinny...Er, Father Forge, thinks I corrupt the souls of innocent women? Because I have made love to a few wo-men?" asked Maxwell.

"A lot," said Wendy.

"That's enough, penguin!" said Maxwell. "I believe I saw some leopard seals in the lake. I wouldn't want to have to throw you in."

"The water's too warm for leopard seals," said Wendy.

"How do you know?" asked Maxwell.

"I'm more intelligent than you are," said Wendy.

"In your dreams, perhaps," said Maxwell.

Wendy ignored the remark. Judith laughed.

"My, you have beautiful lips," said Maxwell, watching the laughter.

"Maxwell! Don't you dare!" exclaimed Lucy.

"I'm sure I don't know what you are talking about," said Max-well.

"You're awfully sure about a lot of ludicrous things, young man!" said Lucy. "But keep away from her lips. They are mine!"

Judith smiled and Lucy thought that Maxwell was right; Judith did indeed have beautiful lips.

"Let's go to lunch," the older woman suggested.

"Yes, let's," said Judith.

"Not a bad idea," said Maxwell, looking at his watch. "Ready to eat, Wendy?"

"Yes, I am."

Judith hoped that she and Lucy would not have to sit with the others and, especially, that Lucy would not sit next to Maxwell like she did at breakfast.

28

As they walked into the hotel lobby, Maxwell looked at the television and saw that Phineas's misadventures were once more in the news. On the screen, an apparently senior police officer stood at a podium littered with microphones.

...no evidence of children having been killed. So far our forensic teams have only found remains of several adult male kroaches. However, this does not change the fact that they were brutally torn apart using some kind of tool as yet unidentified. Although the suspects are highly trained fighters, it would require inhuman strength to tear the kroaches' heads and limbs off.

Questions?

[Reporter 1] Sir, if it is true that only kroaches were killed, would that affect the charges?

[Police officer] Yes, kroach killing falls under different legislation than does human killing, though it also has strict penalties.

[Reporter 1] But surely, if only kroaches were murdered, the nuns will be let off. We all know that kroach killing is not taken seriously in southern Europa.

[Police officer] That is a matter for the courts. Next question, please?

"If it was only kroaches they killed, they'll be out soon," said Lucy.

"And then they'll be chasing after you again, Maxwell," said Wendy, tensing visibly. "I don't want any more of that."

"I can't say I fancy that much either, Wendy." said Maxwell, putting his hand gently on Wendy's back and casting a quick glance at Judith, who blushed.

"What are we going to do?" asked Wendy.

"Fleeing to Erps-Kwerps is surely our best option. I know a couple of high-ranking lasses in the Flemish police, one of whom is still on speaking terms with me. I hope we can count on them to stop Phinny and his nuts."

"Nuns," said Wendy.

"Yes, of course. Nuns," said Maxwell. Judith reddened on hearing this.

"But the car is still being repaired, isn't it?" asked Wendy.

"Yes. And that rather throws rather a spanner into the whole fleeing thing."

"Maxwell! What are we going to do?" asked Wendy.

"Don't worry. I'll check on the car right after lunch. With luck it will be ready and we can go this afternoon."

"What if it's not ready?"

"As I said, Phinny will be expecting us to take the North-South highway to Brussels. He probably reckons we're nearly there by now. He'd never come here looking for us." Maxwell paused for a moment as he eyed Judith. "Unless, of course, you've said something."

Judith turned bright red. "Of course not!" she exclaimed. On the other hand, she had attached the tracking device to the bottom of the Bentley – but Maxwell had not asked about that and she certainly had no intention of telling him. The man was intimidating enough, with his weird behaviour and accusations towards her. She did not want to give him reason to be even more intimidating.

"I hope not," said Maxwell. "If I should suddenly find myself at the gates of Hell in the next day or two, I will personally ask Satan to fetch your soul as well."

"But Maxwell, you don't..." began Wendy.

"Hush, Wendy. Now, let's have some lunch," said Maxwell.

Not surprisingly, Lucy and Judith decided to sit separately from Maxwell and Wendy. Nevertheless, Wendy peered over at them from time to time, ensuring that the younger woman was not on the telephone.

After lunch, Maxwell and Wendy walked the two kilometres into town. The roadside was rich in weeds, with a few signs poking out in order to announced the existence of hotels and restaurants further down the road. As they drew closer, the weeds were replaced with lawns and houses, several of which sported "B&B" signs in front.

As they approached the centre, Maxwell directed them down a small road to a clean but cluttered garage with a handful of cars in various states of dismantlement in front. As they walked inside, they could see the Bentley with its rear end hanging on a pair of jack stands. On the driver's side, the wheel was laying on the ground, together with several pieces of the rear transaxle.

"This does not bode well for fleeing," said Maxwell.

"No, it does not," agreed Wendy.

"Excuse me," called Maxwell.

A middle-aged man slid out from under another car.

"Ah, the Bentley," he said.

"Well, the Bentley's owner," said Maxwell.

"Ha ha. Of course," said the mechanic.

"How is my car coming along? We're in a bit of a hurry to push on, as beautiful as your town may be," said Maxwell.

The mechanic walked over to the dismantled bits of the Bentley and pulled a bent piece of metal off the ground. "It's a simple repair, sir, but the difficult part is finding a replacement for this. We don't see many of these old Bentleys around here. I've ordered the part, but it will be at least next week before it arrives."

Wendy shrieked inadvertently.

"Don't mind her. She's sensitive to long waits. I am too, for that matter."

Maxwell thought for a moment. "If I could get the part to you tonight or tomorrow morning at the latest, could you have the car ready sometime tomorrow?"

"Sure."

"Hang on a moment or three, then," said Maxwell. He pulled out his telephone and made a couple of calls before spending a few minutes happily chatting.

He handed his phone to the mechanic. "Tell this young woman what you need, please."

He explained in detail, followed by two yesses, a no, a yes and his address.

Maxwell took the telephone again. "Can you do that? Excellent! Remember, courier it out as fast as possible. My life depends upon it. Really! Thanks, I owe you one. Oh, but that would be a pleasure, sweetheart. Bye-bye."

To the mechanic, Maxwell said, "the part should be here by nine tomorrow morning."

"Then I'll have it ready by noon tomorrow at the latest."

"Smashing," said Maxwell who pulled €100 out of his wallet and handed it to the mechanic. "For your troubles."

"Thanks," said the mechanic. "Oh, and there's another thing."

"Yes?" asked Maxwell,

"I found this attached to the undercarriage of your car." The mechanic held up the tracking device.

"What is it?" asked Maxwell.

"I'm not sure, but I believe it is a GPS tracking device. I guess you didn't put it there."

Wendy shrieked again.

"You've got an excitable bird there, sir," said the mechanic.

"It's that time of the month," said Maxwell vaguely. "Would you perchance have a sledgehammer here?"

"Sure."

"May I borrow it?"

The mechanic looked at Maxwell, smiled and walked to a storage cabinet. He found a battered old sledgehammer and handed it to Maxwell. "Over there," he said, pointing to a corner of the workshop where a variety of battered car parts were stacked up.

Maxwell walked across the garage, put the tracking device on the floor and smashed it with the sledgehammer. It made a satisfactory crunching sound.

"Thank you," he said, handing the sledgehammer back to the mechanic.

As they walked back to the hotel, Wendy asked, "do you think Phineas put the tracking device on the Bentley?"

"Probably not personally, but I am sure it is his doing. He seems determined to do me in this time."

"What can we do about it?" asked Wendy unsteadily.

"Don't worry about it, old bird. Phinny is still in jail and we'll be out of here tomorrow. Even if he does get out soon, we've got a head start and his gang of nuts won't be able to track us any more."

"But they know we're going to Erps-Kwerps.

"Ah, well, we'll just take the small roads. They're more fun, and if he does get out, he'll be expecting us on the highway."

"Okay," said Wendy, with less unsteadiness.

"But let us not say anything, about finding the tracking thingie to the girl – what was her name?"

"Judith."

"Exactly. Let's not say anything to..." Maxwell burst into a fit of coughing before he could complete his sentence. Then he began coughing some more.

"Are you okay?" asked Wendy.

"I think so. It feels like something is irritating my throat. Perhaps some dust or something from the garage."

"There's a lot of dust about," said Wendy.

"That's probably it," said Maxwell doubtfully.

29

Back in his room, Maxwell opened the window to let in some fresh air and poured himself a glass of water for the cough, which seemed to be getting worse. The water didn't help. If anything, it made the cough even worse. In a moment he exploded into an almost painful coughing fit and felt something rise up his throat, burst out of his mouth and shatter on the floor.

"Lord love a duck and his grandmother!" he exclaimed to himself. "What was that?"

On the floor lay dozens of shards all shimmering away in a disturbingly ethereal way. He had never seen – let alone coughed up – anything like it.

"I do believe I have just coughed up my soul," he said, without knowing why he knew this. At least his cough had gone away.

As he was on his knees studying the pieces of his presumed soul, the door burst open and the angel came in with a case of wine in her arms.

"I have brought us a case of Pingus," she said with obvious pride. "But I had to kill a man to get it."

"What year is the Pingus?" asked Maxwell.

"2018," said the angel.

"Wow, that is a good year. I suppose it was worth killing a man over."

"That's what I thought. He didn't suffer much pain," she said.

"Then I expect it's okay," said Maxwell, who vaguely thought he ought to have rather stronger feelings about the angel's actions. He wondered if it was the lack of a soul, lack of sleep or both that left him indifferent.

Wendy peered into the open door, then walked into the room.

"I have brought us a case of Pingus," said the angel.

"What is that?" asked Wendy.

"Why, it is one of the finest wines in the world," said Maxwell.

"Holy fuck! What has happened here!?" exclaimed the angel, upon seeing Maxwell's soul.

"I think I coughed my soul up," said Maxwell.

"Did it hurt?" asked the angel.

"Just for a moment," said Maxwell.

"How can you cough a soul up?" asked Wendy.

"Well, you just sort of cough a great deal and out it pops. Mind you, this was my first time, so I don't know if this is how it normally happens or not."

"Can you put it back inside?" asked Wendy.

"I really don't know," said Maxwell. "I'm new at this. I've always kept my soul safely inside my body – or wherever it is one keeps one's soul."

"Yes, I think it is possible to put it back," said the angel. "But it is not easy. I think I know someone who can help."

"Well, let me put it in a bag or something until we can find your someone," said Maxwell.

"No, you cannot do that!" scolded the angel. "A bag is too ugly for your soul. We must find something more beautiful." She looked around the room, but saw nothing suitable. "I will go to the market and get you something. Don't go away."

"Okay," said Maxwell. "But don't take too long. And no killing anyone, okay? Do you need some money?"

"Money?"

Maxwell took out his wallet, pulled a couple of €50 notes out of it and gave them to the angel. "Use this."

The angel took the money, walked swiftly to the open window and jumped out. For a split second she fell; then she slowly pumped her wings and flew off towards the town centre.

"Wow, that is impressive," said Maxwell, watching her fly away.

"Yes," said Wendy, with a hint of envy.

Wendy returned to her room. Maxwell put Bach on the sound system and lay back in the bed to think.

The current chaos level was higher than he liked and would only get worse when Phinny got out of prison – which could be any time. Moreover, Phinny could probably trace them to the Valley of Dreams, thanks to the tracking device – but no further, anyway. Maxwell was beginning to regret not having put the tracking device onto a vehicle headed south, but it was too late now. The best thing to do would be to leave the valley and head towards Flanders as soon as possible. Once Maxwell got back to Erps-Kwerps, he would feel safer.

As these thoughts swirled around in his mind, aided by Bach's violin sonatas, he soon dozed off, only to be woken a short while later by a kiss on the forehead and a gentle caress on his cheek.

He opened his eyes to see the angel looking down upon him with a smile upon her face. "My goodness, you look almost motherly from down here," said Maxwell.

"I have bought a box and put your soul into it." The angel pointed to a lacquer box sitting on the bedside table. It was a warm black in colour, with a flowery motif. At its front were two brass latches.

"It's very nice. Thank you," said Maxwell.

"You're welcome," said the angel.

"But it looks awfully small. Were you able to fit all those pieces soul into that box?"

"Do not be ungrateful! Do you think I would throw away some of your soul?"

"No, of course not."

"But I did have to squeeze it a bit to fit it in."

"Oh my! Is that not bad for souls?"

"Not yours. Yours is very...What is the word? Malleable."

"I see. Perhaps that is why it came out so easily."

"Perhaps. Or perhaps you fucked the wrong person. Someone like me."

"Would, um, making love with someone like you be bad for my soul?"

"It could be bad, very bad for your souls."

"Souls?"

"Yes."

"Plural?"

"Yes. Now I must go. I will see you at dinner, no?"

"Yes."

Maxwell wondered where the hell a confused angel would need to go in the early evening.

At dinner, Maxwell, Wendy and the angel decided to walk into the town to look for a place to eat. The found a pleasant pizzeria with outdoor tables looking out on to the town square. Once again, the angel drank prodigious amounts of wine while seeming to remain sober. She ate little. Maxwell also drank considerably, as was his habit, but mopped up the wine with a vegetarian pizza. Wendy opted for a pasta and seafood platter.

Upon returning to the hotel, Wendy and the angel headed upstairs to their rooms. Maxwell decided to take a table at the hotel bar and have a glass of wine before retiring. He had been inspired by the walk through the town and wanted to sketch some ideas before he forgot them. He pulled the notebook out of his jacket pocket and began drawing.

Three pages later, a Japanese woman looked over his shoulder.

"You are very talented. Are you an artist?" she asked.

"Yes, I am," said Maxwell, as he drew three more lines. Then he looked up and smiled at the woman. "And you?"

"Me?" she asked.

"Yes, are you an artist?"

"No," she laughed. "I am an biologist."

"And what brings you here? Studying the strange species that supposedly lurk in the Valley of Dreams?"

"Oh, no!" she smiled, "I am here on holiday with my friend. We are travelling across Europa. I wanted to visit the Valley of Dreams."

"And your friend? Have you dumped her? That kind of thing can happen when you take a trip with a friend. Everything seems hunky-dory to begin with, but time together, differing interests, snoring – they can all drive a wedge between friends and spoil a trip. One day, you pick up a weapon and solve the problem, to your friend's detriment."

She laughed again.

"Oh, no! She is very tired and went to bed already."

"Are you sure? Because there are a lot of open, desolate spaces in the Valley of Dreams. Makes it easy to dispose of a body, you know."

"Oh my God!" she looked at Maxwell, then burst out laughing. "No. No. Really, my friend is just tired. She went to bed. So, I decided to have a drink and see if anyone interesting is here."

Maxwell looked around.

"I'm afraid it is only me."

Once again she laughed. "But you seem interesting."

"I've heard rumours to that extent, but I have my doubts."

"You are being interesting right now!"

"I am? You're sweet to say so."

"Thank you."

"And you've got incredible lips!"

"I do?" she said, touching her lips.

Suddenly, the angel burst in between them, stared the Japanese woman in the eyes and exclaimed in a deep voice: "He's mine, bitch! Keep your hands off!"

The woman fell off her stool, stumbled to her feet and ran back to the bar. Then the angel took Maxwell's hand and said to him, "no fucking tonight. You need a good night's sleep. Come on!" She led him to the lift.

"Egads, Angel!" exclaimed Maxwell. "What's got into you?"

"The fucking determination to get you to bed with no fucking any girls tonight. That's what's fucking got into me." She walked to Maxwell's door, somehow opened it without a key card and led Maxwell to the bed.

"How about you, then? You're very attractive..."

"No!" she roared. She turned around and left – but just before she closed the door, she turned back to Maxwell and said, "and you fucking better not sneak out, or I will rip your head off and mount it to the gatepost of the hotel.

"Yes, dear," said Maxwell, with a trace of sarcasm that completely escaped the angel. Still, he recalled the angel's skill with decapitation and decided not to test the threat.

Once she left the room, the angel said in her normal voice to herself, "that woman downstairs, she wants to be fucked tonight and I shall fuck her gloriously." As she spoke, she transformed herself into a handsome young man, went downstairs to the bar and started flirting with the Japanese tourist.

30

Dan and Sam walked into Frank's office in the Interplanetary Intelligence Agency's station in Madrid. The office was impeccably clean, with merely a desk with one chair behind it and two in front of it. There were no filing cabinets, no papers. There were not even family pictures anywhere.

This last fact was was mostly because Frank's race bred like cats do. When a male senses a female in heat, he simply mounts her then and there, irrespective of where they may be. They have a good mutual orgasm and then both partners go their separate ways. It goes without saying that this behaviour, while normal on Frank's planet, was more than a little disconcerting on Earth, particularly during inter-species meetings.

Not surprisingly, his race was banned from the socially conservative Evangelical States of America, where the public display of a breast is punishable by up to three years in prison – so you can imagine how well public intercourse is received. In short, Frank had no idea or interest in how many offspring he might have, and even less of an interest in putting up their pictures.

"You've found the so-called angel?" asked Dan.

"Yes, I have. She is staying at the Hotel de Memorias Desvanecidas in the Valley of Dreams," said Frank.

"Really? She's just booked a normal hotel room? Like that?" asked Dan.

"You know I am not capable of lying," said Frank.

"Yeah, I know," said Dan. "It's just that I expected her to be in hiding or something, not staying in a hotel. What name did she use to check in?"

"Her room and two others were booked by Maxwell van Mars," said Frank.

"I see. Let's get together a team and bring her in," said Dan.

"I'm on it," said Sam, plucking up a telephone and punching some numbers into it. He spoke for a moment then put his hand over the mouthpiece.

"Do we want weapons?" Sam asked Dan.

"You bet your arse we do," said Dan. "You've seen what it did to those kroaches."

"Heavy weapons?"

"Go for it."

Sam spoke briefly and then rang off. "They'll be ready to move in about a half hour.

"Excellent," said Dan.

31

At breakfast, Maxwell was loading up his plate with various good-
ies from the buffet. He was in a good mood. He had enjoyed a
good night's sleep and in the morning, a phone call to the garage
confirmed that the Bentley would be roadworthy by 10.

"Wow, you really can eat a lot for a skinny guy," said Lucy, who
had just arrived in the buffet and was helping herself to a rather
smaller collection of morning nutrition.

"A high-powered brain like mine requires a considerable
amount of fuel, darling. It's rather like a high-performance car that
requires lots of petrol," explained Maxwell.

Lucy burst out laughing and took hold of Maxwell's shoulder
to retain her balance. It was not so much the audacity of his remark as the sincerity with which he stated it that Lucy found
overly funny this morning. She acknowledged that Maxwell was an
intelligent chap and a very creative one, but knowing that she was
considered a genius herself and that Maxwell would not be able to
keep up with her on any scientific debate made his comment all
the more ridiculous.

"Do you mock me, woman?" Maxwell asked in response.

"Oh, dear me, no," she said, suddenly unable to stop laughing."

"You are causing severe damage to my self-esteem. I lost my
soul yesterday, which was bad enough. To lose my self-esteem
today would break my heart."

"I'm sorry," said Lucy, who had to put down her plate. "I can't
help myself this morning."

"It's probably the scrambled eggs. There's something decidedly dodgy about them, I must say," said Maxwell, touching her arm to steady her.

"That's probably it," said Lucy, who started laughing again.

"Oh, dear! I don't think your girlfriend gets the joke," said Maxwell.

"What?" asked Lucy.

"Look," said Maxwell, nodding towards Judith, who was, as it happened, helping herself to scrambled eggs at the other end of the buffet.

Judith was staring with unhidden dismay at the laughing Lucy, who was once again holding Maxwell. Judith did not like the ease with which Maxwell was able to make her lover laugh, especially when she herself had never made Lucy laugh. This, of course, was because she lacked a sense of humour – but, like most people without a sense of humour, she was ignorant of the fact.

When she saw Maxwell gesturing towards her and Lucy's laughter quickly fading, Judith blushed and focused on the scrambled eggs. Maybe Father Forge was right about Maxwell, she thought. Maybe he was evil. Maybe he would corrupt her darling Lucy and take her away.

"Uh oh," said Lucy. "I'd better see to her. She's had an emotionally rough few days."

"Okay. We're headed off towards Erps-Kwerps after breakfast. I hope we can keep in touch," said Maxwell.

"It'd like that too," said Lucy, "but as friends."

"Friends with benefits?" asked Maxwell.

"No benefits!" insisted Lucy.

"None at all?

"None!"

"That will be difficult, but I'll do my best."

"Very good." Lucy kissed Maxwell on the cheek, picked up her plate and headed over towards Judith.

"Hey, honey. Are you okay?" Lucy asked Judith.

"Yes," said Judith, somewhat icily. Had Lucy looked down, she would have noticed that the serving spoon for the scrambled eggs had been twisted into a spiral. Instead, she led Judith to their table.

After breakfast, Lucy and Judith decided to do some sightseeing in the valley. Lucy wanted to show Judith the sights that had enthralled her as a child. Judith was simply grateful to have alone time with Lucy and eagerly agreed with the suggestion.

At the same time, Maxwell left the hotel and walked into town to fetch the Bentley. However, in a moment of rare sensitivity on his part, he decided to stay back and leave the two women to walk alone a few hundred metres ahead of him.

He arrived ten minutes later at the garage to find the car was ready as promised. Better still, it rode silently and clunklessly back to the hotel. By the time he had returned, Wendy and the angel were packed and ready for the road.

While waiting to check out, Maxwell noticed that Phineas and his gang were once again on the television screen in the lobby.

[A handsome young newsreader with plastic-perfect hair and teeth is speaking.] Members of the Evangelical Church of America who were arrested earlier this week for allegedly slaughtering children were freed this morning after Judge Geraldina Isadora dismissed the case against them.

Following a thorough investigation of the crime scene, no evidence was found of children having been harmed, although the dismembered bodies of several Kroaches were found at the scene. Police were unable to find any evidence demonstrating that the church members were responsible for killing the kroach victims.

Approximately 100 people protested the release outside the Vega de Tera Courthouse. [Cut to scene of protesters with signs such as "Justice for Kroaches" and "Killing Kroaches is Evil, America!"

Meanwhile, at their European headquarters in Cape City , the Evangelical Church of America announced that they would build a kroach school near the kroach encampments on the outskirts of Vega de Tera. [Cut to meeting room in Chruch of America headquarters]...

"Dear me, it looks like Phinny and his nuts got out sooner than I had expected. Good thing the car's done, eh, Wendy?"

"Do you think he'll be able to catch up with us?"

"No way. We've removed the tracking thing and it will take him a day to get up here – that is if the church doesn't call him back over this event. By then, we'll be lost on some beautiful back road. Don't worry. He'll never find us."

Suddenly, the lobby light up in red flashing lights. Maxwell and Wendy looked out the front windows to see that an ambulance had parked in front of the building. Two men pulling a wheeled stretcher with a medical robot mounted to its side dashed in, interrupted an elderly couple slowly checking out and said, "we received a call about someone having an attack."

"Yes, room 311," said the receptionist at the desk. "Carlos, will you lead these gentlemen there?" she added to a bellhop nearby. Carlos did his duty and they dashed off towards the lift.

"Sorry to interrupt you," said the receptionist, "but one of our guests has taken ill."

"Don't worry about it, deary," said the woman. "We're in no hurry." She spoke the truth. It took another five minutes before they collected their bags and headed out to a waiting taxi. Meanwhile, Wendy was becoming agitated. Logically, she knew a few minutes would not make a difference, but she was worried nonetheless.

"We'd like to check out, please, young lady," said Maxwell to the now-available receptionist.

As the receptionist handed Maxwell his receipt, the ambulance crew came back through the lobby. In their stretcher was the Japanese woman Maxwell had spoken to the night before. She seemed to be having some kind of fit. Maxwell could not help but notice that she seemed to be enjoying it. Moreover, he was sure that he had seen women behaving similarly often, but could not place the occasion or reason for a moment.

"What happened to her?" Maxwell asked the receptionist. "Do you know?"

"No idea, sir," said the receptionist. "Apparently, her travel companion found her that way this morning."

Suddenly, Maxwell recalled where he had seen women convulsing similarly.

"By golly, she looks like she's having one hell of an orgasm!" he said.

"Wow," said the receptionist. "Apparently she's been like that way all morning. If you're right, and she does kind of look that way, it really must be one hell of an orgasm."

"Indeed," said Maxwell.

"Hmmm...I wonder what that would be like?" the receptionist asked thoughtfully.

The angel winked at the receptionist as they gathered their bags and began singing "Non, Je Ne Regrette Rien" as they walked to the car.

32

At the front of the hotel, standing before a deep-blue sky full of clouds rushing off into the horizon, stood a determined sign, faded and yet unwilling to be toppled by the eternal winds of Europa. The sign, whose message changed from time to time, today announced an afternoon performance of the modern ballet, "The Angels of Brittany", to be performed by the local high school's dance club.

The ancient Bentley passed the sign and left it in the distance as it accelerated into traffic. A moment later, a small bus delivering a dozen girl dancers, two boy dancers and a skinny, overtired dance coach passed the sign and pulled into the hotel entrance.

Two and a half minutes and three kilometres later, the Bentley decelerated abruptly as Maxwell turned the car into a crowded petrol station. A delivery van pulled up to the pump between the one Maxwell was using and the road. As a result, he did not see the small fleet of sleek, black, unmarked hovercraft, with lights flashing, racing up the same road he had just come down. Nor did the driver and passengers of the lead vehicle see Maxwell's car or the angel they sought.

IIA Agent Sam drove the first of the hovercrafts. Frank sat next to him and Dan was in back. All wore aviator glasses that enhanced the authoritative appearance of the humans and the ridiculousness of the alien. Fortunately for Frank, his race had no concept of ridiculous, but appreciated a bargain – hence the cheap human mask he always wore while working. The aviator glasses were standard issue from the IIA and had been custom designed to enhance authoritativeness.

The hovercraft retraced the path the Bentley had just taken and roared up into the hotel forecourt. The agents opened the gull-wing doors of the first hovercraft and climbed out.

"Holy shit, it looks like there's a gang of those angels inside the lobby of the hotel!" exclaimed Dan.

Sam squinted through the glass entry doors. "Yes, sir. It does indeed. And they seem agitated. What do you suggest we do, sir?"

Dan scanned the hotel and the space around it. "Oh my fucking God!" he exclaimed. "There's a school bus here. There could be young children in the hotel!"

"Shit! And we know those angels are dangerous," said Sam.

" We better contain the situation and apprehend the aliens. Now," said Dan

"Yes, sir," said Sam.

"Yes, sir," agreed Frank.

Inside the hotel, the pupils from the dance club were running around the lobby, full of nervous energy, while the coach repeatedly asked them to calm down, reminded them that the show would start in ten minutes and begged them, for goodness sake, to be careful of their make-up.

Dan gestured to the other hovercrafts, and in an instant a dozen gull-wing doors opened. Men in protective black suits and helmeted visors burst out with high-powered laser weapons in hand. Dan pointed the lobby.

"The alleged aliens are acting in an increasingly agitated manner. We know there are people inside the hotel. We believe there are also young children inside. I want to burst the windows and then take down as many as you can. Use stun. We do not need any collateral damage. Okay?"

"Sir!" they shouted in near unison.

"Then do it!" shouted Dan, stepping to the side.

"Girls! Girls and boys!" shouted the coach as loudly as she could. "The show's going to start soon. Get into the dining room now!"

"Kabloom!" Screamed the plate glass windows in front of the hotel as they exploded in shards of glass, which vaporised as they rained down.

"Holy shit!" she screamed. "Girls, boys, get down!" – but it was too late. The lasers were picking off one pupil after another. The remaining girls, as well as the other guests in the lobby, started screaming and running in various directions, often into each other. Several parents instinctively tried to protect the pupils, but the lasers shot down one after another person until no one was left standing in the lobby.

A hovering sphere buzzed in, spun around slowly and broadcast an all-clear message to Dan's telephone.

"Excellent work!" he shouted. "The drone reports everyone is down aside from one human female hiding behind the reception desk in a puddle of urine."

"Do you want me to shoot her, sir?" asked one of the besuited men.

"Don't be silly. She isn't an alien," said Dan.

"Yes, sir," said the man.

"Okay, gentlemen. Let's go in. But be careful. The angels are an unknown alien race and we do not know how the stun lasers will have affected them," said Dan.

"How many non-human life forms does the drone report?" asked Frank.

Dan flicked some screens around on his telephone. "That's strange," he said.

"What?"

"I'm not reading any unidentified life forms," said Dan.

Several armed men stepped into the hotel lobby and scanned

the situation. "All clear," a captain shouted.

Dan, Sam and Frank stepped in. Dan saw a sign announcing the lunch performance of the "Angels of Brittany" at 13h00. He looked at the clock above the reception desk. Then he looked at the teenage girls, many of whose angel wings were torn from their costumes, laying all over the lobby.

"Oh, shit," he said.

33

Lubidada received a message directly into his brain. Zargonians, you see, had done away with telephones, personal computers and other electronic nonsense a couple of generations before and just sent communications directly into each other's brains.

They had tried to sell this technology to Earthlings, but it was soon discovered that Earthlings thought far too much about sex and tended to send erotic and often pornographic messages to all and sundry. All and sundry were, for the most part, not receptive to such messages and sometimes decidedly unreceptive. Indeed, the customer trial for this new technology was probably the first time in marketing history that participants of a study had to be put into a witness protection programme at the end of the study. However, this historical note bears no relevance to the message received by Lubidada.

"Oh my!" he exclaimed.

"Yes?" asked Snox.

"I've just received a message from our satellite monitoring the tear. It seems there have been curious fluctuations in the dark energy flowing near the tear."

"That is strange. Is anything else happening?" asked Snox.

Lubidada put a tablet on the table between them and mentally requested a view of the tear together with a data-feed.

"No, I see nothing more. Do you?"

"No, but did we not see a similar fluctuation when the object came out of the tear?" asked Snox.

Lubidada thought for a moment. "Yes, I believe you are right.

But I see nothing coming out of the tear."

"Neither do I," said Snox.

At the same time, a vibration ran across the Lake of Dreams, causing a couple of wading children to lose their balance and a few swimmers to stop, tread water and see what was going on. On one quiet shore, the woman in the black bikini waded out. She stopped for a moment, looked around and then walked up a sandy path, which led to a half-full car park. She crossed it, came to the road and looked both ways. To the left, she saw a fuel station and walked towards it, dripping wet.

A black BMW Coupé was parked by the petrol station's shop. Inside the car sat a middle-aged man with a belly that rested atop his legs, an expensive, cuff-linked shirt topped with a neck-tie and an impressive hairdo. The woman tapped on the driver's side window. The man looked round, saw what to his mind was an exceptionally attractive woman and electronically rolled down the window.

"Oh, sorry," said the woman in her soft French accent. "I thought you were my boyfriend."

The man laughed, causing his belly to jiggle. "You have a lucky boyfriend," he said.

"Maybe, but he is not a gentleman to me," she said.

"Well, I think he's a fool. If I had a girlfriend like you, I would treat her like a princess," he said.

"You would?" she asked, then bent down and kissed him on the fat cheek.

"You bet I would!" he said.

She bent down, kissed him again, this time on the lips.

"Oh my God!" he exclaimed.

"This is not so easy, bending over like so," she said. "Perhaps you step out of the car for a moment and we can do this better."

"Sure!" said the man. He opened the car door, stood up and

awkwardly put his hands on her waist.

She put her bare feet upon his highly polished leather shoes, smiled, seductively held his head in her hands and ripped it off. The poor man barely had time to register what had happened before his brain started shutting down, leaving a macabrely surprised expression on his face. She flung the head into the weed-covered field adjacent to the car park.

After taking his wallet, pulling out the cash and credit cards and tucking them into the cups of her bikini top, she lifted the body and tossed it into the field as well. Oddly enough, the only person to witness any of this was a 12-year-old boy in a passing car, who simply said, "cool." He was ignored by his parents in the front seat, who were arguing about whether or not they should have taken the last turn, and his younger sister, who was asleep.

Meanwhile, the bikini-clad woman spotted a water tap by the air pump, washed the man's blood off herself and returned to the car. She opened the boot of the car, found a suitcase and inside it a men's dress shirt. She put it on and tied the tails around her waist. Seeing nothing more of interest, she tossed the suitcase into the field.

She climbed into the driver's seat and found a mobile telephone. Scanning through his text messages, she found his wife and sent her a message: "I'm sorry. I am leaving you for another woman. Goodbye." Then she tossed the phone into the field. She adjusted the seat, rolled up the window and started the engine. After looking long the road both ways, she decided to turn left.

34

Lucy and Judith's first stop was the Crashsite ruins. They bought tickets, nabbed a map and explored. The ruined castle slowly being devoured by vegetation and sitting forlornly upon the mountain ridge would be been beautiful enough in its own right, but this castle now had scattered bits of highly reflective, metallic and clearly alien spaceship embedded into the ruins and the land around it. Most dramatically, a chunk of the hull had pierced through a fat tower, with bits extending from either end, creating a T that stood up against the cloud-rich sky.

"Incredible," said Lucy, awestruck. She had not been to Crashsite since she was a teenager and had forgotten how impressive the ruins were.

"Lucy?" said Judith, whose mind was elsewhere – a preoccupied mind, after all, is not one that is typically receptive to external stimuli, no matter how beautiful.

"Yes, honey?" asked Lucy.

"Do you still love Maxwell?"

"What?!"

"Well, Maxwell used to be your boyfriend, didn't he?"

"Oh, no, honey. Not at all. I prefer girls."

"But you were in bed with him, naked, when I first found you."

"Yes, that's true. But it was not love. It was a one-night stand that didn't even last the night."

"You mean you slept with somebody you didn't love? Why?"

"That's a good question. For fun, I suppose. To remind me of what it is like to sleep with a man and, well, I guess Maxwell is charming in a very seductive way. I broke up with my last girlfriend almost a year ago and, I suppose, I just wanted some good sex with no long-term obligations. A woman would have been better, but Maxwell wasn't bad – especially for a man."

"You mean you could just go to bed and, you know, have sex with someone you did not care about?"

"Not often. But sometimes it's just what the doctor ordered."

"And do you think the doctor will order you to have sex with Maxwell again? You seem to really like him."

Lucy laughed. "Oh goodness, no. I will not have sex with him again, not now. Not when I've got you."

"But he always makes you laugh," said Judith. "Like boys make girls laugh in love stories."

"Yes. He's a funny guy in a totally self-centred, self-absorbed kind of way. It's hard not to laugh."

"But I never make you laugh."

"Do you ever tell me jokes?"

"Well...No. I don't know any jokes."

"There you go. But we still have laughs together. Remember our bubble bath last night?"

"Oh, yes." Judith smiled.

"Maxwell is just a funny guy. I like him. He's clever and and entertaining. But there is nothing special between us."

Judith thought about this for a moment. "Do you love me?"

"It's too soon, honey. I like you very much. But love takes time. That's one reason I wanted to take this drive with you: to give us some time."

"Do you think you could love me?"

"I'm sure I could. Just, let's get to know each other better first. You may discover over time that you don't really love me."

"But I do love you," Judith insisted, as a tear formed in her left eye.

"Oh, baby," said Lucy, hugging Judith. After a moment, Lucy

took Judith's shoulders in her hands, held her back and looked into her eyes. "Let's just give this relationship a little time and try and get to know each other better. Then love will follow naturally. True love. Okay, Judith?"

"Okay," sniffed Judith. "And you won't run off with Maxwell?"

"Of course not!"

"Okay."

They continued walking through the ruins, holding hands but not speaking, until they came to the more modern museum building adjacent to the castle. They went in and examined the exhibits, which were mostly glass-encased papers, photos and trinkets about the castle, the crash, the planet Fynsha and the Fynshans themselves.

Judith's telephone rang, which caused her to jump.

"Excuse me," she said to Lucy as she walked outside to answer the call. This was partly out of good manners to the handful of tourists also in the museum and largely because she had been taught always to take phone calls in private. Although much of what the ninja nuns had to do was sanctioned by the church, police authorities outside of evangelical America tended to take a dimmer view of many of the nuns' activities. Discretion was advised.

"Hello?" she said.

"Sister Judith! This is Petra," said an excited ninja nun on the other end of the phone connection.

"Oh, Sister Petra," said a somewhat less-excited Judith. "How are you? Where are you?"

"We were released early this morning. The case against us has been dropped."

"You were? It was?" asked Judith.

"Yes, isn't it wonderful?" asked Petra.

Judith really wasn't sure, but knew saying as much was not an ideal response under the circumstances. "Yes, of course it is!"

"Oh, Judith, the prison was so terrible! It was full of homosexuals! One of them even tried to kiss me like a husband and wife do, so I flung her across the room!"

"You did?" said Judith.

"Yes, of course I did. You know what the Bible says about homosexuals," said Petra.

"What does it say?" asked Judith.

"That they shall burn in Hell!" said Petra.

"Does it?" asked Judith.

"Of course it does. Why all the interest? Do you think I would let a lesbian do things to me in prison or something?" asked Petra.

"No. No, of course not," said Judith.

There was some talking in the background, though Judith could not make it out.

"Sorry, got off topic there. Father Forge says that the tracking device is no longer working and wants to know if you've been able to track down Maxwell."

Given the option, Judith would have liked to have had a day to think about the question and, more specifically, how to respond to it. She loved Lucy (or at least believed that she did), but hated Lucy's closeness to Maxwell. Moreover, Lucy did not yet love her. What future did she have with Lucy, Judith wondered. And would that future be threatened if it included Maxwell? What if Lucy dumped Judith. After all, Lucy was so intelligent and experienced. What could she see in a naïve and ill-experienced woman with no figure like Judith?

"Judith?"

"Sorry, it's a bad connection. What did you say?"

"Father Forge wants to know if you know where Maxwell is."

Judith made a split-second decision to solve her own Maxwell problem.

"He was in the Valley of Dreams this morning and is headed towards Erps-Kwerps."

"That's excellent! Do you know which road he is taking?"

"I'm not sure, but he expects you to be looking for him on the North-South Highway, so, I think he will leave the valley at the northern end and take, maybe, that highway through the French provinces. Which is it? Route 103, I think."

Judith could hear Petra repeating what she had just said. There was then a bit of a scuffling and Father Forge was on the line.

"You have done a marvellous job of following Maxwell, Sister Judith," said the priest.

"Thank you, Father," said Judith.

"And where are you now, Sister?"

"Um, I'm in the Valley of Dreams."

"Watching Maxwell no doubt. I am proud of you, young lady."

"Thank you, Father."

"You still have the truck, don't you?"

"Um, yes. Father."

"Good. Good. Now, I want you to follow Maxwell's route to Erps-Kwerps. If you get a chance to expedite him to Hell, you go ahead and do it, now. If not, we will meet up in Erps-Kwerps and take care of him together. Have I made myself clear?"

"Yes, Father."

"Excellent. I shall see you in Erps-Kwerps, Sister. Now, God-speed, you hear?"

"Yes, Father."

"Bye, now."

"Goodbye, Father."

Judith stood motionless on the concrete platform between the museum and one of the ruined castle walls. She looked out at the valley floor below. The warm wind jostled her hair. The only sound was the faint rustling of the branches, disturbed from time to time by small groups of tourists moving between the buildings.

She had made a decision. She was not sure if it was the right one. In fact, she rather suspected it was the completely and totally wrong one, but with Maxwell gone, her life would be simpler. Maybe he was a demon.

She pulled out her telephone and tapped in a message to Lucy: "I'm sorry. I have to go. Maybe" She intended to delete the last word and replace it with another, but accidentally pressed send instead. Too late. The message was sent.

She walked out to the car park, climbed into the SUV and started her long drive to Erps-Kwerps.

After receiving the message, Lucy searched the museum. Not finding her young lover, she quickly walked through the ruins of the castle, without success. Finally, she looked in the car park where the only SUVs were the wrong colour, size and marque.

"Damn it to hell!" she shouted. She tried calling Judith, but there was no answer. She left a voicemail: "Hey honey, what's wrong? Have you run away? Are you coming back? Let's talk about this. I'm walking back to the hotel now. I hope to see you there."

She began walking.

35

Although the walk from the Crashsite ruins to the hotel was a beautiful one recommended by several guidebooks, Lucy was not admiring the stunning landscape of green-covered mountains that rolled off into the horizon. Nor was she impressed by the tall, multicoloured plants growing by the roadside and blowing happily in the wind. She even failed completely to see the giraffe that watched her walk past. The amazing mixture of smells that rode upon the breeze was equally unable to gain her attention.

Rather, she was wondering what the hell happened with Judith, and when she wasn't doing that, she was wondering what the hell happened to herself. Really. Running off with a homicidal and repressed nun 16 years her junior was simply daft. That the girl only ran away should be seen as a good thing. When Lucy first saw Judith, the latter was seriously attempting to kill a man. The girl could have tried doing the same to her. Indeed, surely it was better she was gone.

She was also sexy as all fuck. And that was the problem.

Unfortunately, Lucy was not even clear on Judith's message. Did the girl have to go take care of business – though, Lucy would prefer not to dwell on the nature of a ninja nun's business – or was she going away for good? Would Lucy see her at the hotel or another time or never again? Did Lucy even want to see her? Maybe it was best to get the girl out of her life altogether and focus on relationships with reliable, professional women like herself?

The more she thought about it, the more she thought the girl was gone for good. And maybe that was for the best. But if that was the case, why the fuck was Lucy crying?

To clear the tears, she tried focusing on her next steps. She was stuck in a hotel outside Crashsite. She had no car and she wasn't sure where to go. She should probably go back to Cape City – but she had started on a journey and was rather in the mood to complete it. On the other hand, was there any point in going to Erps-Kwerps alone? Was Judith going that way? Or was she going back to her convent?

Judith! Damn her. Lucy felt tears coming on again.

"Hello? Are you okay?" said a soft, French-accented voice that caused Lucy to jump. She had not even heard the black BMW Coupé pull up beside her, in spite of the deep growl of the car's engine. The bikini-clad woman, now also wearing an oversized shirt tied at the waist, stretched across the seats and smiled at Lucy. "Can I give you a lift?" she asked.

Lucy thought a moment. She had walked about half way back to the hotel after being on her feet all morning. She was tired. A lift suddenly seemed an awfully good idea.

"Yes. That's very kind of you," she said.

"I'd enjoy the company," said the bikini woman. "It's been a bad day."

"You too?" asked Lucy, climbing into the cool, air-conditioned car's leather seat.

"Yep," said the woman. "It's a long story."

"I'm just going to the Hotel de Memorias Desvanecidas, down the road and then to the right," said Lucy.

"I know the place. It is a very beautiful hotel, I think," said the woman.

"Yes, it's lovely. I used to visit it when I was a child," said Lucy.

"What? Alone?" asked the woman.

"No, no. With my brother and parents," said Lucy, laughing gently.

The woman laughed as well. They rode in silence for a moment until the woman asked, "excuse my abruptness, but have you eaten?"

"Uh, no, I haven't, actually."

"That makes two of us," said the woman. "I propose we have some lunch and share our stories. I think we both have a need to share." She pulled into the car park of a small, lakeside restaurant with tables outside. "This looks like a nice place, do you think so?"

"Well..." said Lucy, surprised by the woman's openness.

"Oh, I am sorry. You are perhaps in a hurry. Shall I take you back to Hotel de Memorias Desvanecidas immediately?"

Lucy thought for a moment. There really was no reason to hurry back to the hotel. She was reasonably sure Judith was gone for good, but even if the girl came back, there was no reason why Lucy should race back for her. On top of that, this woman had a compelling charm.

"Sure, let's have something to eat here."

"Wonderful! My name is Legna, by the way."

"Lucy."

The restaurant was quiet in an off-seasonish kind of way. A few of the tables were occupied. Many more were lonely. The two women chose a table slightly removed from the rest, pressed up against a railing dividing the concrete patio from the rocky lakeside. A cool breeze blew up off the lake, caressing the women's hair and causing Legna's oversized shirt to billow.

Legna laughed as she pulled the shirt closer. "This is the evidence of my bad luck. I went for a swim in the lake this morning. I came out and my clothes, they were gone. Only the car keys were still in the sand."

"Oh my!" said Lucy.

"Yes. I think it was some kids causing mischief. Fortunately, I have found one of my father's shirts in the car. It is his car. But, as you can see, I think, he is a big man," said Legna, stretching out the open ends of the shirt. "I think there is enough room for both of us in this shirt."

"Well...Tied up like that, it looks good on you," said Lucy.

"Thank you," said Legna. "But this story is only the end of a sequence of bad luck. Yesterday, my girlfriend left me...For a man!"

"Oh, shit. I expect that hurt," said Lucy.

"Yes, very much. Then, I guess I am thinking too much about her and I crashed my car. This is why I am driving my father's car."

"Oh, you poor thing!" said Lucy.

"Yes, but I think that bad luck comes in threes. The stealing of my clothes is number three. Now it is time for good luck. Maybe meeting you is good luck."

"Oh, I don't know," said Lucy. "But talk about coincidences: my girlfriend left me today too. In her car!"

"So that is why you are walking."

"Yes. We were at Crashsite. We drove there in her car. Then she got a phone call and suddenly ran away – like that!"

"Like that?"

"Yes."

"May I ask, did you have the fight first?"

"No, but in fairness, she's young, has been through a very difficult time lately and we don't really know each other very well. Maybe it's been too much for her emotionally."

A waiter came and took the women's orders: two Salads Niçoises and a carafe of the house white wine.

"Do you think she might come back?"

"Perhaps. I don't know. I don't think so."

"And so, what is next for you?"

"To be honest, I was trying to figure that out when you stopped and offered me a lift. I think I will try and get a flight or lightning train back home to Cape City. "

"I am going towards Santander. I can give you a ride to the airport or train station if you would like."

"That would be very kind of you, if it's not out of your way, but I need to get my things from the hotel first."

"It is no problem. I am not in a hurry. I propose we have a leisurely lunch. Then we go to the hotel. You get your things and then we go to the airport."

"You're very kind. Thank you," said Lucy.

"It's my pleasure. Perhaps you would like to check on flights? You have a phone?"

"Yes, that's a good idea," said Lucy. "Excuse me a moment."

"Of course," said Legna as Lucy fiddled with the screen on her telephone, checking flight options.

"There's a flight from Santander to Madrid at half past five and a connecting flight that gets me into Cape City later than I'd like, but it will work.

"Excellent," said Legna.

As they ate, Lucy gave a very abbreviated account of her situation with Judith, omitting the bits about the girl's professional history and the details of how they met. Legna was sympathetic, affectionate and – as much as Lucy hated to admit it just hours after losing her new girlfriend – very good looking. Indeed, Lucy found herself becoming increasingly enchanted by Legna. It was not only the woman's looks, but her voice, her smell, her eyes. Especially her eyes. The scientist in Lucy wondered what was happening. This was not normal – it was stimulating and exciting, but not normal.

After lunch they drove to the hotel. It was a mess. Police cars were at the front, although all visible police officers seemed to be milling about professionally, rather than doing anything productive. A cleaning crew was busy tidying up broken glass. A number of people, hotel guests and locals presumably, stood in small circles talking among themselves.

"What the fuck happened here?" asked Lucy.

"I have no idea. Do you want me to go in with you?" asked

Legna.

"Yes, I'd like that," said Lucy, who thought a moment and then added, "assuming Judith has left her clothes in the room, we can probably find something for you to wear, if you'd like."

"That would be very kind," said Legna.

As they entered the hotel lobby, they saw a large sign indicating that the hotel apologised for any inconvenience that may have resulted from the "police action" that morning and that all guests would be given a drink on the house.

However, what caught Lucy's attention was the television showing a repeat of the news report about the Reverend Forge and the nuns being freed. "Just a minute," she said to Legna, taking her hand.

So that's what happened, she thought. Judith must have learned that her sisters had been freed and felt compelled to join them. Perhaps they pressured her. After all, Judith disappeared after taking a phone call. Lucy was thinking that maybe she should travel up to Erps-Kwerps after all.

"Is everything okay?" asked Legna.

"Yes, sorry. I was interested in that news story."

"No problem. Take your time."

"You know, I think I might stay here one more night to think about my options. I can get a train to Santander easily enough in the morning, but let's see if we can find you some clothes."

The two women took the lift up to Lucy's and Judith's room, where they found Judith's carefully packed bag still carefully packed. "You can help yourself to anything in there that fits you," said Lucy.

Legna rummaged around and found a pair of panties, jeans and patterned T-shirt.

"I think your ex-girlfriend is a tiny bit bigger than me, but perhaps these will fit."

She took off her swimsuit top. Lucy was impressed.

"Holy shit, you've got incredible boobs! They're symmetrical. I've never seen such symmetrical tits."

"Maybe they look the same, but I do not think they feel the same. One is softer than the other. Here, feel them." She took Lucy's hands and held them against her breasts. "What do you think?"

"Oh, my," said Lucy, feeling Lenga's nipples becoming firm and penetrating into the palms of her hand, something that always turned her on – and she was getting turned on in spite of her intention not to. She had made love to Judith in this same room the night before.

But the sensations moving through her hands were incredible and, a small part of her mind warned her, scientifically implausible. Meanwhile, her nose was being enticed by Legna's smell, which was like the clean, cool, spring breeze in a wood. Suddenly, Lucy felt crushing desire like she had not felt in years.

When Legna leaned forward to kiss Lucy on the lips, Lucy kissed back with passion, a passion that was reminiscent of her brief, experimental flirtation with hallucinogenic drugs in university. Once again, the back of her mind was really trying to warn Lucy that something was not quite right about the intensity of feelings she was experiencing – but the thing with intense feelings is they are seldom swayed by logic, especially when sexual desire is an integral part of those feelings.

The women hurriedly and awkwardly undressed each other while passionately kissing. Legna pushed Lucy down on to the bed and straddled her, kissing her on the lips and working her way sensually down Lucy's neck, chest, abdomen and pelvis, sending powerful pulses of pleasure up and down her body.

Then Lucy felt Legna's tongue caressing her clitoris, bringing her to further heights of hallucinogenic sexual pleasure. The tongue, that incredible tongue, somehow continued to caress her clitoris while simultaneously going deeper and deeper – impossibly deeper – into Lucy, tickling and then caressing her g-spot before going further in.

"Ha, I warned you something was not right here," the rational bit of her mind said.

"Fuck off. This is brilliant," the rest of her brain said as she became impossibly close to climax and feeling a combination of pleasure and desire building to levels that she had never before experienced.

Suddenly, her mind and body exploded in the most incredible orgasm she had ever known. She clenched her body, grabbed Legna's head in her hand and screamed silently with joy.

Bizarrely, as most of her mind was simply having an orgasmically great time, a small part of it was replaying her experiences with Maxwell, observing him in more detail in memory than she had in reality.

This is because Legna's tongue had done more than Lucy realised. It had stretched deep inside her and then extended into microscopically thin tendons that connected to Lucy's brain. Legna then looked for memories of Maxwell and absorbed them. This accomplished, the tongue retracted back down through Lucy's reproductive system, nabbing a couple of eggs as souvenirs, and returned to its normal size.

The memories of Maxwell abruptly faded into the pulsing, orgasmic pleasure, leaving Lucy exhausted on the bed. Legna kissed Lucy's body, working her way upwards to her lips. Lucy kissed back, wondering if she had the energy to return the favour, when Legna said, "no, no. It is not necessary. I climaxed watching you, feeling you climax. It was so incredible! Now the time, it is very late. I must go now. But I think we will meet again soon." She kissed Lucy, who was fast fading into sleep, dressed in Judith's clothes and blew one last kiss at Lucy before stepping out the door.

By the time the door clicked shut, Lucy was asleep.

Moments later, Legna climbed into her car, started the engine and drove away from the hotel, following the route Maxwell had taken earlier that day.

36

It was the end of what was probably the best weekend in Fabio's adult life. The week before, he had won a middling prize in the lottery. Rather than put the money away, he decided to blow it on a marvellous, selfish weekend. He hired himself a Ferrari and took off for weekend of gambling in Estoril. Surprisingly, he broke even and still had a lot of cash left over, so he drove the sports car up to the infamous whorehouses outside of Santander. After looking at several, he chose to blow his money in the House of Mystic Pleasure – an ancient stone manor house with a glaring neon sign bolted to the roof – because he liked the way it looked.

Inside, he purchased the expert services of not one but two young women with silicon-enhanced breasts that made them look top heavy to anyone with decent aesthetic tastes, and comic-book sexy to the sort of man who values big tits above all else in a woman. Nevertheless, as professionals, the two chesty lasses were very good at their work, ensuring that Fabio had the best sex of his life. Indeed, even his lewdest adolescent fantasies could not compare with the creative pleasures he enjoyed that afternoon. The bottle of champagne certainly helped – particularly as Fabio drank most of it. The young women knew better than to drink on the job.

Two hours later, with a wonderful buzz in his head and a feeling of sexual satisfaction that he had not experienced since he lost his virginity, Fabio climbed into the hired Ferrari. It was time to return the car, go home and resume his life as a bank clerk. He fired up the engine, backed out of the parking space and drove out of the car park. At the exit, a sleek-looking businessman with an expensive haircut and a high-end Mercedes saloon was waiting for an opportunity to pull into traffic.

"Smug bastard!" said Fabio to himself as he revved the engine of his hired car and grinned at the other driver. Seeing a space in the traffic, he stomped on the accelerator, popped the paddle shift into gear and burst forward. As he yanked the steering to the right, in order to achieve a screeching turn onto the main road, the left side of the car imploded into him. The window smashed itself over his head, the roof caved in and a massive wheel crushed his skull.

In a small way, he was lucky. Earlier that day, his wife had worked out that he was not, as he had claimed, going on fishing trip with Mario and Eduardo. She did a little investigating and quickly worked out what had happened. She was waiting for him. When he returned home, she intended to make his life hell. She probably would have succeeded. Instead, Fabio died so quickly, that the last thought on his mind was a heavenly double blow job.

The low-slung, wedged shape of the Ferrari was sufficient to send the SUV that had hit it – which happened to be the vehicle in which Phineas was riding – into the air at an angle that resulted in a series of messy somersaults across the highway. Ivan, the driver, had only enough time to hit the brake pedal at the same instant that the SUV hit the Ferrari that had burst out in front of him. He received a fatal blow on the head when the top of the big vehicle hit the road on the second bounce. Phineas was knocked unconscious. Two other cars were damaged in the crash, though no one else was hurt.

The nuns, meanwhile, brought their two SUVs to a screeching halt and raced back to check on their leader. They were trained in basic first aid, in order to help their sisters in combat, and quickly ascertained that Ivan was dead, but that Phineas did not appear to have any broken bones or other severe injuries, though there was a big lump on his head.

They carried him into the House of Mystic Pleasure. The manager, seeing his condition, had a woman from behind the bar open one of the "Heavenly Delights" bedrooms on the ground floor. The nuns carried him in and set him down on the bed. The room, in keeping with the heavenly theme, the ceiling was painted sky blue and dappled with wispy clouds.

The manager brought an ice bag in and placed over the bump on Phineas's head. As she did so, she could not help but feel she knew this bruised priest, though she could not place him. This was hardly surprising. She had known in various, intimate ways a lot of men, including many members of the clergy, over the years. But she felt this guy was from another part of her life.

Phineas came to on a soft bed beneath a heavenly sky. A woman was looking down on him. Hers was a familiar face. It was...By the mercy of God, it was Cathy's face, albeit a little older than when he had last seen her. She had the same curly hair and hourglass figure. Age had carved out her cheekbones and made her look more elegant and less virginal than he had remembered.

But that did not matter. What mattered was that his true love had finally come to him in this time of need, when he was laying beneath this bizarre, unchanging sky. Was he in Heaven? Was he in a field back in America? Indeed, he wondered what had happened and why he was laying here. He tried moving. His body hurt and his head felt terrible, but he could move easily enough.

"Take it easy there, Father," said the manager.

"Cathy?" asked Phineas, weakly.

"Do I know you?" the manager asked. She squinted at the priest on the bed, again trying to place him. Three of the ninja nuns were also in the room and were more than a little puzzled as to how their Reverend Forge knew a brothel manager.

"Cathy, have you come back to me?" asked Phineas.

"I'm not sure. Who are you?" asked Cathy.

"Have you sought forgiveness in Jesus Christ, our Lord?"

"What?!"

"Don't you remember, Cathy? You used to be my fiancé."

"Father!" shouted one of the nuns, in shock.

"I what?! Who the hell are you?"

"I am Phinny...Phineas Forge, my darling Cathy. We were to be married." Phineas, regaining his strength, sat up in the bed.

Cathy had been trying to place the priest's moustache, but was unable to do so. Finally, she mentally erased the massive bit of facial hair and a memory stirred.

"Phinny?" she said.

"Oh, yes, dear, dear Cathy."

"But we were never engaged. Hell, we never even shagged."

"What?! Why, of course not. We were not married. But I saved myself for you and I know you saved yourself for me, my dear."

"No, I didn't."

"That's because Maxwell corrupted your soul through your, ah...Your womanly parts."

The nuns were riveted. This was the most exciting conversation any of them had heard since they managed to sneak out of the convent and watch a soap opera on television a year before.

"What!? Who?! What the hell are you talking about, Phinny?"

"Don't you remember, dear Cathy? I heard your calls for help in the art studio at the university and I came to save you. But I was too late. Maxwell was doing something vile and perverted and filthy to you. It corrupted your soul and sent you on a path of sin."

"What the fuck?"

"But I always knew you were pure in your soul and that if you opened your heart to Jesus Christ, you could be saved and become my wife."

"Oh, do you mean Maxwell the artist? I remember him. He gave good head."

"I know that he violated you and did terrible, truly terrible things to you, but if you bring God into your heart..."

"No, Maxwell wasn't terrible. He was rather..."

"God will cleanse and purify your soul so that you can be my wife."

"Your wife!? Holy shit, Phinny!" She took his hands in hers. "I think that concussion has confused you. You're not making any sense at all."

The nuns were fascinated. This just got better and better.

"I am not confused, Cathy! Don't you remember? You were such a pure virgin in university. We were going to get married. You were going to stand by my side and..."

"Virgin!? Phinny, my cherry got popped when I was 14. I loved – and still love – sex. I slept with dozens of boys at the university. Maxwell was just one of many."

"...have my children and raise them to be good, God-fearing Christians."

"Oh my God!" said Cathy, taking her hands away. She was beginning to realise that Phineas's delusions pre-dated his concussion by nearly 20 years.

"But then that vile demon, Maxwell, tore off your clothes and corrupted you."

"He did nothing of the kind. He sculpted me and I got turned on by the way he looked at me, the way he so brazenly desired me, while he worked. The sexuality he put into the sculpture..."

"And I know that since then you have lived a life of misery and sin."

"Phinny, listen to me!" she shouted. "You don't know what you are talking about."

"No, Cathy, you listen to me. That is Satan talking. But if you accept Jesus Christ into your heart and cast away the demon Maxwell planted in your heart, you can be my wife. Raise my children. Keep my house."

"Are you out of your mind?! Now, listen to me, Phinny. Listen to me! I have never loved you and never wanted to marry you or anyone. I've always wanted to live my life my way and not the way some man tells me. I've wanted to be able to shag whomever I wanted to shag and not have some needy man clinging to me."

"Oh Cathy, that is Satan talking, not you."

The nuns, who had far too much experience of not being listened to in their lives in the church, were empathising more and more with Cathy.

"No! It's me talking, Phinny. It's me! Now look around you. This whorehouse you're sitting in is mine. This is my life. I built it up. I slept with the first customers. I still sleep with my favourite regulars and even some of the girls here – training, you know."

The nuns giggled.

"And I've both enjoyed it and I am proud of what I have built. There's no way I am going to give this up to be the slave of some deluded, selfish man."

"But Cathy, Cathy! Don't you see? Maxwell did this to you when he defiled you. That's why I have been trying to kill him. To save your soul. Now let us pray together, please!"

The nuns gasped.

"Kill him? Are you out of your mind? Maxwell *did* nothing of the kind. I am what I am."

"But Maxwell..." began Phineas, feeling lost in the same way that he had in that art studio so many years ago.

"Oh, for fuck's sake, Phinny. What is this? Some kind of twisted jealousy trip? Can't you just leave Maxwell...and me be?"

One of the nuns, Gabriella, finally spoke up.

"Father Forge, is this true? Is this why we have been trying to expedite Maxwell to Hell?"

"Oh my fucking God!" said Cathy, who was beginning to grasp that this was much, much more than a twisted jealousy trip.

Just then, there was a gentle rapping on the door and a uniformed police officer looked in.

"Excuse me, ma'am; is that the passenger from the SUV who was injured in the crash?"

"Yes, it is," said Cathy.

"Do you mind if we have a word with him? We'd like to ask him a few questions about the accident. We've also got ambulance crew here. They should take a look at him too."

"By all means," said Cathy, "but good luck getting any sense out of him. He's completely deluded."

"Thank you, ma'am."

Cathy walked out of the room. The nuns watched her, looked at each other and then, one by one, walked out after her.

37

The Bentley left the Route 103 for the centre of Lyons, in the French region. Although the zombie invasion that wiped out the population of the city had taken place years before, the city remained remarkably desolate. People seemed reluctant to return to the city that had been home to Europa's greatest post-war bloodbath. As a result, it had an odd, desolate beauty that appealed to arty types like Maxwell.

Maxwell, Wendy and the angel found a small, traditionally decorated hotel on the outskirts of the city. It offered a magnificent view over the ruins of the nearby Roman amphitheatre. Three adjoining rooms were available and booked. After settling in, the three ventured down into into the ruins.

With a cold breeze blowing across the landscape, Maxwell wore a tweed jacket and long wool scarf that danced together with his curly hair in the wind. The angel also had a long white scarf wrapped around her neck; a long white, linen dress that neither Maxwell nor Wendy had seen before; and a white shoulder bag. Wendy, being a penguin, was comfortable in her feathers. Indeed, she preferred the cooler weather.

As they walked across the amphitheatre's stage, Maxwell saw the angel take a swig from a bottle of wine.

"Good gracious! Is that a bottle of the Pingus?" has asked.

"Yes," said the angel.

"And you're drinking directly from the bottle?"

The angel examined the bottle for a moment. "Yes."

"Is that morally justifiable?" asked Maxwell.

"Have you brought glasses?" asked the angel.

"No," admitted Maxwell.

"Then there is not much we can do, is there?" she asked, handing Maxwell the bottle.

He sniffed from the open end of the bottle, failed to get more than a hint of the smell of the wine and took a medium-sized swig.

"Holy dancing wombats! That is good wine!" exclaimed Maxwell. "Imagine how nice it would be poured into a decent glass."

Two crystal wine goblets appeared on the waist-high ruins of a column in front of them.

"That's jolly good imagining," said Maxwell.

"Pingus can be very inspirational," said the angel as Maxwell splashed wine into the two glasses.

"I reckon it can be. Cheers," said Maxwell.

"Cheers."

Uninterested in the wine, Wendy walked up past the amphitheatre's stone seating and a further staircase in order to get a view of the ruins from higher up. As she did so, she saw a black BMW Coupé drive up the access road that led up behind the seating area.

The car pulled into the car park, stopped straddling two parking spaces and Legna stepped out. She was wearing an elegant long black dress more suited to a late-night cocktail party than a sunset in Roman ruins. She looked at Wendy for a penetrating instant before walking slowly down the stairs towards the stage.

"It is you," said the angel, drinking down the last of the wine in her glass. She set it down.

"Yes, it is me," said Legna.

"Lord love a duck," said Maxwell. "I thought you swam out of my life forever."

"No. I would need your soul in order to do that," said Legna.

"I'd rather keep it," said Maxwell offhandedly before remembering that, in fact, his soul was not in his possession at the time, and adding, "oh."

"So you did fuck her," said the angel.

"I'd rather think of it as love-making," said Maxwell. "'Fucking' just sounds so tawdry."

"You love her?" asked the angel.

"Well, no," said Maxwell. "Look, this conversation is getting too deep for one glass of wine; do you think you could pour me another? And, out of civil decency, we really should offer your friend a glass."

"Yes, sister," said Legna, who miraculously had a wine goblet in her hand. "I think a glass of Pingus would be perfect just now."

The angel poured the remainder of the wine into each of their glasses then tossed the bottle away.

"Maxwell, you should go over there with Wendy. This situation could become ugly."

"Thanks for the warning. You do ugly in a particularly ugly way," said Maxwell. He walked up past the seating area to the top row where Wendy was now standing and watching. The angel and Legna slowly approached each other.

The angel said something to Legna in a language that sounded like French to Maxwell, but wasn't the French with which he had a passing acquaintance.

"What are they speaking?" he asked rhetorically.

"I don't know," said Wendy.

The sound of Joan Baez singing a medieval chant sneaked up behind them. It was followed by the mechanical accent of a machine translator.

"It is a variant of Old French," said Lubidada, who then held up a litre bottle of water and added, "would you like some water?"

"Um, no thanks. But where have you come from?" asked Maxwell in surprise.

"The planet Zargon. I thought you knew that," said the Zargonian. "Wendy, would you like some water?"

"No, thank you," said Wendy.

"You are as obtuse as she is," said Maxwell, nodding towards Wendy. "I meant, what has brought you here just now?"

"Our vehicle." Lubidada pointed to a Zargonian hovercraft parked behind the Coupé.

Before he could reframe the question for a third try, he noticed that the two women – or angels or whatever they were – had begun to slowly circle each other. Each was crouched over with arms raised and eyes staring at the other. As he watched, a pair of wings burst out of Legna's dress.

"They look like two angry cats sizing each other up for a fight," said Maxwell.

"Yes, they are adopting combat mode," said Lubidada.

"What are they?" asked Wendy.

"That is difficult to answer, in part because we are not completely sure. However, we believe they are humans resulting from a different evolutionary track than humans like Maxwell."

"They are from Earth!?" asked Maxwell.

"Not this one," said Lubidada, waving his arms to indicate the planet around him. "Rather from an alternative Earth, a very different Earth from this one. Not only have they followed a different evolutionary track, but it is clear they have inherited elements which are not of your Earth at all."

"But how did they...?" Wendy cocked her head in thought for a moment. "From the tear?"

"We believe so."

"How do you know they are alternative-track humans?" asked Wendy.

"We do not know for certain, but they look broadly human, they smell of a combination of human and cat and, most interestingly, their language is remarkably close to Old French. They are not of this Earth, but the odds of beings from another planet sharing so many characteristics with you humans are statistically non-viable."

The angel and Legna continued circling each other while arguing passionately in their curious near-French language. From time to time, one would making a peculiar hissing sound or even swipe her hand at the other.

Maxwell, watching the growing aggression below, asked Lubidada, "can you follow their argument with that translation thingie?"

"Much of it, but not all of it. The translator is still learning the language. But they were initially arguing about who has the right to your soul, Maxwell."

"Surely I do!" said Maxwell.

"Be that as it may, it is not an option they are considering. Your angel believes it is hers because she has it in her possession. The other believes it is hers because she enticed it out through an act similar to sexual intercourse, but which is not entirely clear to me."

"Maxwell, can't you keep your penis to yourself?" said Wendy. "So many of your troubles are a result of its misuse."

"If God wanted me to keep my penis to myself, she would have given me a vagina," said Maxwell.

"But you don't believe in God," said Wendy.

"I'm not sure I understand," said Lubidada.

"Don't worry about it," said Maxwell. "Wendy has certain issues with my sex life. Anyway, what's happening down on stage?"

"It is confusing. If I understand correctly, they are challenging each other with complex mathematical proofs to show who has the right to your soul."

"Curious," said Maxwell.

"That cannot be right!" said the translator as Lubidada shouted passionately in his own language.

"What's wrong?" asked Maxwell.

"I believe the one in the black dress has just put forward a theorem that questions the reality of our existence. If that's correct, we exist only in her imagination. But maybe I have misunderstood."

The angel considered Lenga's words for a moment, then smugly said a few words that caused Legna to jolt backwards as if hit by a massive gust of wind.

"Is the woman in black crying?" asked Wendy.

"You've got incredible eyesight," said Maxwell.

"Yes, it seems your angel has torn apart the other's theorem and therefore destroyed her entire argument."

The angel laughed. "Fuck you and the horse you came in on!" she said, in accented English, to Legna. Head held low, shoulders hunched and hair billowing in the wind, Legna had transformed from a remarkably elegant young woman to a tired, much-older woman sporting an incredible pair of wings.

The angel took the bag off her shoulder, unravelled the scarf from her neck and stepped out of her dress. Naked, she reached into the bag and pulled out the lacquer box in which she had put Maxwell's soul and held it against her chest with crossed arms. Her wings began to flap with increasing speed. She took off into the sky, moving with phenomenal speed.

"You could have taken the lake, you stupid fuck," said Legna. She flew up to her car, climbed in and started up the engine. With a roar, the car backed down the road with increasing speed until it performed a screechingly elegant 180-degree turn and raced away.

"Hey, that's my soul you're taking off the planet!" shouted Maxwell.

Ignoring his shouts, the angel accelerated rapidly as she soared into the sky. She folded her wings to her side and pointed her nose forward. A bronze-like shell formed around her body and soon began to glow in the intense heat of atmosphere being ruthlessly flung aside by her body's velocity. Flames licked across her bronze face, but she seemed unperturbed.

The flames faded as she left the atmosphere and entered the near-vacuum of space. He face was a statuesque fixture of determination in burnt bronze. Her speed increased and increased and increased. By the time she passed Saturn's orbit, she had reached 90 per cent of light speed, yet she kept accelerating in the direction of the tear in the fabric of the universe.

38

The Zargonians stood at the top of the ruins, their various eyes watching the angel's path into the sky; Maxwell and Wendy walking away; and each other. After a moment, Snox said to Lubidada, "what did she mean by 'you could have taken the lake'?"

"I was puzzling over the same matter," said Lubidada.

"Do you think there may be a portal on this planet?" asked Snox.

"I suspect there may be. We will follow the one who spoke of the lake. If this second portal exists, she will soon go to it."

"Yes."

"Wait a moment...I believe we have visitors."

The fleet of IIA hovercrafts blew into the access road and parked near the aliens. Dan, Sam and Frank jumped out of the lead vehicle.

"Interplanetary Intelligence Agency. I'm Dan."

"Pleased to meet you, Dan. I am Lubidada and this is my partner Snox."

"We have reason to believe there is a violent, unregistered alien in the vicinity."

"We are Zargonians. Our race is not only registered with the Galactic Registry of Sentient Life Forms, we co-founded it. We are also both registered with the Europa Government as resident aliens," said Lubidada patiently.

"I know that," said Dan impatiently. "This is a new alien. Never seen before and dangerous."

"We have not seen anything like that here," said Lubidada.

One eye on each of the Zargonians looked down the access road to see a small group of white vehicles with flashing lights approaching. Another eye on each looked into the eye of the other, conveying an expression of *this situation is clearly going to become significantly more chaotic; we should consider our socially acceptable escape options*, an expression that two Zargonians can readily convey to one another discreetly. Students of Zargonian social psychology have suggested that this simple facial expression may be a key reason why the Zargonians are the oldest surviving intelligent race in the galaxy.

"Are you sure? The unregistered aliens are highly human in appearance,;however, they have large fleshy wings and appear to be reminiscent of angels," said Dan.

"Ah, the angel," said Lubidada, as the police vehicles drew up.

"So, you have seen the alien," said Dan.

"No," said the Zargonian as the vehicles came to a stop.

"But, you said..." said Dan.

"Yes, there was an 'angel' here," said the Zargonian. "But she was not an angel. She was a human."

"Humans don't have wings!" said Dan.

"She was from an alternative reality, but she was genetically human." said the Zargonian as the doors opened on the lead police vehicle and a couple of officers climbed out.

A senior police officer walked over and nodded politely at the Zargonians. They had met earlier. The Zargonians had introduced themselves to the local police when the arrived in the area, something they often did, especially when visiting smaller towns where the locals' reaction to aliens was unpredictable.

The officer stopped in front of Dan.

"What the hell are you doing here, sir?" he asked.

"Excuse me, officer?" asked Dan.

"I said, what the hell are you doing here?" said the officer.

"I am with the Interplanetary Intelligence Agency, on official business."

"Your Interplanetary Intelligence Agency has been shut down, sir," said the officer.

"That has not been confirmed," said Dan, suddenly looking a little less authoritative.

"Yes it has, sir. It seems a team of idiots shot up two dozen schoolgirls in Crashsite today, I gather it was the last straw."

"We used stun guns. We didn't kill anyone."

"It was you?" said the officer.

"Yes, we had good reason to believe there were dangerous aliens in the hotel."

"Let us leave without saying goodbye," said Snox discreetly to Lubidada.

"Yes, let's," said Lubidada.

"The only thing dangerous near that hotel was you and your gang of thugs!" said the officer.

"But the guns were set to stun. No one was killed!" said Dan.

"You don't need to argue this with me. All I know is your agency was shut down today. After a spate of disasters, shooting the schoolgirls was too much. The Europa government launched an emergency measure to shut the agency down., Take it up with your ex-agency."

"I don't think I like your attitude, officer! We were trying to save innocent people," said Dan.

"More like shooting them up. Several of the girls were seriously injured," said the officer.

"Collateral damage," said Dan. "Shit happens."

The two Zargonians quietly stepped back, hopped into their hovercraft and raced off into the twilight, unnoticed by the arguing officials.

39

The police officer spoke with Phineas for about a quarter of an hour, but it soon became apparent that the priest remembered nothing of the accident. Because it was clearly the now-deceased driver of the Ferrari who was at fault, the officer let Phineas go, albeit with a recommendation that he see a doctor – a recommendation Phineas had no intention of following. He would feel fine once Maxwell was in Hell.

He walked out of the room of heavenly delights and into the quiet lounge area, where a scant few customers, most accompanied by professionally attractive young women and most with their hands all over said women, were having a drink. In a corner to the side of the bar, he saw the nuns sitting.

As he walked towards their table, he saw the nun Gabriella talking with apparent seriousness to Cathy. As he drew closer, he could see that the nun was crying.

"Don't you worry about me, Sister Gabriella," he said. "I am just fine. And don't you worry, Cathy. Once we have dispatched Maxwell to Hell, I believe you will see the error of your ways and I will be back for you."

Had Phineas been capable of reading people, he would have noticed that Cathy tensed up perceptibly when he spoke, but she realised there was no point in trying to talk with him. At least she had been able to talk to the nuns for a few minutes – though what she learned upset her even more.

"Come along, now, sisters," he continued. "We need to get going. Maxwell is gaining on us every minute we spend chit-chatting here."

"We are not coming with you, Reverend Forge," said Gabriella formally.

"What do you mean you're not coming with me?" said Phineas.

"Just what I've said, Reverend," said Gabriella. "The sisters and I have decided to return home."

"Why, you cannot do that, Sister. We have our holy and divine duty to God to kill Maxwell."

"That's just it. We don't believe this is about divine duty. We believe that this is about jealousy and personal issues. It's nothing to do with God or the church or corrupting women!"

"Oh my God, you have been corrupted, too!" said Phineas. "Has Cathy done this to you? Has the evil within her, which I know is from Maxwell, corrupted your souls too?"

"No, Father."

"Then get yourselves into the trucks now and let's be going!"

"No, Father. Too many people have died over this thing. Our sisters, the man in the car out front. Those Kroaches. I am not sure God will forgive us for those things, but at least they were accidents. If we kill Maxwell in cold blood, then I am sure God will not forgive us."

"Don't be ridiculous, woman! God wants us to expedite Maxwell's journey to Hell. You know that. Deep down in your heart, you do."

"Phinny," said Cathy. "It's you who's being ridiculous. These girls are staying here with me tonight and then will go back to the convent."

"Except me. I want to stay and work here," said one pert nun.

"Anyway," continued Cathy. "I want you to leave now. I think it would be best for you to go home, see a doctor and get some rest – but I don't care. I just want you out of here now!"

"But Cathy, don't you understand?"

"Phinny, do you see those two big men over there by the

door?"

"Why, yes I do, Cathy."

"They are bouncers. I keep them here for dealing with unruly customers. If I flag them over here, they will physically throw you out of the building."

"But, Cathy..."

"Now, Phinny!"

"Girls? Sisters? Isn't anyone coming with me?"

"Sorry, Father," said Gabriella.

"May God have mercy upon your souls," said Phineas, shoulders slumped and making his way to the door. He stopped, turned around and headed back.

"If you attempt to coerce the girls, my bouncers will also deal with you," said Cathy.

"I just want the keys to one of the trucks," said Phineas, attempting to muster any remaining dignity he could find in the situation, which was precious little.

"Sister Cordelia," said Gabriella. "Please give the Reverend the keys for your truck."

Sister Cordelia did as she was told. Phineas took them, turned and held his head high as he walked out the door. It took him 10 minutes to find the SUV. He didn't dare return to ask where they had parked the trucks. He started up the engine and headed towards Erps-Kwerps.

Meanwhile, the nuns felt a sense of relief they had not experienced since childhood. Cathy, touched by their innocence, indulged them. They shared a small suite and three bottles of Prosecco, which facilitated their enjoyment of three pornographic films on the whorehouse's video system, an incredible pillow fight and some adolescent-like mutual sexual exploration.

In the end, the nuns stayed for three days and two of them decided to stay on and work in Cathy's business, albeit as bar staff rather than prostitutes.

Had Phineas known of any of this, he doubtless would have blamed Maxwell. But it would not have mattered. He was already more determined than ever to kill Maxwell.

40

"Well, I reckon it's just you and me for dinner tonight," said Maxwell to Wendy. The angel, Zargonians and IIA agents had all gone their separate ways and the remaining two friends were standing alone as dusk descended upon the Roman ruins and cast the evening into shades of grey.

"That will be nice," said Wendy. "We've not had a quiet dinner with just the two of us in a long time."

"Indeed, old friend. Indeed," said Maxwell, putting his arm around Wendy and leading her back towards the hotel. Halfway there, they passed a bistro with a terrace offering a decent view of the ruins. Although it was quiet, with just two other tables occupied, the staff served up better than local fare. They both ordered *quenelle* – with fish for Wendy and a vegetarian version for Maxwell. After a long debate with the proprietor about whether or not a red wine would overpower the delicate flavour of the *quenelle*, and following repeated assurances that the house Beaujolais would not be too much for the Quenelle, Maxwell ordered a half bottle, a decision he did not regret.

The two friends were content to eat in silence while serenaded by crickets and leaves rustling in the ever-present wind. As darkness fell, the shadows of the ruins grew ever longer, until the historical sight disappeared into their own shadows.

After finishing dinner followed by exceptional coffees, they walked back to the hotel, the dark road lit only by the half moon and the lights from an occasional house. Only one car passed them, a banged-up old Renault that gave them a wide berth – a local, presumably.

Once they got back to the hotel, Wendy went up to her room to read. Maxwell decided to have one last glass of wine in the hotel bar. He was inspired by the angels and wanted to sketch some ideas before they faded from memory entirely.

He ordered a glass of a local Beaujolais, pulled out his notebook and scribbled three pages of ideas. At the same time, a woman reading something on a tablet looked up. She was an attractive, curly-haired brunette seemingly in her early 30s. Their eyes met for a second and the brunette started.

"Hey, you look like this Maxwell van Mars guy," she said, looking at her tablet.

Maxwell started to say something witty, about that Maxwell van Mars guy looking like him, but he knew where that would go – to someone's bed – and he was thinking about Wendy's remark regarding his penis getting him in trouble. For a penguin, she should could sometimes be very perceptive, and he really did not want more trouble. Not tonight.

"Yes, a lot of people tell me that," Maxwell replied instead. He drank the last gulp of wine, bade the woman good night, went to his room and retired to bed with a novel which, indeed, kept him out of trouble, at least for the night.

The next couple of days, however, would be a very different story.

41

In the uncertain wee hours of the morning, Lucy awoke naked and tangled up in the duvet. The previous day's events fluttered across her mind like autumn leaves on a windy day. She was conflicted. She was hurt by Judith's sudden departure, but could not help but also to feel a sense of freedom – like those leaves no longer tied to their trees. This was a sensation she knew all too well. She had a tendency to jump too quickly into a relationship, only to be surprised at the exhilaration she sometimes felt when the relationship died. Nevertheless, this was one of the shortest-lived relationships she had ever had – discounting her apparent recent propensity for one-night stands.

Then there was Legna. It was hard to think clearly about her – almost as if Lucy had been stoned or something, but she had not touched recreational drugs since university and even then had not done a lot. She valued her mind too much to want to mess with it.

She wondered if Legna had slipped her something – not that it would have been necessary. The woman was good looking, charming and a hell of a seductress. There was no denying that the previous afternoon she had enjoyed the best sex in her life. But she also felt funny, unsettled by it – almost violated, in the same way she had felt in school when a boy tried to put his hand in her pants way too early in the dating game. But where the boy's hand was unwanted and inappropriate, Legna's seduction was scrumptious.

"Ah, you are awake, Dr Heisenberg," said a matronly voice.

"Fuck," said Lucy, scrambling – or at least attempting to

scramble – to get up and wrapping the duvet around her chest. She squinted around the darkened room, but did not see anyone.

"Who are you? What are you doing in my room?" she asked.

"I am an electronic agent projected by your tablet. On behalf of the Zargonian Mission in Brussels, I would like to communicate with you."

Lucy switched on the reading lamp by her bed and saw a matronly woman standing in the middle of the room. Looking closely, she could see the woman looked more nebulous than the average matronly woman. She was not real, but a projection.

Nevertheless, Lucy did not feel at ease sitting on her bed, wrapped in a duvet and looking, she was sure, dishevelled. On the other hand, she knew it would be silly to excuse herself, comb her hair and put on some clothes, as much as she wanted to do so.

"Yes. What do you wish to communicate with me?" she asked instead.

"The Zargonian Mission requests an appointment with you as soon as possible in order to discuss the tear in the fabric of the universe."

Lucy considered this for a moment, and a short moment at that. She had been dumped by her girlfriend, seduced by a strange woman she'd probably never see again, was naked in a hotel in Crashsite and lacked transportation. A free flight out of her current situation seemed an awfully good idea.

"I assume the Zargonia Mission will provide aeroplane tickets and accommodation in Brussels," said Lucy.

"A Zargonian flyer is parked in the field adjacent to the hotel car park. It will take you directly to the Mission. Afterwards, the Mission will arrange transportation back here, to Cape City or anywhere else. A five-star hotel room near the Mission will also be provided for the duration of your stay."

"Not bad," said Lucy. "When do we leave?"

"As soon as you are ready. There is breakfast for you on the flyer if you'd like."

"Yes, that would be lovely. Give me fifteen minutes to shower and get ready, please."

"Very good. I will communicate with the Mission. Thank you." The matronly woman disappeared.

Lucy showered, dressed and collected her things. She put Judith's belongings into her suitcase, wrote "help yourself to any or all of this" on a piece of hotel stationary and left it on the younger woman's bag. Hopefully, the maid would find some of her ex-lover's stuff useful.

Downstairs, it took a moment before a sleepy young man appeared at the desk to check Lucy out. Country hotels are not used to guests leaving at four in the morning. Nevertheless, he was polite and professional.

Walking out of the hotel, she saw the flyer standing on three extended feet on a field next to the hotel. It was a metallic and bulbous vehicle that looked like a caricature of an overweight fish. A side door was open and light shone out.

Lucy walked over to the flyer and peered in. There was a sofa against one wall, four seats around a table and two more seats facing forward. However, there was no evidence of the pilot – which seemed strange. The hotel lobby had been empty, aside from her and the receptionist.

"Hello?" she called hesitantly.

"Hello," said a soft, feminine voice from within the flyer.

"Where are..." Lucy started to ask, before she realised that the flyer lacked a cockpit. It must fly itself, she thought.

"Could you please repeat your question?" asked the flyer.

"Never mind. I am ready to go."

"Then please enter the flyer, take a seat and fasten your seatbelt, Dr Heisenberg," said the flyer.

"Okay, thanks." said Lucy, choosing one of the chairs at the table. As the door closed, she realised there were no windows, which was a claustrophobia-inducing thought, to say the least.

"Would you like a forward view?" the flyer asked as Lucy was getting worked up by the lack of windows.

"Oh, yes, please," said Lucy.

Suddenly, the front half of the egg-shaped cabin seemed to become transparent.

"Flight time to Brussels will be 38 minutes. Please fasten your seatbelt and we will take off. Once we're levelled off, you may help yourself to coffee, tea and breakfast from the kitchenette." A cabinet on the wall at the back of the cabin lit up briefly.

The flyer rose straight upwards to 12,000 metres, levelled off, then shot forward suddenly. Although Lucy felt some weight from the acceleration, it was not as much as she would have expected.

"We are cruising. Please feel free to help yourself to breakfast at any time. There are a collection of films available should you wish entertainment. The toilet is at the rear of the flyer."

Lucy helped herself to a cappuccino and a croissant. She sat in one of the seats facing forward and thought about the past few days while watching the sky whiz past. The 38 minutes were insufficient for any real thought, and before she knew it, the flyer was landing.

<h1 style="text-align:center">42</h1>

The Zargonian Mission to Europa was in an old building at the edge of the government district of Brussels. The flyer landed neatly in a courtyard behind the building. The door opened to reveal Lubidada and Snox, who greeted Lucy with the formality that characterised all interactions between Zargonians and humans. This was partly because the translation tool rendered discussions more formal than the participants often intended, and partly because humans and Zargonians had very, very different notions of what was socially the right thing to do.

They walked quickly inside, past a reception desk managed by a human, up a grand staircase and through an oak door into an ultramodern hallway that seemed at odds with the classical style of the building. The corridor was a dull grey with pictures of Zargon and Zargonians on the wall, as well as door-sized rectangles of frosted glass flush upon the walls. At one such glass rectangle, the Zargonians stopped. The glass disappeared with a whoosh and they walked into a small meeting room occupied by a single round table, four chairs and a curious potted plant by the exterior window. Upon the table was a bottle of water and a single glass.

"Would you like something to drink? Some water, perhaps, Dr Heisenberg?" asked Lubidada.

"No, thank you," said Lucy.

"Have a seat, please," said Lubidada.

"Thank you."

"We have asked you to come here because we believe something significant will happen with respect to the tear in the fabric of the universe."

"Significant?"

"Yes. There is a being racing towards the tear with the intellectual essence of a human."

"Essence of a human?"

"Yes. You might also call it a soul"

"A soul? A human soul? And the human owner of the soul?"

"Still on Earth."

"Alive?"

"Yes."

"I see," said Lucy thoughtfully – but after a moment's thought, added, "no, actually, I don't see at all."

"We believe this being has somehow removed the soul of the human and is taking it to the tear."

"Okay. And how can I help you?" asked Lucy, reaching for the water after all.

"You are a highly regarded astrophysicist and the leading human expert on dark energy."

"But we humans have nowhere near the knowledge you Zargonians have. You're the ones who explained it all to us!"

"Yes, but you have been intimate with the human whose soul was taken."

"Intimate? Who is she?"

"Maxwell."

"How the...How did you know about our, um, intimacy?"

"We saw you and him go to his room at the Splendouria. Your smell and behaviour indicated that you intended to be intimate. Have we misunderstood?"

"No," said Lucy, who was coming to regret more and more her fling with Maxwell. "I *was* intimate with him, but not any more."

"You are also familiar with the being who has his soul."

"I am?"

"Yes. She is the one whom Maxwell and the others refer to as 'the angel'."

"'Familiar' might be overstating the case. What exactly is she? An alien?"

"We are reasonably certain she is a near-human from an alternate reality somewhat divergent from this one."

"Presumably, she comes from the reality that exists on the other side of the tear."

"We believe so."

Lucy contemplated this for a moment. "So, this angel is taking Maxwell's soul to the tear in the fabric of the universe, probably to pass through and bring her souvenir to her universe?"

"Souvenir?"

"Maxwell's soul."

"This is what we surmise, based on our evidence."

"Evidence? Perhaps you should tell me what happened."

"Yes, that would be best," said Lubidada, who described the events in Lyon.

"Wow!" said Lucy. "Do you have any video of this? Particularly the angel's takeoff?"

"Yes, we do. One moment, please." Lubidada drew a square in the air with his hands, leaving a hazy outline floating above the table. He then gave the square a push. It floated gently to the wall where it stopped, grew larger and showed a video of the fight between Legna and Angel and the latter's take-off.

"Oh my....Could you play that one more time, please? From the beginning?" asked Lucy.

The Zargonian did as requested. Lucy walked closer to the video display on the wall.

"I think I know this other woman who is duelling with the angel," said Lucy.

"She is also a being from the angel's reality," said the Zargonian.

"Fuck me," said Lucy.

"That is not anatomically possible," said Lubidada.

"Sorry. It was an exclamation, not an invitation."

"Oh. I smell your meaning. Why the exclamation?"

"I know...Or, rather, I have met this being," said Lucy. "I am surprised to learn she is not human."

"How do you know her?"

"She picked me up while I was walking back to my hotel, after – well, you don't need the details. Anyway, I was walking to the hotel and this woman stopped and gave me a lift. We chatted a bit. She said her name was Legna...Oh, my!"

"You are surprised by your own story?"

"Yes, I've just realised: assuming she spells her name L-E-G-N-A, then it is simply the word 'angel' backwards."

"That information smells interesting, but I am not sure in what way. Excuse me while I discuss this with Snox," said Lubidada. The two spoke in Zargonian for a few moments.

Once they stopped, Lucy asked, "well?"

"Snox agrees that it smells interesting. It indicates that she knew about the angel's arrival on your Earth and her relationship with your friends."

"Perhaps," said Lucy. "Incidentally, spelling angel backwards could be construed as being anti-angel."

"Yes. Let us keep this in mind," said Lubidada. "Meanwhile, we will have a meeting at 11 to review the situation and what must be done. We'd like you to attend the meeting. We would also like you to telephone Maxwell and Wendy and learn what you can from them regarding the tear and the incident you have just watched."

"That's a good idea," agreed Lucy.

"Very good. We will leave you in privacy and return five minutes before the meeting. You may use our telephone, if you wish."

"Thank you."

"You're welcome."

The aliens left the room. Lucy opted to use her own telephone. "Ring Maxwell," she told her telephone, which obeyed, as telephones are wont to do.

"Never fear, Maxwell's here," the telephone answered in Maxwell's cheerful voice a moment later.

"Thank goodness for that," said Lucy with a touch of sarcasm in her voice.

"Lord love a duck! Is that, um...?"

"Yes?"

"Hang on. It starts with an L, doesn't it?"

"Yes, but you're going to have to find a few more letters of it if you intend to impress me."

"Lucy!"

"Bravo!"

"You've decided to change your sexual orientation and live a life of peaceful sexual depravity with me, get married and live happily ever after?"

"No, actually, that's not at all why I've called you."

"A dirty weekend then?"

"I like my weekends clean."

"I can do that, too. What are you staring at, penguin?"

"What!?" said Lucy.

"Sorry. Wendy was giving me one of her judgemental looks," said Maxwell.

"Maxwell, could you please focus for a few moments. I want to ask you some questions about the angel and the incident in Lyon," said Lucy.

"You know about that?"

"Yes. I am with the Zargonians. They've told me."

Through questioning and answering, Maxwell described the loss of his soul in a coughing fit, though found it difficult to explain how he knew it was his soul. He described the angel's finding a nice container for it. He gave his impression of the duel between the angel and Legna.

Finally, under some questioning from Lucy, he admitted that he had had sex with Legna on the island. To her credit, Lucy admitted her own fling with Legna. Notes were compared, though the only point in common seemed to be the incredible seductiveness and performance of Legna. Indeed, Lucy observed that Legna seemed able to sense the best approach in both her seductions and wondered aloud if she had seduced any other humans besides the two engaged in the telephone conversation. Maxwell said there was no way to be sure. As Maxwell spoke, Lucy made occasional notes in the notebook she was in the habit of carrying about in her handbag.

"Thanks, Maxwell," said Lucy, after nearly an hour of talking."

"My pleasure," said Maxwell. "Say, did you say you are with the Zargonians?"

"Yes."

"At their Mission in Brussels?"

"Yes, I am."

"If you've got nothing on, why don't you come to Erps-Kwerps when you are finished for the day? It's a short drive or train ride from Brussels and there's a bit of a bash on tonight."

"Well..."

"You can stay in my house. I've got guest bedrooms coming out my ears and domestic robots that are bored to their bolts."

"And will you behave?"

"Towards you, impeccably, unless you give me written permission to do otherwise."

"That's an awfully tempting invitation, Maxwell. I'll try to make it."

"Marvellous! I'll tell the staff at the house to expect you."

"Maybe."

"To maybe expect you. No, that won't do! It's terrible!"

"Why!?"

"I've split an infinitive."

"What? Oh! Okay, then, tell them maybe to expect me."

"Yes, that works."

Lucy rang off and saw from the clock on her telephone that it would still be another half hour before the meeting started.

"What am I going to do in a half hour?" she muttered out loud.

"You could use me," said the room.

"What are you?" she asked.

"A computer. I can work with spoken commends, gestures and typed commands," it said. A keyboard layout lit up on the desk in front of Lucy.

"Can you show me the tear?" she asked.

"Yes," said the computer. The room darkened and an even darker cube of about a metre per side appeared on the table. Inside she saw a shimmering shape.

Lucy assumed that was the tear. "Can you highlight the tear?" she asked. The tear immediately became brighter. She walked around the cube to look at it from different angles.

"I am equipped with electro-stimulation. You can touch the elements of the projection and manipulate them if you wish," said the computer.

Lucy reached into the dark cube, which felt cooler than the room – though far from the near-absolute zero of the deep space – and touched the tear. It was warm and seemed to have a faint vibration. She turned it round slowly.

"Can you show me how the tear looks from the other universe – the universe on the other side of the tear?"

"Yes, I can. However, please be aware that it is based on images and analysis from a probe that explored the tear two days ago and that my data from the other universe is limited."

"I understand. Please show it to me."

The blackness of the cube disappeared for a second then

seemingly reappeared, but the tear looked different. Lucy reached in, touched it and ran her finger along part of it.

"Huh," she said thoughtfully, and then added, "can you fold the image into the 10th dimension?"

"Yes. How do you wish the data?"

"Numeric."

Lucy studied the numbers. "Fuck me," she said.

A muscular man wearing only a revealing swimsuit shimmered into existence in front of her.

"What the...? Oh, no! That was an exclamation, not a request," said Lucy. The image disappeared.

Lucy studied the numbers for several minutes, reflected on their meaning and scribbled down some notes. Then she spoke to the computer.

"I am attending a meeting about the tear in," she looked at her watch, "seven minutes. Do you know if I will have access to your services during the meeting?"

"Yes, I will be available."

"Thank you. Do you have a music library?"

"Yes, including music from Earth."

"Do you have "Adagio" by Samuel Barber?"

"Not as performed by him, but I have several other musicians' interpretations."

"Leonard Bernstein's?"

"Yes."

"Play it, please – and, if possible, ask that I am not disturbed until it finishes."

"I can do that, but cannot guarantee that the request is followed."

"Fair enough."

Slowly, the sound of strings filled the room and Lucy's mind. She sat back, closed her eyes and let her mind dance with the music.

Once it ended, the door opened and a small, bearded man in his late 60s or early 70s peered in.

"Dr Heisenberg? Your meeting is convening now. May I show you to the room?"

He led her down a couple of corridors to another flush glass door, which disappeared with a whoosh. Inside was a small auditorium of the kind she had often lectured from at the university. Around 20 people and six Zargonians occupied the seats. Lubidada was at the door to meet her.

"Please come in, Dr Heisenberg," said Lubidada.

Lucy walked in and made to take a seat in the third row from the front.

"Excuse me, Dr Heisenberg," began Lubidada.

"Lucy. Call me Lucy, please."

"Okay. Excuse me, Lucy, but we believe you have made a significant discovery."

"Um, yes —but how did you work that out? Have you been monitoring me?"

"Yes, of course we have been monitoring you, but we also expected you to find the answer. The maths were very much in favour of your doing so."

Lucy was felt a sudden twinge of annoyance at the intrusion into her privacy, but remembered that Zargonians had no concept of privacy or indignation, so any attempt to become indignant at the loss of privacy could only lead to confusion. Instead, she focused on the second statement.

"The maths were very much in favour of my solving the problem?" she asked.

"Yes, that's why we asked you here. By yesterday afternoon, our calculations indicated a 98.965 per cent chance you would solve the problem by this time today. Have you?"

"Yes."

"Then would you be so kind as to share your discovery with all of us?" asked Lubidada, gesturing with an eye towards the stage.

Shrugging her shoulders, Lucy walked up to the stage. As she stepped upon it, spotlights shone upon her and two young blonde women in low-hanging skirts and bikini tops took her by the arms. Lucy was torn between being appalled by implied sexism of attractive women being exploited for their appearance, and excited by the undeniable sexual desirability of both girls.

Lucy wondered why on Earth the Zargonians had modelled her presentation on silly game shows. It only got worse.

The round stage upon which she and the blondes stood began slowly to rise upwards into a plexiglass dome hanging from the ceiling. Once the stage was surrounded by the dome, it came to a stop. From the dome, Lucy heard a jazzy tune, rich in saxophone and bass, playing away. A burst of steam appeared to Lucy's left and out of it crept a wheelchair carrying a young man with long, straight, red hair that fell over his face. He looked over Lucy's shoulder, avoiding eye contact altogether, and suddenly started speaking not through his mouth, but through a speaker mounted to the wheel chair. All the while, his eyes stared over her shoulder, studiously avoiding meeting hers.

"Dr Lucy Heisenberg, have you uncovered the secret to the tear in the fabric of the universe?" asked the voice synthesiser in a voice too deep for the tiny body on the wheelchair.

"Yes, I believe I have," said Lucy, trying to work out what the fuck was going on all around her. As she spoke, applause combined with a chorus of voices, not all of them human, erupted. Looking around her, Lucy saw that the dome above her was full of screens displaying a wide variety of beings – humans, Zargonians and a number of other aliens, at least three species of which Lucy had never seen before. They were all watching her, reacting to her. The blondes were doing a little dance in the background.

"Wait, what's going on here?" asked Lucy.

"You have – allegedly – solved a problem that has been puzzling the best brains in the galaxy," said the speaker on the wheelchair. "Now those brains want to hear your story."

"And these two women?" asked Lucy.

"Dance interpreters," said a voice seemingly coming from the top of the dome. "Every good story must have a dance."

"You may begin," said the man in the wheelchair.

As he said this, Lucy finally recognised him. He was Simon Havik, one of the Earth's great physicists – who was also autistic and had only been able to communicate his brilliance when wired into a computer in his late teenage years.

It was rumoured that his awareness existed in another higher dimension and he was unable to communicate in simple human terms without the computer connection. Lucy had long had doubts about that theory. However, now that she was with him in person, she could not help but feel there was something more to this young man's genius than a still body in a wheelchair, with thoughtful eyes that stared off into the distance.

"Dr Havik?" she asked.

"Yes I am; but it is you, not me, who is interesting just now, Dr Heisenberg."

"Lucy."

"Simon. Now tell us what you have discovered about this tear in the fabric of the universe, this tear caused by one of your lovers."

Lucy was ready to get indignant about the romantic association of her with Maxwell, but realised it was a lost cause. The more she fussed about it, the more likely it was people would focus on a silly fling rather than her intellect.

"Actually, Maxwell did not cause the tear; at least, he was not ultimately responsible for it," said Lucy. A series of gasps and alien equivalents resounded throughout the dome.

"The penguin, then?" suggested Simon.

"No, the tear was initiated in the other universe, the one on the other side of the tear." Another multilingual gasp rang out.

"But the tear occurred when Maxwell's ship raced around Gateway – too close to its Schwarzchild radius. Is this just a coincidence?"

"Not really. More a matter of bad luck on Maxwell's part. You see, I believe the angels –as we are calling the alternate humans on the other side – weakened the fabric of of the universe as much as possible, but did not break it." Lucy paused for a moment, then asked, "computer?"

"Dr Heisenberg?"

"Could you please display the tear?"

"Of course," said the computer. A black box, a metre to each side, appeared and hovered to Lucy's right.

"Here it is. Now, computer, please display the tear from the other side." Lucy moved her hand as the computer performed this operation, giving the impression that she pulled the tear inside out.

"As you can see," she continued, hoping her audience was sufficiently knowledgeable to grasp what she was demonstrating, "this shape clearly indicates substantial stress in the fabric of the universe – and it originates on the angels' side of the tear.

"At first I thought the angels had tried to break through from their universe to ours, but had not succeeded. Then I folded the stretched fabric into higher dimensions until I reached 10."

Lucy paused for a moment, then asked the computer, "please display the 10th dimensional analysis."

She paused again, allowing her audience to review the numbers.

"As you can see, the angels seem to have stretched the fabric of their universe in dozens – if not hundreds – of directions, and each direction is towards a different reality."

"Why?" asked one of the faces on one of the monitors.

There was a rustle of conversation in the audience. Lucy waited for it to die down before she continued.

"I believe they are setting traps for technically advanced humans in other universes. Because Gateway is our portal into hyper-space, it is a focus of space travel in our solar system. It is also the area where hyperspacecraft enter and exit hyperspace. As you know, this puts additional stress on the fabric of the universe in the vicinity. So, it was only a matter of time before someone like Maxwell stretched the already-stretched space-time area enough to break it. We know that a Gateway also exists in the angels' universe. Presumably it exists in many alternate universes, especially those most similar to ours and the angels'."

"Why would the angels set up such complex traps?" asked Simon amid a rumble of radically multilingual background discussion.

"I assume that they are only interested in technically advanced humans. Making traps that could only be opened by spacecraft would be a way to achieve this goal," said Lucy.

"And why are they interested in trapping technically advanced humans?" asked Simon.

"To widen their gene pool both physically and intellectually," said Lucy.

"What?" said Simon, his eyes actually turning towards Lucy for an instant before shifting away quickly.

"We, well, I, know that one of the angels has had sexual intercourse with at least two humans from this Earth – a renowned artist and scientist. Very possibly, she has had sex with others."

"But if she is human, she would only carry the child of one of the humans from this Earth, would she not?" asked one of the video images.

"Yes, but assuming advanced technology on their side is on a different developmental track to ours, it is possible that she was somehow storing genetic material: sperm and eggs from those she had sex with. She was certainly seductive, or so I have heard."

"Tearing the fabric of the universe seems a drastic step to take in order to broaden the gene pool."

"I agree, and I suspect something has happened in that other universe, or at least on their Earth, that has reduced the gene pool dramatically."

"What happened?" asked the video image of a human.

"I have no idea. It is only supposition."

"But..." began the same image.

"You said expand the intellectual gene pool," said Simon, interrupting the image.

"Yes; this is both more interesting and more complicated," said Lucy. "As you may know, current theory states that dark energy is the intellectual reservoir of the universe, that every sentient being's intellect flows within the dark energy – and that dark energy powers the intellect."

Several video images started to protest.

"Yes, I know that is a very simplified explanation, but it will suffice. I will go into greater detail later, when I better understand. But the key issue here is that I believe that in this other universe, there are far fewer sentient beings. I believe this alternative Earth has far fewer people than ours, either as the result of some catastrophe or because few people were born. Moreover, I note that we have seen no aliens coming through the tear. If it were this universe, surely the Zargonians, or one of their robot probes, would have crossed over."

There was a murmur of discussion. Lucy paused for a moment before continuing.

"As you know, a being we call the angel is moving towards the tear at a phenomenal velocity – in excess of 99 per cent of the speed of light. She is carrying the soul of a human artist, Maxwell van Mars. I believe she wishes to add his soul to the dark energy of her universe in order to diversify it. A second angel had sexual intercourse with Maxwell. She could be carrying his child or his genetic material in some way."

"Why only one human from your Earth?" asked one of the

images. "Surely, it would make sense to take a variety of humans – or at least their souls and babies – in order to increase the diversity."

"Yes, but bear in mind that when a man ejaculates, he creates many sperm cells. It is possible that one angel is carrying not a child, but a sperm collection."

"Are you suggesting that she might be carrying millions of foetuses fathered by Mr van Mars?" asked an alien Lucy did not recognise, though its head was reminiscent of an insect.

Lucy was about to swear, then thought better of it.

"The notion of millions of little Maxwells is too frightening for words. In any event, I doubt that is the case, though she may be carrying a large number of sperm to fertilise other women on her Earth."

"If so, that would increase the genetic diversity, of course. But sperm from multiple humans would create even more diversity," said the voice.

"Yes, that's true. It may be that there are other angels on our Earth collecting souls. It may be that the angel will make multiple trips – though that seems inefficient. But bear in mind that they have created dozens of traps in the fabric of the universe. Not all of them will succeed, of course. In many of the other universes, humans will not have hyperspace transport. But, many will presumably succeed. I am guessing that the angels are going for a higher level of diversity, collecting a small amount of genetic and intellectual material from each universe. Moreover, they are probably targeting interesting people. Maxwell, for instance, is considered one of the most creative artists alive today."

"Why is it that the dark energy of our universe and theirs does not mingle at the tear and bring diversity that way?" asked another image.

"Because dark energy exists on a complex web of dark matter. It does not flow across empty space. Indeed, it is this web that is torn that has created the hole, opening the two universes to each other."

"In your informed opinion, does this situation pose a threat to our universe?" asked one of the images, a Zargonian.

"No. I believe their aim is to improve their own universe, not to harm ours. Once they have accomplished their task – and that will be soon, I believe – they will close the tear. All in all, the threat to our universe is so negligible as to be non-existent."

"What about this artist, Maxwell? What effect is this having on him?"

"That is outside my expertise, but I expect he'll exist between both universes for a short period of time and that the event will have a powerful effect on his sanity, though that is already of debatable quality."

"Sorry? He's insane?"

"I don't know. But like many artists and creative types, he's not exactly sane."

"And will he be harmed by this?"

"Emotionally? Very possibly. Physically, I doubt it. But I could be wrong."

43

Phineas was awoken by something pressing against his cheek. He opened his eyes to see a young man with long dark-brown hair, a full beard and a glowing circle behind his head. The man, who held Phineas's cheek, was wearing robes and sported the most benevolent smile Phineas had ever seen.

"Jesus Christ?" he asked.

"Why, yes, my son. I am Jesus Christ. At your service," replied the self-proclaimed Son of God in a Southern American accent remarkably similar to Phineas's.

"Oh, Jesus," said Phineas, tears welling in his eyes.

"Do not worry, my son," said Jesus. "I know of your mission to rid the world of Maxwell and make it a safer place for women. I want you to know that it is a good and noble mission. God and I are really and truly pleased with you, Phineas. You can expect special treatment in Heaven when your time comes."

"You are? I can?" said Phineas.

"Of course, my son, of course. But you have much driving to do to get to Erps-Kwerps and dispatch Maxwell to Hell. You had better get moving, my son."

"Yes, Jesus. Oh, yes!" said Phineas, looking for the keys to the SUV. They were not in the ignition and not in his pocket.

"Oh, Jesus, I cannot find the keys," cried Phineas.

"Look harder, my son. Heaven and Earth are waiting for you to rid the world of Maxwell."

"I am looking, Jesus, I am looking!" cried Phineas, with tears streaming down his cheeks.

"Why, Maxwell is probably having perverted sex with Cathy right now," said Jesus. "And here you are on the highway looking for your keys. Have God and I made a mistake in trusting you?"

"No, Jesus, no!" cried Phineas.

"Then find the goddamned keys, my son. You cannot drive a truck and accomplish your mission for God and I without the damned keys!"

Phineas was wakened by something pressing against his cheek. He snorted and jerked upright. He had fallen asleep against the door panel of the SUV. A cool breeze wafted in the slightly opened windows of the vehicle but failed to clear Phineas's head.

"Praise be to God! Jesus has spoken to me in a dream!" cried Phineas. "I knew He supported my holy mission." Looking at the steering column of the SUV, he saw that the keys were still in the ignition. "And He has found my keys. Oh thanks to the Glory of God!!" he cried.

Phineas stepped outside to pee into the verge and splash some bottled water onto his face. He hopped back into the truck, fired up the engine and drove off towards the horizon. At the junction, he got on the road to Frankfurt, pushed the accelerator down and raced off.

Sadly, he should have taken the road to Paris if he wanted to get to Erps-Kwerps quickly. Frankfurt was in the wrong direction.

44

Judith awoke to a bell chiming and found herself on a small cot in a sparse brick room. It took her a moment to remember that she was in a convent in Tours. Then the previous day's events came rushing back to her.

While driving past Toulouse, she had received a call from Sister Gertrude, who was her closest friend in the ninja training convent. Judith pulled over and parked the SUV so that she could focus on the conversation.

Gertrude told Judith about the accident and the revelations about Father Forge. It was clear to the sisters that he was a deluded man, jealous of Maxwell and exploiting the nuns in order to get revenge over an affair Maxwell had many years ago with a woman that Father Forge was in love with — though she was not in love with him. While Maxwell was no Christian, he was not a demon either — just an irresponsible man with some poor values.

Judith started to protest that maybe Maxwell really was demonic and was tricking them, but when pressed to explain herself realised that any explanation she could offer would involve admitting that she had not only had premarital sex, but had done so with a woman and enjoyed herself beyond words.

Well, maybe she would not have to go into details about the 'beyond words' bit, but she'd have to divulge more information about her recent behaviour than she wanted to do at the time. Even her dear friend Gertrude might not understand, let alone condone, premarital lesbian sex.

Or so Judith assumed. The truth was that Gertrude was con-

sidered by a small handful of the sisters to be something of a con-
noisseur of premarital lesbian sex. Her probing fingers, it was said,
enabled many a young woman to see the Father, Son and Holy
Ghost, not to mention nirvana, simultaneously. However, Gertrude was sensitive to Judith's charming naiveté and, although
occasionally tempted, had never seduced Judith, nor even mentioned her sexual pastimes.

After the call, Judith sat in the SUV and stared at the road for a
while. She really did not know what to do. She wanted to go back
to Lucy; to be held and kissed and comforted by the older woman,
but having run away from Lucy, she was not sure she would be
welcome in those wonderful arms again.

Why had she run away? What was she thinking, leaving Lucy?
Then again, Lucy did not love her. What would an intelligent, suc-
cessful scientist like Lucy want with a silly ex-ninja – but still a nun
– like her? A nun who was feeling kind of stupid, in fact.

Lacking any better ideas, Lucy decided to revert to the plan she
had discussed with Lucy in Cape City a few nights before. She
would go to Tours and hope to be accepted into the convent there.
She did not anticipate any problems. Convents are pretty good
about accepting nuns, especially nuns willing to help out with
chores.

Once she made her decision, she started the engine, put the
SUV into gear and drove all the way to Tours, stopping only for
petrol. She arrived at night but, as she had expected, she was
warmly welcomed at her one-time home. She was exhausted. After
prayers, she collapsed in the comfortable cot in the small but cosy
bedroom and within seconds had fallen asleep.

As she lay in the cot the following morning, the past few days'
events resurfaced in her mind. She felt emotionally overwhelmed.
She had tried, and nearly succeeded, to kill a man. She had lost her
virginity to a woman. She had fallen in love. She also felt vaguely
responsible for the accident that had killed Ivan.

She reckoned she should pray for forgiveness, but she was not entirely sure which bits of her activities had been sins and which were cool with God. Her church had told her that it was a good deed to kill Maxwell, but wrong to have sex before marriage and worse to have sex with a woman. But time alone with Lucy had been magical and more spiritual than anything she had previously experienced. That could not be so bad, could it?

But, of course, she had run away from Lucy. Should she go back and beg for forgiveness? Would Lucy take her back? Lucy didn't love her. Maybe Lucy had gone back to Maxwell.

No, she would not think in that direction. It only hurt. But it was hard. The best thing to do, she decided, would be to call Lucy and apologise. To talk to her.

Judith got out of bed, found her handbag, dug out her phone and rang her lover. There was no answer. At the tone for voice-mail, she could not think what to say until the line disconnected. Not much of a voicemail. She'd try later.

In the meantime, she'd have a go with prayer and meditation and hope that God could help her answer some of these questions. She knew God talked to important people in the church, like Father Forge (but was he important? If not, why did God talk to him?) and the other senior priests and nuns, but God had never spoken to her. Nevertheless, she would pray hard and listen for divine advice.

As she prayed, she wondered what God's voice would sound like and whether or not she would even recognise it.

45

After a buffet breakfast in the hotel dining room, Maxwell collected the angel's possessions from her room using the keycard that was in her bag. He found a toothbrush, a couple of dresses and the remainder of the case of Pingus.

"The selfish thing drank a couple of bottles without me," Maxwell muttered to himself.

He and Wendy checked out without incident. In the car, he cried, "home, Mrs Miller," to the GPS unit and waited for it to locate the necessary satellites. Maxwell's prodding that they were most likely in the same orbit they had always occupied was ignored by Mrs Miller, who took her time finding them. Through perseverance, she succeeded, and told Maxwell to turn right out of the hotel car park. Within moments they were on the highway.

Maxwell pressed the accelerator pedal to the floor, loving, as he always did, the growl of the big engine. In no time, the French countryside was whizzing past the windows of the car while the clouds above hurried past in quite another direction, pressed by the eternal wind of Europa.

"You know, Wendy..." said Maxwell.

"Rather a lot," said Wendy, looking up from *Science and Human Behaviour* by BF Skinner. "Be more specific."

"A strange thing happened to me in the hotel bar last night," said Maxwell.

Wendy arched an eyebrow, not sure whether or not she really wanted to hear more. Maxwell seemed to have a particular talent for getting into trouble in hotel bars. But curiosity got the best of her. "What was that?" she asked.

"Nothing," said Maxwell.

"Oh my, that is strange," said Wendy. She contemplated this for a moment, then asked, "did you remember to inform the household staff we would return today?"

"Of course," said Maxwell.

"Stranger still," said Wendy.

"Indeed," said Maxwell. "I'm thinking perhaps I should have a medical check-up when I get back."

"In 1.6 kilometres, keep right," said Mrs Miller. And Maxwell, feeling oddly compliant towards the old GPS, did precisely that.

The remainder of the drive was smooth enough as the car raced across the French regions into Wallonia and finally into Flanders in the late afternoon. A series of winding back roads brought them to the ruins of the village wall and south gate of Erps-Kwerps.

As they passed through the gate, they saw a sign posted in front of the ruins of the old gatehouse announcing a "Welcome Home Maxwell Party" in the village square tonight.

"That didn't take them long," Maxwell said to Wendy.

"Indeed," said Wendy, looking up from her book.

"It's always touching to be loved by one's townsfolk," commented Maxwell.

"I should think the substantial annual contribution from your family to the village coffers helps," said Wendy.

"Wendy, cynicism does not suit you!" said Maxwell.

"We penguins are not cynical. It is just an observation," said Wendy.

"Are you saying you were accidentally cynical?" said Maxwell as he steered the car though the local roads.

"Could be," said Wendy.

The iron gates at the entry drive to the family castle opened automatically and the carved marble lions atop the gate posts roared in delight (they were an early sculptural effort by Maxwell) as the Bentley approached.

Maxwell drove through the gate and down a cobblestone drive lined with overgrown vegetation. In a moment they came to the circular drive, with a fountain at the centre, in front of the main entrance to the castle.

On the steps, Mr and Mrs Suárez and three robots stood waiting. The robots, modified by Maxwell some years ago, looked like young women wearing medium-length skirts and no tops. Their skin, however, was unblemished sky blue all over – even the lips and nipples. Each had yellow curly hair, dark blue eyes and pointed, elfin ears.

The property had been in Maxwell's family for less than a century. His great-grandfather had won the old castle from the Duke of Kwerps in a notorious poker game. Although this pleased the locals – they found van Mars's polite eccentricities far more appealing than the Kwerps's haughty superiority – the Duke and his descendants were pissed off about the incident, at least until Maxwell's father married the Duke's great-granddaughter. By that time, the Kwerps family had fallen onto hard times, their wealth blown on dodgy investments and poor risk-assessment in poker. So, they were only too pleased to marry into the wealth of Maxwell's family, who had done particularly well in off-Earth businesses.

Maxwell, combining genes from his van Mars and Kwerps lines, always felt an affinity towards the old family castle and considered it his home. As his parents, sister and her children all lived on Mars, he largely had the castle to himself.

Maxwell brought the Bentley to a halt at the bottom of the stairs and climbed out. The three robots curtsied in unison as Mrs Suárez said, "welcome home, Mr Maxwell."

"Thanks, Mrs Suárez. Jolly marvellous to be home!" said Maxwell. "It's been a challenging journey, to say the least. And how are things here? I see the old building is still standing. Always a good sign."

"Yes, Mr Maxwell. However, we have had to do some renovations to the south wing. Hannes will show you the costs," said Mrs Suárez.

"Best bring me a generous glass of Valpolicella first," said Maxwell. "You know I need a drink before I deal with money." He dreaded the meeting with Hannes, who was a fine accountant, but lacked a sense of humour and became painfully serious when dealing with big numbers.

"The burgemeester invites you to the table of honour at the village celebration this evening. He suggests you arrive at eight, ideally sober," said Mr Suárez.

"I'm always sober at that hour," said Maxwell. "Unless, of course, my sister is visiting. She always brings out the worst in me."

"Yes, sir," said Mr Suárez.

"My sister isn't hiding around here, is she?" asked Maxwell, suddenly concerned.

"Actually, she is, Mr Maxwell," said Mr Suárez.

"Oh, dear," said Maxwell.

"She is in Antwerp on business today, but promises to be back for the party," said Mr Suárez.

"That's something, then," said Maxwell. Looking at his watch, he added, "Wendy, we've got a couple of hours. I suggest a rest, shower and clean clothes before we join the bash. Mrs Suárez, please tell the burgemeester that we'll be there."

"Very good," said Mrs Suárez.

"I hope so," said Maxwell.

The village square was alive with festivities. The local bars and restaurants had set tables outside in the cool, spring evening, and nearly all of the tables were surrounded by local Erps-Kwerpsers drinking and chatting the night away. On a makeshift stage on the square, a jazz band blasted out lively tunes to which a dozen or so couples were merrily dancing away.

In the centre of the square, a large bonfire roared while a tofu buffalo on a spit was slowly roasted.

"They really do take your vegetarianism seriously, don't they?" said Wendy.

"They do indeed. And I love them for it," said Maxwell.

"Love us for what?" asked the burgemeester, a large man with a larger, beer-enhanced belly. His round face and smile-induced wrinkles were evidence of his joviality. His seemingly polished head with large ears poking out on either side enhanced the image of a cheerful, easy-going chap in late middle age – which summed the old fellow up rather well.

"For the tofu buffalo," said Maxwell. "I am touched that you go to the trouble to appease my vegetarianism."

"Oh, that's because your Mrs Suárez insists," said the burgemeester, with a laugh.

"And one does not want to get on her wrong side," said Maxwell.

"Indeed not," laughed the burgemeester. "Oh, and I've nabbed a couple of virgins from Veltem-Beisem. I thought we could sacrifice them to the volcano in honour of your return, old son."

"What?!" said Maxwell in alarm.

"You know, toss a couple of virgins into the old volcano. Appease the gods. I've read in a book that it's a super thing to do for good luck," said the burgemeester.

"May the gods have mercy upon you, old fruit! What kind of book extols that kind of thing in this day and age?" asked Maxwell.

"A very old book," admitted the burgemeester.

"Get a newer book then! You know I disapprove of the slaughter of innocent young people for outdated, twisted rituals," said Maxwell severely.

"But they're from Veltem-Beisem, not Erps-Kwerps," explained the burgemeester.

"Be that as it may," said Maxwell. "It's still not on. Please let the lasses free and invite them to join the party as my guests," said Maxwell.

"Okay," said the burgemeester grudgingly.

Maxwell patted the man on the back and walked to the nearest bar for a new glass of wine. While waiting, he saw a familiar face.

"Lord love a duck!" he exclaimed.

"I'm sure She does love ducks and all birds," said Lucy.

"You've made it," said Maxwell.

"So it seems," smiled Lucy.

"And you've decided to throw away your lesbian lifestyle and explore the joys of heterosexuality with me," suggested Maxwell.

"You wish," said Lucy.

"I do indeed," said Maxwell.

"Sorry, darling, but I've had my hetero experience for this decade," said Lucy.

"Wasn't I convincing?"

"No, darling, not quite."

"Well, I'll blame your genetic makeup for that appalling lack of taste on your part. Now, come, let me introduce you to a few people – but don't give the burgemeester..."

"The whom?"

"The burgemeester. The...Um...Mayor. Don't give the mayor the impression you might be a virgin."

"What? Why not? It's hardly any of his business."

"He's got this thing about flinging virgins into the village volcano during festivals. Thinks it appeases some god or another."

"Primitive."

"The natives are old fashioned here and he's completely off his rocker. It's part of the village charm," said Maxwell.

"Who's off his rocker?" boomed a woman's voice. Lucy looked around to see that the substantial voice belonged to a rather insubstantial woman: tall, very thin and supporting herself on a cane. As she walked towards them, she gave the impression that she was weighed down by invisible weights and needed the cane to remained upright.

She had long, wavy hair, a prominent nose and wore clothes that subtly suggested wealth and aesthetic good taste, a combination far rarer than it should be. She also looked familiar, in a moderately famous kind of way, but Lucy could not place the face with a name.

"Vivian," said Maxwell, kissing the woman on the cheek and giving her a platonic hug. "I'd heard a rumour you'd come to Earth with the intent of harassing me."

"I have far better and more productive things to do with my time than to harass a useless older brother who wouldn't listen to me anyway. Now, are you going to find any of those good manners Mum and Dad attempted to instil in you and introduce me to this lovely woman?" Vivian smiled at Lucy. "Or are you going to continue to be a cad?"

"Sorry, Sis. I was overwhelmed with emotion upon seeing you again and temporarily forgot my manners – which, I assure you, are tattooed upon my soul. Vivian, this is my friend Lucy. Lucy, this is my sister, Vivian."

The women exchanged pleasantries. Then Vivian said to Maxwell, "actually, as I understand it you're short a soul these days. No wonder your manners are appalling."

"My manners are impeccable, but yours could certainly do with some improving. Not criticising your brother in public would be a good start," said Maxwell.

As the two bickered, Lucy made the mental connection she had been struggling with a moment before. Vivian was, in addition to being Maxwell's sister, the CEO of the Martian Mining Company and, arguably, one of the most powerful people in the solar system. As one popular tabloid had written some years before, this was a position slated for Maxwell, who was the first born child in the socially conservative family. However, he had little interest in running a company, particularly as his sculptural work was beginning to sell. Moreover, his irresponsibility was legendary and often fodder for the selfsame tabloids.

Fortunately for the family, his younger sister demonstrated the financial and business aptitude necessary for the further success of the company. As their father grew older, Vivian proved her business acumen by running teams, then divisions, then business units. She even set up a division to exploit Maxwell's fame by selling models of his sculptures, posters and other paraphernalia. As a result, the company actually earned more income from Maxwell's work than he did, which was a point of contention, albeit a silly one; Maxwell's shares in the Martian Mining Company ensured that he had money coming out his ears and would continue to do so for the rest of his life – no matter how irresponsible he was.

At the same time as she was proving her worth, their father was losing his mind and ability to manage the show, thanks to a rare neurodegenerative disease. He was still sharp, but not sharp enough to manage a business that spanned multiple planets. Fortunately, his daughter had inherited the family business sense and was eventually made CEO. Father was promoted to president and gave the occasional speech, but this was more a position of prestige than operations.

Of course, Lucy realised, this was why Vivian used a walking stick and seemed to struggle with her weight. Here on Earth, she weighed almost three times as much as she did on Mars.

She was also, Lucy thought, awfully good looking. She had some of the features that Lucy had found attractive in Maxwell, but in a much nicer woman's body. Lucy promptly wiped this thought from her mind. She'd had more partners this week than she had the previous year – and she really wanted romantic simplicity in her life, not complexity. Moreover, Vivian did not seem to be a lesbian.

As friends, however, the two women got on like wildfire. They were similar in age, intelligent and equipped with complementary senses of humour. Indeed, Maxwell soon felt left out of the conversation. So, he left the women with a bottle of wine and dove back into the party, with the aim of finding a suitable recipient of his flirtations.

Maxwell, being Maxwell, did not require a great deal of time to achieve this aim.

46

Maxwell woke up the next morning on the chesterfield sofa in the library with an ex-virgin from Veltem-Beisem tangled up in his arms and legs. Their clothes made an indirect path back from the door to the sofa. Three empty wine bottles were scattered among the clothes.

"Lord love a duck," said Maxwell.

"Wat heeft je gezegd?" mumbled the ex-virgin.

"Nothing, baby. Go back to sleep" said Maxwell in strongly accented Flemish, as he untangled himself as gently as he could. He followed the clothing trail to his trousers and donned them. Next, a cappuccino was sorely needed in order to jump-start his brain for the day.

After breakfast and vague promises – that both sides knew would be ignored – to meet up again soon, the ex-virgin took off for neighbouring Veltem-Beisem.

"I reckon she wasn't a virgin, even before last night," said Maxwell.

"Sorry?" asked Wendy, looking up from the latest issue of Nature, which she was reading while breakfasting on herring and toast.

"Nothing, sorry. I was speaking to myself," said Maxwell.

"Ah, then I'll leave you to it," said Wendy.

"Actually, it was a short conversation that came to a prompt conclusion. The advantage to talking to one's self is one seldom disagrees with one's main points," said Maxwell.

"It was less confusing when you were talking to yourself," confessed Wendy.

"No worries, old bird," said Maxwell. "I'll make sense now."

"That's good," said Wendy, wrinkling her eyes into a smile.

"It's a beautiful day outside," said Maxwell. "And the wind is bearable."

"Unusual," said Wendy.

"Indeed. I suggest we exploit the situation and take the bicycle out for a spin."

"I'd like that."

"Me too."

"And you almost never get into trouble when bicycling."

"No, I don't," agreed Maxwell. "And I've had quite enough trouble this week. I'd like to avoid it for a while."

"A good plan."

While Wendy finished her breakfast, Maxwell went out to the bicycle shed and pulled out a curious-looking tandem. The front half looked very much like the front halves of the vast majority of bicycles-built-for-two. The back half, however, had been radically modified in order to seat a penguin. The saddle was optimised for a penguin bottom, the handlebars were easily reached by penguin wings and the peddles were just beneath the saddle. Maxwell wiped the bicycle down, oiled the bits that required lubrication and peddled over to the front entrance to the castle where Wendy was waiting.

They cycled along the winding lanes that ran through the nearby farming villages. The sky was a deep blue, surprisingly lacking in clouds. Even the ever-present wind was gentler than usual, though it still made peddling significantly harder — or easier, depending on which direction they were moving.

It was behind them, pushing the bicycle gently but quickly, when they peddled into Erps-Kwerps village centre. Maxwell waved to people out for their morning shopping or, as was the case with many of the older folk, simply out and about in order to run into neighbours and strike up conversations. They whipped past the old, now deconsecrated, church upon which a signboard still announced Maxwell's reception party of the night before as well as a disco dance tonight.

As the bicycle veered to the right to go down the hill past some of the nicer houses in the area, there was a thunderous crack that filled the air. At the same time, Maxwell's chest exploded and blood splattered across Wendy. Maxwell was thrust backwards and to the right, throwing the bicycle to the left. Maxwell hit the ground with a thud and somersaulted chaotically, like a rag doll bouncing along the road. As the bicycle fell, so too did Wendy – head first, though she took most of the fall on her shoulder. Nevertheless, by the time she stopped bouncing, her beak was cracked badly and her wing-bone snapped..

In the street, a silence filled the air, as it does when an unexpected and bloody accident happens. Wendy looked up and crawled towards Maxwell. She couldn't walk. Something was wrong with her legs and every movement hurt. But she knew Maxwell was hurt much more. She only hoped he was still alive. A disturbingly large amount of his blood had hit her. A great deal more seemed to be in the growing puddle in the street. She did not think there could be much more remaining inside her friend – her irritatingly irrational but best friend.

Someone screamed. A couple of men pointed towards a dishevelled priest holding a large shotgun and crying "Jesus?" A portly woman who had been laughing a moment ago dropped her shopping and marched swiftly and purposefully towards Maxwell.

Wendy finally crawled as far as Maxwell's body, though the pain was unbearable. She put her good wing over Maxwell's bullet wound, then did the only thing she was capable of: she passed out.

The portly woman arrived and dropped to her knees. "It's okay, dear," she said in a motherly voice to Wendy as she moved the wing gently. "I'm a doctor. I'm just going to check your friend's wound."

A police siren could be heard in the distance. The priest was now holding the gun loosely at his side. He looked at the bodies of Maxwell and the penguin and then looked around him nervously as if trying to find someone or something. He suddenly looked pathetic and unlikely to shoot anyone else. A couple of burly farmers who looked like they could each lift a medium-sized tractor marched slowly towards the preacher. The sirens grew louder. The priest suddenly ran towards the church.

"He's still alive," the portly doctor said to a skinny man, "but I don't know if he's going to make it. Has someone called an ambulance?"

"Yes, darling," said the man. "It's on the way."

The woman who ran the handicrafts shop nearby ran out with a couple of quilted blankets and pillows for Maxwell and Wendy.

47

The previous day, Phineas had driven as far as Heidelberg before Jesus suddenly reappeared in the passenger seat of the SUV and told the priest he had been driving in the wrong direction.

"Where the heck are you going, Phineas? You don't want to go this way! You've got to drive towards Cologne, and then Brussels," explained the Son of God.

"Oh, Jesus, you came back," cried Phineas.

"Yes, I did, my son. God said you might need a little help," said Jesus.

"I do," said Phineas.

"Well, first you've got to take the exit ahead and get on the road to Cologne, Phineas," said Jesus.

Phineas followed the advice, veering off the highway and following a series of curves, merges and lane changes until he was on the Holy Son's suggested route. He drove as far as Koblenz where, late at night, he dozed off at the wheel of the SUV and very nearly smashed into a big Mercedes.

"Better pull over and get some shut-eye, big boy," said Jesus.

Phineas did so and asked, "couldn't you drive for a while?"

"No can do, Phinny. I haven't got a driving licence," said Jesus.

"Oh, okay," said Phineas, who was asleep by the final syllable of his reply.

"Hey, wake up, Phinny!" said Jesus the next morning. "You've got to take care of Maxwell. Why, he's probably defiling a virgin or two right now while you sleep!"

"Oh my God! Yes, of course, Jesus," said Phineas with a start. He immediately began driving again. By mid-morning, he was in Erps-Kwerps. In the village square, he found a billboard with a map of Erps-Kwerps. He pulled over, hopped out of the SUV and studied the map.

Jesus followed a moment later and examined the map as well.

"Do you think it shows Maxwell's house on this map?" he asked with what Phineas felt was a trace of sarcasm.

At the same time, two teenage girls walked past the sign.

"Oh look!" said one to the other, pointing down the road. "Check out that bicycle. It's Maxwell and his penguin. It's, like, such a cool bicycle."

"Cool!" laughed the other girl.

"Did you hear that?" asked Jesus. "It's Maxwell! Look! You'd better get ready."

"Ready?" asked Phineas. The two girls looked round to see a dishevelled priest, with a massive moustache, talking to himself.

"Yes, ready! There's a gun in the car, Phinny. You can take care of the Maxwell problem once and for all – right now!" said Jesus.

"But..." sputtered Phineas as the girls picked up their pace and moved on, glancing worriedly behind them.

"What's wrong, son? Scared to do God's work? Has my Father misjudged you?" demanded Jesus.

"Oh no! Of course not," said Phineas.

"I did not hear you!" said Jesus.

"No, my Lord! I am not scared," shouted Phineas

"Then get the damned gun and do what you need to do, son," exclaimed Jesus.

Phineas returned the SUV, found the shotgun and pulled it out just as the unusual tandem bicycle approached. That was definitely Maxwell riding it.

"Shoot, you idiot. Shoot!" shrieked Jesus.

Phineas pointed the gun and fired a single haphazard shot

which, amazingly, managed to hit Maxwell in the chest.

"Oh, look, Jesus! Look, I have done your work! I have hit Maxwell with my first shot thanks to your help," he shouted in tearful joy to Jesus. But Jesus was not there. He had disappeared.

"Jesus?!" Phineas called. There was no reply. He was confused. Jesus was gone. People were shouting. A siren could be heard in the distance. He did not know what to do. He did not know why Jesus had abandoned him.

Some big men were walking towards him.

Looking around frantically, he saw the church and ran towards it. Surely, he'd find Jesus there, he thought – and, if not, he'd have a word with God about His irresponsible son. Phineas shoved at the door for a moment. It wouldn't budge. The sirens were getting louder. He heard strange, unchurchlike music behind the door. Why would would the door not open? Of course! He needed to pull on it. He grabbed the handle and pulled. The door opened.

He stepped inside and was enveloped in warmth. Glowing, glittering lights swirled around the room like tiny angels moving along with the odd music. Surely, they were angels dancing to the glory of Jesus. God was welcoming Phineas for his holy deed. Phineas dropped to his knees as the colourful angels swirled around him.

"Oh, God, I have come to you," said Phineas.

"Huh? Who are you?" God thundered in return, His voice resonating above the music and throughout the church.

"Why, I am Phineas Forge, God! I have done what you willed of me in Your name."

"Um, what exactly have you done?" thundered God.

"Are you testing me, Lord?"

The music throbbed in the background. The angels swarmed. But God took a moment to speak.

"Yes, I am. What have you done?"

"Why, I've killed Maxwell – dispatched him to Hell for you!"

"You've what?!" God thundered even louder than before.

"I've killed Maxwell, as was Your will."

"Maxwell? You mean Maxwell van Mars, the artist?"

"Yes, my Lord! Yes, he will never defile another woman again!"

"Yes, that sounds like Maxwell..."

"I beg your pardon, Lord?"

"You've really killed him?"

"Yes. He must be burning in Hell now."

"What did you say your name was?"

"Phineas Forge," said the priest, feeling that this was not how he expected a conversation with God to unravel.

"Phineas Fudge?"

"Forge, God, Forge."

"Oh, sorry. Phineas Forge, what you have done is a very bad thing."

"What? But it's what you asked of me, Lord!"

"I did not ask you to kill Maxwell."

"He is evil!"

"He can indeed be an irritating bastard at times, but he's not evil."

"Lord?"

"You have done a very bad thing, Phineas Forge."

"But, Lord..." Phineas was weeping now. This was not how he expected things to work out. He wanted God to embrace him, to thank him. But God seemed upset with him. And even the angels seemed to be mocking him.

"Phineas Forge!"

"Yes, Lord?"

"I want you to step outside now and give yourself up to the police."

"Lord?"

"I do not want you to kill anyone else, okay, Phineas Forge?"

"Yes, Lord."

"Now, Phineas Forge!"

"Yes, Lord," said Phineas. Shoulders slumped, moustache drooping, the priest slowly walked out the door to find a dozen armed police officers awaiting him. He dropped his gun and raised his hands. Immediately behind him was the sign announcing the disco tonight in the "Old Erps Church" which, as everyone in the village knew, had been deconsecrated years ago and was now used for school plays, discos and other community activities.

Wim, the man whose voice, broadcast through the sound system, Phineas believed to be God's, was a local DJ testing the sound system for the night's disco.

"Do you reckon he's really killed Maxwell?" he asked Pieter, who was taping down the wiring.

"I hope not. I kind of like the bastard," said Pieter.

"Me, too," said Wim, switching off the disco lights and thus making Phineas's dancing angels disappear.

48

The university city of Leuven sits not far from Erps-Kwerps, and in that city sat Vivian and Lucy, enjoying a coffee in the Grote Markt, beneath the slowly encroaching shadow of the nearby town hall. Vivian had a long list of shopping to do while on Earth and Lucy was happy to join her. Nevertheless, neither of the woman were keen shoppers and after a couple of hours decided to enjoy coffees in the old square.

"I've been thinking, Lucy," said Vivian.

"Yes?"

"The University of Mars is planning to set up a department of astronomy. It's still a young university and small, of course, but the thin air makes for good viewing. Thanks to the company, the University also has a share in a couple of telescopes orbiting the Earth."

Vivian's telephone began ringing. She looked at the screen, decided not to answer and continued. "I know they are looking for someone to head up the department. Now, I know it's a lot smaller than Cape City, where you are now. And it's on Mars, which is not everyone's cup of tea. But, I reckon you'd do a great job with it, and you would be in charge."

"Is that a job offer?" asked Lucy.

"Not exactly. I can make a recommendation to the university, which they will take seriously. But the decision is up to them."

"It sounds very appealing. I could do with a change and a new challenge. It seems like that position would offer me both in one convenient package," said Lucy.

Vivian's telephone began ringing again. She muttered under her breath and ignored it.

"Mars has a rapidly growing population, and a clever one. I reckon it's because there were a lot of scientists among the early colonists and their brainy genes have been passed on to the new generations. To be fair, Maxwell reckons it's because there's nothing to do but read, study and go to parties and, again by his reckoning, the parties are not nearly decadent enough," said Vivian as her telephone began ringing again. "Good grief," she exclaimed.

"Maybe you should answer it," suggested Lucy.

"Yes, it's the only way we'll get any peace. Sorry about this," said Vivian to Lucy. Into the telephone, she said, "hello? Vivian here."

Her face dropped dramatically. "Oh, my..." she said, then listened further, before adding, "okay. Thank you so much for calling. I'll head over there right away. Thanks again. Bye." She clicked off the telephone.

"Some nut has shot Maxwell," she said to Lucy.

"Holy shit! Really?" said Lucy.

"I'm afraid so. Will you excuse me? I'm going over to the hospital." She stood up shakily.

Lucy took her arm. "Why don't I come with you?" she asked. "Unless you'd prefer to be alone."

"No, no. I'd like it if you came with me. Thanks," said Vivian, who promptly called the driver, who brought the car around. Within minutes, they were at Leuven University Hospital, a scant few kilometres up the road from where they had been enjoying coffee.

From the reception they were directed to the intensive care unit and there a nurse informed them that Maxwell was alive, albeit barely, and was being operated upon while they spoke.

"And Wendy, the penguin who was doubtless with him?" asked Vivian.

The nurse looked at his computer and flicked his fingers across the screen three times. "She's been sent to the Sentient Non-Human Terrestrial wing of the hospital. It seems she suffered a number of injuries as well, but she's not in ICU," he said.

"How long do you expect Maxwell to be in surgery?" asked Vivian.

"At least another two or three hours. We've got two top robots assisting the doctor, but the damage is severe," said the nurse.

"Why don't we go visit Wendy?" Vivian suggested.

Lucy agreed and they wandered the extensive corridors of the hospital for some time before they came to a sign welcoming them to the Sentient Non-Human Terrestrial Unit (SNHTU). They walked over to the reception window, which was vacant except for a cat dozing on the ledge. The women peered in to see three desks, each with a computer and several stacks of paper sitting on it. The women looked at each other. Vivian checked her watch. Lucy stared at the cat, a curious addition to a hospital.

"Can I help you? Or do you intend simply to hang out on my window all afternoon?" asked the cat.

Lucy jumped and even Vivian gave a start. "Oh, sorry, I didn't realise..." she trailed off.

"That I was a talking cat?" asked the feline.

"Yes, as a matter of fact," said Vivian.

"You are aware this is the Sentient Non-Human Terrestrials Unit, are you not?" asked the cat.

"Yes, of course," said Vivian.

"Well, that's pretty much talking animals," said the cat.

"You strike me as having an attitude problem," said Vivian, attempting to take control of the discussion.

"Have you ever met a cat who doesn't?" asked the cat.

Vivian laughed for the first time since the phone call. "That's true," she said.

"I'm glad we've cleared that up, human. Now, I assume you are enquiring after one of the patients, since both of you look human," said the cat.

"Yes," said Vivian. "Wendy, a kairuku penguin."

The cat hopped from the ledge to one of the desks, where she moved her nose around on the computer screen.

"She received a number of injuries, including a cracked beak, broken wing bones and a fractured ankle. The doctors have fixed her up and she's resting now."

"May we see her?" asked Lucy.

"Yes, but not for too long. She needs her rest."

They found the room in question and peered in. In the bed was a bandaged Wendy connected by a black cable to several machines whose displays seemed to indicate that things were happening inside the penguin's body. Her beak was in some kind of cast. Crisp, clean blankets covered the rest of her.

"Wendy?" asked Vivian.

Wendy nodded her head slightly and the two women walked in.

"How are you doing, old friend?" asked Vivian.

Wendy crinkled her eyes slightly.

"Hi, Wendy," said Lucy, feeling slightly awkward; she had only known Wendy a short time, but liked her and respected her tremendous knowledge.

Wendy crinkled her eyes again.

"We've just been to the ICU. They are operating on Maxwell now. So, he's still alive, and we both know he's a tough bastard when he has to be. I'm sure he'll pull through."

A tear welled up in one of Wendy's eyes.

"Don't worry, old friend," said Vivian, gently brushing Wendy's cheek. "He'll be okay. It may take a while, but he'll be okay."

The women sat with Wendy for a half hour. During that time, Lucy talked about current research into the lattice structure of dark matter, which seemed to cheer Wendy up.

When the cat came in to shoo them away, they both bade

goodbye to Wendy and promised to keep her updated on Maxwell's situation.

In the ICU waiting room, they waited another hour and a half before Dr Ihonen came out. "You are Maxwell's sisters?" she asked.

"I am," said Vivian. "This is Lucy Heisenberg, a family friend."

"Very good," said the doctor, a pale woman whose granny glasses and dark dreadlocks gave the impression of being more of a hippy than a doctor.

"As you know, your brother has been very seriously injured. He was shot in the chest, shattering a rib, breaking another and damaging one of his lungs. He also fractured his skull when he fell from the bicycle. The good news is that the bullet missed the heart.

"As we speak, a team of robots is removing bullet and bone shrapnel as well as repairing the lung using artificial tissue. Once that is functioning, we'll graft an artificial rib into the stub of the shattered rib."

"And will he....?" began Vivian.

"We hope so. I reckon he has better than a 50 per cent chance," said the doctor.

"That's, well, something, I guess. When can I see him?" asked Vivian.

"The operation will take three or four more hours. Then he'll be in an artificial coma until we can replace the rib. You can come during visiting hours tomorrow, but he won't be conscious."

A buzzing sound emitted from the doctor's jacket pocket. She pulled out a phone, read the screen and raised her eyebrows just enough to be observed by a sensitive Lucy.

"Oh, dear. I've got to go," said the doctor.

"Is it Maxwell?" asked Lucy. But it was too late. The doctor had already disappeared back into the innards of the hospital.

"I don't have a good feeling about that," said Vivian, nodding towards the door through which the doctor had just walked.

"Neither do I," said Lucy, "but there's nothing much we can do for now. I suggest we go have a drink. It's been a long day."

Vivian looked at her watch. "But it's not even the aperitif hour."

"Never mind," said Lucy, taking Vivian's arm.

The doctor returned to a computer terminal inside the operating chamber. It displayed a series of numbers representing Maxwell's various vital signs. Unfortunately, the numbers were slowly but determinedly sliding towards zero.

The robots were calmly attaching a series of tubes to Maxwell's chest. Robots were good that way. They could work intricately, never tired and stayed calm no matter what happened. The doctor watched them for a moment and then checked the data on the computer screen. That 50 per cent she cited in the waiting room suddenly seemed optimistic.

49

Lucy and Vivian returned to Erps-Kwerps and had a couple of drinks at Central Café. However, their hearts were not into it. After a beer, Vivian decided to return to the family castle for a nap. She was exhausted. Lucy stayed on at the bar, deciding to leave Vivian be for a while. She ordered another beer just as her telephone rang.

"Lucy Heisenberg," she said into the phone. There was no reply. "Hello?" she asked. Again, there was nothing. She was about to ring off when she heard a faint voice at the other end.

"Lucy?"

"Yes, it's me. Is that Judith?"

Pause. "Yes."

"How are you doing, Judith?" she asked.

"I don't know. I'm very confused," said Judith.

"Well, you kind of confused me when you fucked off on me a couple of days ago," said Lucy.

Tears. Sniffling. "Oh, I'm sorry, Lucy. I didn't mean to run away on you. But..."

Lucy waited quietly.

"But..."

"Yes?"

"I thought you wanted to be with Maxwell."

"I told you, I am not interested in him. He's a man. I prefer women. Of all the people to be jealous of, he was a poor choice on your part. Anyway, it seems your friend the priest shot him this morning."

"What!?"

Lucy repeated herself.

"Oh, no. Oh my God."

"Isn't that what your fellow nuns and that priest wanted?" asked Lucy, feeling a bit spiteful and slightly ashamed of herself for reacting that way.

"Yes, I thought so. But I talked to my friend Gertrude last night. She said it was all a mistake. She said that Father Forge was super jealous of Maxwell because Maxwell had premarital sex with his girlfriend – but she wasn't even interested in Father Forge."

"Holy shit – is there any woman in Europa Maxwell hasn't fucked?"

"Me!" said Judith and, after a moment's thought, "and Gertrude. I think Gertrude is still a virgin."

Lucy stifled a laugh. "That's good to hear. Go on. You were saying about your Father Forge?"

"He's a virgin, too!"

"What?" said Lucy.

"Father Forge is a virgin, too. You see, he used to love this woman named Cathy, but when he found Cathy and Maxwell having premarital sex, he vowed he would never have sex. So, he's a virgin and I'm not!"

"How old is he?" asked Lucy.

"In his 40s, I think. Maybe older," said Judith.

"Talk about repressed sexual frustration," said Lucy.

"What?" asked Judith.

"Nothing. Go on with your story."

"Well, it seems Father Forge was on some kind of revenge trip because he lost his girlfriend to Maxwell and, it seems, lots of other people. You see Cathy is – what did Gertrude call her? – a nymphy...A nompha..."

"A nymphomaniac?"

"Yes, I think that was it. Anyway, Gertrude said that we have all been chasing Maxwell and trying to kill him because Father Forge is crazy jealous and not because Maxwell has committed any great sin – though he has sinned a great deal, but that's different, I guess."

Lucy absorbed all of this while also reviewing her feelings towards Judith. Truth be told, those feelings were not very strong any more. Judith had a fucking cute, athletic body and was remarkably agile in bed. It had been a fun few days, but now that she was gone, Lucy really did not fancy trying to get back together again.

"What do you want now?" Lucy asked cautiously.

"I think I need some time to find myself."

"That's probably a good idea. Where are you?"

"I'm in the convent in Tours. Praying for answers."

"Have you received any yet?"

"No, actually I haven't. I don't know why God seems to answer the prayers of loud men who already know what they want, like Father Forge, but He ignores my prayers."

"I think you've answered your question."

"Huh?"

"Don't worry about it. Keep praying."

"I will."

50

Halfway to the tear, the bronze, metallic angel rotated 180 degrees and began decelerating at the same phenomenal rate at which she had previously been accelerating.

It may be worth noting that a young graduate student who had been following the angel, from the moment she raced past an orbiting telescope that he had been using to monitor objects in the Oort Cloud, was inspired to change his doctoral thesis theme "Organic Compounds in Icy Deposits in Long-Period Comets" to "Ultra-High Acceleration Techniques in Extra-Solar System Transportation Devices". His professors thought the paper excessively fanciful, poorly argued and unacceptable. Rather than rewrite the thesis, the student dropped out, set up a company to exploit the ideas from the thesis and became stinking rich. However, this has absolutely nothing to do with our story.

By the time she reached the tear, the angel had slowed considerably, to a few thousand kilometres per hour. She entered the tear, which to her seemed like a long, dark tunnel with a few stars visible at the far end. In a moment, she exited the tear in her own universe. Slowly, her wings spread outward, followed by her hands. Her knees bent and moved apart slightly. As this was happening, flakes broke off her bronze-like exterior and trailed behind her like a glittering comet tail. She decelerated further, causing much of the debris to speed past her.

Once her speed had dropped to a mere couple hundred kilometres per hour, she began spiralling as she moved forward. She opened the box and let out sparkling pieces of soul that trailed behind her spirals. The box empty, she pushed it aside, brought her arms, legs and wings together and accelerated rapidly towards an Earth, which from space looked very much, but not exactly, like Maxwell's. Beneath the clouds upon almost familiar continents lived a population of angels that numbered in the scant millions and who lived in stone and brick buildings reminiscent of Medieval Europe.

Meanwhile, the pieces of soul slowly dissolved into space and into the latticework of dark matter. At the same time, the tear in the fabric of the universe slowly came together and mended itself like a cut in the flesh.

Something that was almost a sound resonated across this universe. It was oddly reminiscent of a burp.

51

Maxwell awoke on a hospital bed beneath a deep blue, lightly clouded sky with a miscoloured rainbow stretching from horizon to horizon. In the background, he heard a gentle, rhythmic splooshing sound. Add to that a vague taste of saltiness, and Maxwell could not help but be reminded of the seaside.

He sat up and discovered that he was, in fact, on a hospital bed on a deserted beach. Gentle waves lapped at a shore that was surprisingly devoid of footprints, rubbish and any evidence that the beach had recently been visited. He stepped down and found that he felt perfectly fine. He was pleased. He had a vague sense of something terribly bad having happened to him recently, but could not recall what it was.

He walked to the shore, squatted down and felt the water; it was cool, but not cold.

"Ah, you're here," said a slightly raspy, but friendly voice.

Maxwell looked up to see a thin woman who looked to be in her 70s. She had long silver hair simply tied behind her head, fine cheekbones and deep, deep blue eyes. She was wearing a simple, long white gown that swayed gently in the light wind. The wrinkles in her face enhanced a sweet yet knowing smile.

"So it seems," said Maxwell getting up. "But where is here?"

"Well, it's Earth, but it's on the other side."

"Other side! Lord love a duck. Have I died and gone to Heaven?" asked Maxwell, again remembering that something very bad had happened to him recently, something seriously detrimental to his health, though he still could not recall any details.

"Not yet," said the elderly woman. "Come, let us walk along this beach for a bit." As she turned, Maxwell saw that she sported a magnificent pair of wings similar to the angel's, though they looked older.

"Is this the angel's planet?" asked Maxwell.

"Angel? Oh, I expect you mean Helena, the one who went to you."

"Probably. She didn't know her name. Indeed, she seemed a confused lass when I knew her – and a dangerous one."

"Mmm. Travelling between realities is not easy. The new reality begins to take hold over you until you become a part of it – and lose the connection to your original reality."

"Does this kind of thing happen often?"

"Rarely, thankfully."

"And you are?" asked Maxwell.

"I am – it is difficult to explain. I am the sum of all humanity across all realities."

"You're God?"

"Well, not exactly God. Most of your religions, at least the monotheistic ones, perceive God as the creator of the universe and humanity. However, I am the consequence of the universe and humanity."

"The universe created you?"

"Yes, that's about right."

"Pity."

"Why is that?"

"I am imagining a crazy priest I know, Phinny Forge. If he knew God was a woman, it would burst his feeble brain." As he mentioned his foe's name, Maxwell felt a brief but incredible pain in his chest. He briefly wondered if he was having a heart attack, but realised the pain was on the wrong side of his chest for heart misbehaviour.

"I understand his brain is a lost cause at this time," said God.

"I'm not sure it was ever entirely found," said Maxwell.

"Be that as it may, it surprises me that so many men like Phineas worship their mothers, yet believe that God is a father. Do they really think a man can manage a family the size of several universes?"

"Actually, I am an atheist, or at least I was until now. You are presenting some pretty compelling evidence against my philosophy in that department."

"Don't worry, Maxwell. You can go on being an atheist. I may well not exist."

"I see," said Maxwell who was not sure whether or not he really did.

They walked along the beach in silence for several minutes. On the right, opposite from the water, Maxwell could see a walled town growing with each step they took. In time they came to a path that led from the beach to the town. The path led past some dried-out vegetation and a few tired palm trees to a wooden gate in the town wall.

The woman turned and looked at Maxwell. "In your reality, you are hovering between life and death, with death being the easier option."

"Oh, dear," said Maxwell, concerned.

"I cannot do anything about that. However, you have some time in this reality. Do what you need to do in order to make peace and prepare yourself." She took Maxwell's head in her surprisingly soft, warm hands and kissed him on the forehead. Then she opened the gate for him and gestured that he should walk through, which is precisely what Maxwell did. As he passed, he turned to the elderly angel and asked, "I suppose you are rather all knowing, are you not?"

"Very nearly."

"Tell me, then, what is the meaning of life?"

"Why, it is to fuck, of course. If you don't reproduce, you

won't last two generations."

"I thought as much. Thanks."

"My pleasure."

Maxwell allowed the gate to shut behind him as he walked into the walled town, a tightly packed collection of mostly faded white-washed stone buildings, though a few pastel-coloured buildings were scattered about. Plant pots that once presumably held colourful flowers now provided a home base to an anarchic variety of equally colourful weeds, some of which climbed up the sides of the buildings, while others fell to the cobblestone road below. With no separate footpaths, the buildings bordered upon the street itself. A smell of wet stone and vegetation circulated in the gentle breeze, a refreshing change from the strong winds that blew across most of Europa.

When it was full of people, the town must have been stunningly beautiful, thought Maxwell. Even now, its desolation gave it an aesthetic dignity of timelessness.

As he walked the streets, wondering how on Earth to make peace – particularly when he was not on his own Earth – he started to hear a faint, almost musical sound. Walking towards it, the sound became clear. It was Zargonians talking. He paused and slowly turned his head to scan the town. It sounded like they were in the church. It sounded as though there were several of them, which was unusual. In his experience, the Zargonians typically hung out in pairs. He walked over and quietly opened the door.

Inside were not the expected aliens, but a dozen angels singing a medieval chant, their voices eerily reminiscent of Joan Baez's. Each wore a long white dress that fluttered as they swayed to their own song.

The stunning sight and hypnotically beautiful music held Maxwell's attention for several minutes, which was why he failed initially to see that nailed to the cross hanging above the altar was Phineas Forge wearing a cowboy suit.

"I am dying for your sins here, Maxwell!" he shouted, seemingly unfazed by the nails that had been driven into his hands and legs.

Maxwell started. "I've never asked you to do that, Phinny. I have always been willing to take responsibility for my own misbehaviour."

"It is not your choice to make, you vile sinner! It is God's choice!"

"As it happens, I was just chatting with her," began Maxwell.

"Her! How dare you blaspheme in His name?"

"Would you believe it? I told Her you might respond like this. Anyway, I think She's happy to let me do my own thing, Phinny, so there's no need to die on my behalf. To tell the truth, I find your behaviour rather embarrassing."

"Ha! It does not matter what you want or how much you blaspheme, Maxwell! I have already killed you!"

"Will you shut the fuck up!" an angel shouted at the priest.

Maxwell looked at her and recognised his angel: Helena. She stepped away from the other angels, smiled at him and embraced him. Her accent was the same, but there was greater alertness in her voice and eyes than he had remembered. On Earth, his Earth, she had always seemed a little stoned. Here, she looked sober, alert and more attractive than ever.

"Do you wish to pray to God?" she asked. Maxwell looked at that alter, surprised to see that the crucified Phineas had been replaced by a carved wooden angel smiling down upon him.

"No, thanks," said Maxwell. I chatted with her just a few minutes ago."

"She's nice, isn't she?" asked the angel. She looked at Maxwell a moment, smiled, then took his hand. "Come."

Dusk had fallen when they exited the church, casting deep shadows across the narrow lanes; leaving some buildings vaguely lit and some in mysterious, almost sinister darkness. Helena led

Maxwell by the hand along the lanes until they came to Hotel Lusco Fusco on a picturesque street corner. The angel pushed the door open and they walked in. After climbing up three flights of stairs, she came to an unlocked door, which she opened. The room was scantly furnished, with a canopied, wrought-iron bed covered in white blankets to one side. A white sofa and a couple of up-holstered wooden chairs were on the other side. Open windows let in a gentle breeze setting the white curtains aflutter.

The angel turned and kissed Maxwell on the lips, gently at first but with slowly growing passion that Maxwell returned. This was indeed his idea of making peace with the world. If he was dying, making love to an angel would be a jolly good way to go, he thought.

The angel slowly pushed him towards the bed, pulling off his clothes with remarkable dexterity. She pushed him down on the bed, pulled off her dress and tossed it to the floor.

For three hours, they engaged in the most incredible love-making Maxwell had known – and he had known rather a lot, having made the acquisition of carnal knowledge one of his major goals in life. They utilised the bed, the cool wooden floor, the sofa and the chairs. At one point, the angel flew while Maxwell penetrated her, her arms and legs holding his body just below hers.

Eventually, exhausted and orgasmed out, Maxwell collapsed on the bed while the angel caressed his chest and played with his hair.

"You are not a bad fuck," she said softly.

"Gosh, thanks. You're not bad yourself," said Maxwell fading into sleep and out of the world he had temporarily occupied. It was time to return to his Earth and, unfortunately, fight for his life – not something Maxwell had ever had to do before.

52

"That's the first time I have ever seen someone have a wet dream while in a coma," a doctor checking on Maxwell commented to the assisting intern. "But it seems to have helped. Look at his vitals."

And, indeed, Maxwell's vital signs had improved considerably. Though the senior doctor would not go so far as to feel optimistic, she began to feel hopeful. After the trauma of surgery, many patients showed initial improvement before going downhill again.

On the other hand, she had never seen someone orgasm while in a coma. She hoped it would be a good precedent.

53

Two weeks later, Maxwell was out of the ICU unit and in a very comfortable room in the hospital. He was laying in his bed with the back raised so that he was sitting up. Sitting on one of the chairs by the bedside was Wendy. One of her wings was in a sling and her beak was wired shut, but the worst of the bruising had gone down. She was reading an anthology of contemporary American philosophers writing on religion in their country.

On the sofa across the room sat Lucy and Vivian, who were talking about Mars. On the small table in front of them was one empty and one nearly full bottle of Valpolicella. Each of the humans had a glass of said wine within easy reach. Wendy had a cup of warm tea with a straw by her side.

The nurse came in, looked at the wine and looked at Maxwell.

"Are you drinking again, Maxwell?" she asked.

"It is a necessity of life, Nora," he said. "Humans need to drink."

"But they do not need to drink alcohol!" said Nora.

"This is not just alcohol, young lady," Maxwell insisted. "This is Valpolicella, probably the friendliest wine on the planet. Valpolicella would never hurt a fly, let alone me. It has my best interests at heart. I'd trust it with my life!"

"But you are recuperating from a very serious injury, Maxwell. You are taking medication."

"And the Valpolicella only enhances that medication. And that's because it cares deeply about me," said Maxwell.

"But Maxwell!"

"You're right. I am being thoughtless. Would you like a glass?"

"You are not thoughtless. You are hopeless!" said the nurse, laughing and leaving the room.

Wendy crinkled her eyes into a smile. She would have liked to have scolded Maxwell for drinking in the hospital herself, but the wire around her beak prevented it. She wrote Maxwell a note, but it was hard to debate in writing when the other party could retaliate verbally. In any event, Lucy and Vivian were also drinking, so there was little point in arguing.

Vivian kept her drinking tightly under control. She ran the family businesses and realised that was a job best done sober, but when she was not working, she drank nearly as much as Maxwell. Years ago, Wendy had asked Vivian why she did not try to encourage Maxwell to drink less, she replied that if he drank himself into an early grave, it would only increase her inheritance. Wendy reckoned that she was joking at the time, but was never quite sure. Maxwell's family had a curious sense of humour.

Not long after the nurse left, the burgemeester walked into the hospital room.

The two women greeted the man. Maxwell waved, then said, "Lord love a duck, this place is more popular than my last show."

Wendy turned to dispute the statement. There were a lot of people at his last show, she thought. Many more than in this room.

"Ha," said Maxwell to Wendy. "You'll just have to accept my statement irrespective of its lack of merit."

Wendy threw her drinking straw at Maxwell.

"Anyway, crazy penguin, you know it was an exaggeration to make a point."

Wendy winked at Maxwell and returned to her reading.

"Am I interrupting anything?" asked the burgemeester.

"No. I've just finished demonstrating to Wendy that wit trumps facts in any discussion," said Maxwell.

Wendy glanced around her, looking for something to throw.

Maxwell picked up the straw from his bed. "Would you mind giving this to Wendy?" he asked the burgemeester. "I believe she would like to throw it at me again."

"I must say you're looking a lot better today, old son," said the burgemeester. "We thought we were going to lose you for a while there."

"Yes, at one point I thought I had died and gone to Heaven, which was an awfully picturesque place, but doubtless would have got boring over an eternity."

"Well, thank the gods you didn't stay there," said the burgemeester.

"Indeed."

Vivian poured another glass of wine and handed it to the burgemeester.

The burgemeester took a deep sip. "The doctor tells me you'll be out of here in a couple of weeks. I think we should have a party to celebrate the return to health of our favourite son."

"That's jolly decent of you," said Maxwell.

"Le Cannibale Ancienne is already preparing a tofu buffalo to roast," said the burgemeester.

"Le Cannibale Ancienne?" asked Lucy.

"It's a local vegetarian restaurant," explained Maxwell. "And that's marvellous," he added to the burgemeester.

"The lesbians..."

"Jan!" scolded Vivian, aware of Lucy's sexual preference, but unsure of her sensitivity about it. "They have names."

"Sorry. Eva and Anna at Noordcafé have ordered several cases of some of Alentejo's finest wines."

"Brilliant!"

"And, on this occasion of your surviving a near-fatal gunshot wound, I really think we should sacrifice a virgin to the volcano."

"Oh, Jan," said Vivian. "Why do you insist on sacrificing virgins?"

"Indeed," added Maxwell. "What have they ever done to you?"

"It's not about me. It's about the volcano gods. We need to appease them. Indeed, if you had let me sacrifice one of those Veltem-Beisem virgins to the volcano, you probably would not have been shot. You displeased the volcano gods and have suffered the consequences. Thankfully, the gods have offered you a second chance," said the burgemeester.

"I'm reasonably sure at least one of those lasses was not a virgin," said Maxwell.

"Really?" asked the burgemeester, shocked. "Somchai assured me they were virgins."

"Somchai?" asked Vivian.

"He runs the Jet Set Club," said the burgemeester.

"He's an alcoholic gangster who was thrown out of Siam for reasons unclear and he runs the village's only brothel," said Maxwell. "I'd not trust anything he says."

"Anyway, you know this village has a long history of working with the volcano gods in exchange for our prosperity. And your family is our most prosperous," said the burgemeester.

"I like to think we earned our fortune through hard work rather than the whims of a volcano god," said Vivian.

"And a bit of gambling," added Maxwell.

Lucy laughed. "Speaking of virgins, that reminds me. You know the priest who shot you, Maxwell?"

"He's rather hard to forget under the circumstances."

"Apparently, he's still a virgin. Can you believe it? A man his age?"

"Perhaps sexual frustration drove him to try and kill me," said Maxwell thoughtfully. "If I go without sex for more than a week or so, I get a bit unstable myself. Imagine going more than 40 years without."

"You're hardly normal," said Vivian.

"I know. I like to think of myself as being above normality. I am an ideal to aspire to," said Maxwell.

The burgemeester's face lit up.

"Why, I think we have a solution to all our problems. Why don't we toss the priest into the volcano?"

"Works for me," said Maxwell.

54

Phineas awoke in the middle of the night, confused. In the distance, he could hear the dull roar of voices and the beat of popular music played by a live band. Probably another festival, he thought.

But he was in a jail cell. It always took him a moment to get used to that, to remember why he woke up in a jail cell – though sometimes, he was pretty sure, he woke up in Heaven. When he tried to remember those specific occasions, his memory failed and his head began to hurt. All this was certainly not how he had expected things to work out after he expedited Maxwell to Hell. No one besides Jesus showed any appreciation for his noble deed.

Well, attempted noble deed. Yesterday, he was unsettled to learn from his lawyer that Maxwell had survived the gunshot wound. Worse, the lawyer seemed to think this was good news. "As a result, your charge will be attempted murder," she had explained.

What would a woman know about noble deeds, thought Phineas.

He was miserable, alone and had not even entirely succeeded in his holy task, though he was sure Maxwell must now be reflecting back on his life of sin and be preparing to improve himself in the eyes of God.

"Why does no one appreciate what I did?" shouted Phineas in frustration.

"God appreciates it, Phineas. And I do, too. Well, sort of. You could have aimed better," said Jesus.

"I'm sorry, Jesus," said Phineas. "I tried. I really tried."

"Don't you worry about it, Phinny, my son. You'll get another chance."

"I will?"

"Of course you will! God and I are setting it all up for you."

"You are?"

"That's right, Phinny."

Phineas wondered when and why Jesus started calling him "Phinny". He was a victim of that nickname in school; he had never liked it and had been glad to be rid of it as an adult.

"But Phinny, you have got to stop whining so much about your situation."

"I am not whining, am I?"

"You are, Phinny. And martyrs are not whiners."

"No, of course they aren't. I'm sorry."

"And stop apologising! Did you see me whining when the Romans nailed me to a cross?"

"No, no, Jesus. Of course I didn't. I'm so..."

"Don't you fucking say sorry to me again after I told you to stop!" shrieked Jesus in a voice so loud Phineas was sure it would draw complaints.

"I am beginning to wonder if my Father and I made a mistake in entrusting you to do this, the holiest of holy tasks in the 21st century."

"No, of course not. You can trust me. I'll be better now. But maybe you could..." Phineas looked around. Jesus had disappeared. Then he heard footsteps on the corridor outside. He wondered why Jesus always disappeared when one of the guards came. He also wondered if he would be in trouble for all the noise – even if it was Jesus who was making the noise. Well, if he was, never mind. He was going to be a good martyr. A damned good martyr. Let the guards beat him. He'd show Jesus and God what a good martyr he could be.

In fact, it was not one guard, but two of them who opened the door and announced in near unison, "come along, Forge."

"Where are we going?" asked Phineas.

"To see a volcano," said the guard.

55

Two days after the village party to celebrate Maxwell's return to life and health, he and Wendy were tossing bags into the boot of the ancient Bentley. They climbed in, waved good-bye to Mr and Mrs Suárez and headed down the drive. As Mrs Miller came to life and enquired as to where they were going, Maxwell said, "direct me to Prague, please, Mrs Miller. The town hall, if you will."

"Calculating," said Mrs Miller.

"I've been invited to make a sculpture for the city, you see," said Maxwell, though the GPS unit seemed uninterested in this detail.

"In 400 metres, turn left on Droomstraat," said Mrs Miller.

Maxwell turned right and floored the accelerator. The engine's 12 cylinders roared with delight at being able to apply some muscle to the crankshaft and the wheels squealed as they dug into the road and propelled the old car forward. The road ahead was a winding, indirect route, but jolly good to drive along.

"Recalculating," said Mrs Miller.

"I appreciate it," said Maxwell.

"You don't act like you do," said Mrs Miller.

To Wendy, Maxwell said, "I'm thinking we should aim to have a slightly less-eventful trip this time."

"That's a good plan," said Wendy, pulling Cicero's *On the Good Life* out of her satchel and opening it. "But I am pessimistic."

"So am I, old friend. So am I. But at least we'll share whatever twisted events fate throws at us."

"Actually, it's usually you who throws twisted events at us," said

Wendy.

"Me?" asked Maxwell.

"Yes," said Wendy. "But I'm glad to share those events with you too, as long as they do not involve being eaten by kroaches."

"No, that would not be any fun at all," said Maxwell.

"Or your being shot," said Wendy.

"Also best avoided," agreed Maxwell.

"In 400 metres, turn left onto the N2," said Mrs Miller.

"I feel oddly compelled to do so," said Maxwell.

"Go on, then," said Wendy.

And he did.

About the Author

Jeffrey Baumgartner has done a great many things in many places, including studying art in London, teaching English in Lisbon and writing magazine columns in Bangkok. He's also launched an early Internet company, advised the European Commission on e-commerce, and given creativity workshops throughout the world. These days, he lives in Erps-Kwerps, Belgium with his patchwork family comprising his two sons, his sweetheart and her son – who all think he's bonkers, but in a kind of charming way.